THE MOST DANGEROUS WOMAN IN THE UNDERHIVE HAS A PRICE ON HER HEAD AND DOZENS WILLING TO COLLECT...

D'onne Ulanti is an outlaw and a maniac, known amongst the scum of Necromunda as "Mad Donna", as her uncontrollable and violent nature makes her a dangerous and unpredictable ally.

However, it looks like time has finally caught up with D'onne when a figure from her mysterious past approaches her, but all he reveals is that she's been sold out. Barely escaping with her life, D'onne is mad as hell and hungry for vengeance. The Underhive will shake to its foundations as D'onne seeks to even the score.

If you want to stay breathing, stay out of her way!

*More storming action from the
Necromunda Universe*

SALVATION
C S Goto

Coming soon

BLOOD ROYAL
Will McDermott & Gordon Rennie

JUNKTION
Matt Farrer

NECROMUNDA
SURVIVAL INSTINCT

ANDY CHAMBERS

To my twin gods, momentum and inertia, to dogs and cats and to everyone who never said a discouraging word.

A BLACK LIBRARY PUBLICATION

First published in Great Britain in 2005 by
BL Publishing,
Games Workshop Ltd.,
Willow Road, Nottingham,
NG7 2WS, UK.

10 9 8 7 6 5 4 3 2 1

Cover illustration by Clint Langley.

© Games Workshop Limited 2005. All rights reserved.

Black Library, the Black Library logo, BL Publishing, the BL Publishing logo, Games Workshop, Necromunda, the Necromunda logo and all associated marks, names, characters, illustrations and images from the Necromunda Universe are either ®, TM and/or © Games Workshop Ltd 2000-2004, variably registered in the UK and other countries around the world. All rights reserved.

A CIP record for this book is available from the British Library.

ISBN 13: 978 1 84416 188 1
ISBN 10: 1 84416 188 9

Distributed in the US by Simon & Schuster
1230 Avenue of the Americas, New York, NY 10020, US.

Printed and bound in Great Britain by
Bookmarque, Surrey, UK.

No part of this publication may be reproduced, stored in a retrieval system, or transmitted in any form or by any means, electronic, mechanical, photocopying, recording or otherwise, without the prior permission of the publishers.

This is a work of fiction. All the characters and events portrayed in this book are fictional, and any resemblance to real people or incidents is purely coincidental.

See the Black Library on the Internet at
www.blacklibrary.com

Find out more about Games Workshop
and the world of Necromunda at
www.games-workshop.com

In order to even begin to understand the blasted world of Necromunda you must first understand the hive cities. These man-made mountains of plasteel, ceramite and rockrete have accreted over centuries to protect their inhabitants from a hostile environment, so very much like the termite mounds they resemble. The Necromundan hive cities have populations in the billions and are intensely industrialised, each one commanding the manufacturing potential of an entire planet or colony system compacted into a few hundred square kilometres.

The internal stratification of the hive cities is also illuminating to observe. The entire hive structure replicates the social status of its inhabitants in a vertical plane. At the top are the nobility, below them are the workers, and below the workers are dregs of society, the outcasts. Hive Primus, seat of the planetary governor Lord Helmawr of Necromunda, illustrates this in the starkest terms. The nobles – Houses Helmawr, Cattalus, Ty, Ulanti, Greim, Ran Lo and Ko'Iron – live in 'The Spire', and seldom set foot below 'The Wall' that exists between themselves and the great forges and hab zones of the hive city proper.

Below the hive city is the 'Underhive', foundation layers of habitation domes, industrial zones and tunnels which have been abandoned in prior generations, only to be re-occupied by those with nowhere else to go.

But... humans are not insects. They do not hive together well. Necessity may force it, but the hive cities of Necromunda remain internally divided to the point of brutalisation and outright violence being an everyday fact of life. The Underhive, meanwhile, is a thoroughly lawless place, beset by gangs and renegades, where only the strongest or the most cunning survive. The Goliaths who believe firmly that might is right; the matriarchal, man-hating Escher; the industrial Orlocks; the technologically minded Van Saar; the Delaque whose very existence depends on their espionage network; the firey zealots of the Cawdor. All striving for the advantage that will elevate them, no matter how briefly, above the other houses and gangs of the Underhive.

Most fascinating of all is when individuals attempt to cross the monumental physical and social divides of the hive to start new lives. Given social conditions, ascension through the hive is nigh on impossible, but descent is an altogether easier, albeit altogether less appealing, possibility.

excerpted from Xonariarius the Younger's
Nobilite Pax Imperator – the Triumph of Aristocracy over Democracy.

1: GLORY HOLE

TALK. SOME SAY Underhivers do nothing but talk, that they chatter like reprieved convicts coming out of solitary. Fact is, to them, talking is all about survival: where the lashworms have taken root, where the waste spills are toxic, who's top dog, where to find trade or scav, who's new in town. It's an unwritten law that nothing is taboo down here. A refusal to answer just about any question is a tacit invitation for a fight, not that it's uncommon to see it used as such.

So it is that the drinking holes and slop shops are always filled with a hubbub of gossip that hangs in heavy clouds like the twisting obscura smoke and the greasy fumes of tallow candles.

So when *she* walked into Hagen's place, everyone, and I mean everyone, already knew that Mad Donna was in the settlement of Glory Hole.

It wasn't like in the pict-shows; the music didn't stop, everyone didn't shut up and stop what they were doing to stare. But there was a discernable dip in the noise and a dozen subtle shifts in body postures betrayed curiosity or fear or bravado or guardedness in the crowd. She gazed brazenly at the inhabitants of the shadowy bar with her brilliant blue eye, zapping them with a billion volts of bad attitude. You get a tough crowd in Hagen's place, but few were brave enough to meet her gaze and no one was about to challenge her right to be there.

Outlaw. Psycho bitch. Renegade noble. With a multiple choice of reasons like that to choose from, it was easy to hate or fear Mad Donna. Her gory reputation had spread through Badzones like a twenty-kay rad-cloud in the five cycles she had been below. She was easy on the eye with a dancer's long legs and a set of bewitching curves more flaunted than obscured by her body-casque. Her face would have been beautiful if it wasn't etched by hard lines of cruelty and despair. Legend had it that she'd torn her own eye out years before when a barkeep had told her she was pretty, and now one socket was covered by a glittering, unblinking bionic. Truly there was more softness and compassion in that metal eye than the remaining real one. She carried well-worn weapons on her curving hips, two pistols and a slender chainsword she called 'Seventy-one' for the number of fingers and toes it had chopped off in its time. A dozen pairs of eyes in Hagen's place quickly found other places to be.

She ordered Wildsnake and was greeted by two Escher gangers – Tola and Avignon – emerging from a side booth looking like they didn't really want to be there. The three had obvious deal-talk to conduct: Tola was speaking fast and waving her hands, Avignon chiming in, Donna nodding occasionally. No doubt they wanted to hire Donna's renowned fighting skills as insurance for some scav-run, gang fight or turf war.

Meanwhile tongues were wagging amongst the assembled Underhivers and fighters, telling and re-telling the old stories about Mad Donna. There was the one of how she had murdered her noble husband in the Spire.

'With a silver fish fork no less,' Akas Fishbelly had added knowingly. 'Gouged out 'is eyes.'

Then how she had fled to down-hive to escape her father's wrath, somehow staying one step ahead of the enforcers and bounty hunters all the way. How she had even ghosted through the impenetrable mass of security at The Wall to get from the Spire into Hive City. How she had killed her own sister, how she had skinned a Goliath who crossed her once, how she had carved out a killer reputation in half a decade of gang fights and craziness.

Gradually thoughts turned to other things and cups rose, dice rattled and chips fell once again. That was when it happened. A new voice was heard above the murmur of talk in the bar, and what it said produced that immediate black hole of silence so beloved of storytellers.

'D'onne Ulanti?'

The speaker found himself with Mad Donna's laspistol pressed between his eyes in an uncoiling blur that was almost too fast too see. She spoke in a husky, murderous burr.

'No one has dared use that name around me for five years, so you'd better have a damn good reason for using it now.'

The man at the edge of death was a scrawny young pit slave. A Merchants Guild ownership stud in his forehead winked nervously a millimetre above the laspistol's hungry muzzle.

'I-I have a message from Guilder Theodus Relli for D'onne Ulanti,' he bleated. 'Please don't kill me.'

Donna scanned around the bar without moving the gun and wondered which sack of pus had named her to this hapless rube. Many faces flinched away at her icy glare, but none revealed themselves as the potential sump-stirrer. She holstered the pistol and pointedly turned her back, opening her gloved hand palm-up in front of the slave's nose. After a moment's hesitation a grimy scroll was pressed into her hand and the slave fled.

'What the frik?' said Tola, gazing at the authentic-looking guilder seal embossed in metallic inks on the pale roll of hide.

'Someone wants your attention,' observed Avignon wisely, an effect she ruined only marginally by dripping Wildsnake over her chin as she swigged back another shot.

'Someone is asking for a kicking,' said Mad Donna and dropped the message on the slop-pooled bar top.

'Aren't you going to read it?' asked Tola.

Mad Donna shook her head. 'No, I'm going to finish this bottle and then find Guilder Theodus frikkin' Relli and break it over his no doubt fat and balding head.' Her gaze was distant. 'No one has messages for D'onne Ulanti to hear. She's long dead.'

'Can I read it?' Tola was nothing if not impetuous, little more than a juve really, an effect enhanced by her close-cropped, dirty-blonde hair.

Donna gazed at her evenly for a moment. 'Sure.'

Avignon gave Tola a long-suffering 'I-can't-believe-you-just-did-that' look but Tola was too busy breaking the seal and unrolling the scroll to notice. Her lips moved unconsciously as she read the words. Avignon impatiently snatched the scroll out of Tola's hands and laid it out on the bar for them all to see.

It was handwritten. The practiced pen strokes of a scribe were now growing soft-edged like patches of mould as the pale hide drank up puddles of cheap alcohol, but it had been nicely written. It read:

To the esteemed nobledam D'onne Astride Ge'Sylvanus of the House of Ulanti,

Please forgive this unwarranted intrusion but a matter has come to my attention regarding your past that I felt you should be apprised of with immediacy. I feel it would be unwise to communicate the matter in a simple letter, but I feel sure that such knowledge could be conveyed in person for a suitable consideration. I can be contacted via Strakan's warehouse on the third tier should you wish to pursue this matter further.

Yours in faith,

Theodus Relli
Of the Merchants Guild

'Trap,' belched Avignon.

'No, blackmail. He wants to get a payoff,' said Tola. 'What he's saying is "pay me off or I'll tell someone else about it and they'll pay me off instead".'

'Could be either, or both,' said Donna. 'Most likely the worm has already sold me out and wants to double his money.' Her blue eye was hard and bright with interest. 'It's been tried by bounty hunters before, but never by a guilder.'

The Merchant Guild formed the tenuous threads that stitched the scattered settlements of the Underhive together, moving from place to place trading their wares. They were powerful enough to enjoy as much of a protected status as anyone could claim in the Hive Bottom, the sole supplier of essentials and comforts that were unobtainable otherwise: flak cloth, lumebulbs, protein supplements, data slates, pict slugs, power packs, air filters, fuel rods. They had their fingers in lots of pies and it didn't bode well to make an enemy of one. Guilders had a habit of sticking together and could swing enough credits to put out a bounty so big it would mean a death sentence for just about anybody. Common wisdom was that when guilders took an interest it meant bad things were right around the corner.

'You gonna go?' Tola asked.

Donna shook her head. 'I'd have to be crazy to fall for it.' She wadded up the letter and threw it at Hagen. 'More snake! And make it good or there'll be hell to pay.'

And that was that.

THE SETTLEMENT OF Glory Hole was called that because it *was* a hole: a fungus-like outcropping of trade posts, hovels, workshops, rickety gantries, palisades and trailing cables clustered around a sixty-storey drop between two half-collapsed domes. Centuries ago neglect and unimaginable loads from Hive City above had caused this part of the Underhive to splinter and crack like old bones. A hab-dome that was once half a mile high and six across had been crushed down to a quarter of that size, and the falling debris opened a hole to a larger, older dome beneath that had been previously sealed off by an unbreakable floor of thick ferrocrete.

Underhivers are great survivors by nature; those that aren't get killed off too quickly to find out why. After pulling themselves out of the wreckage they soon investigated the giant hole. The freshly opened dome turned out to be a cornucopia of scav and scrap buried in a vast sea of dust and detritus that was dubbed the

White Wastes. People came from all over to try their hand at plumbing the depths, so the settlement of Glory Hole sprang into existence to supply their needs and relieve them of their newly found wealth. Some of the boldest fortune hunters came back with archeotech hoards big enough to buy a place in the Spire, or so the stories went, and some didn't come back at all.

The White Wastes below had long since been tapped out by Donna's day, but the settlement of Glory Hole hung on just because it was there. Most of the gambling holes and flesh joints had closed down, but enough people stayed around to make it a community. Fungus farmers and rat herders brought their produce there, guilders took their cut, gangs and hired guns generally passed right on through and the authorities generally stayed away. That's just the way the Underhivers liked things.

Mad Donna made her way unsteadily across the second tier, its rusty patchwork of metal plates and mesh grilles creaking every step of the way. She was contemplating the fact that a little less Wildsnake and bravado earlier on would have made things a lot easier for her now, but she was definitely intrigued. It had taken a while for it to settle in but it was there now and nagging like a loose tooth.

What she hadn't told Tola and Avignon were the two things that stood out in Relli's letter. Firstly, it had followed the correct uphive forms of address for herself as a spyrer: nobledam was an old term that just emphasised that nagging fact. Then there was the big one. Relli had used her full name – D'onne Astride Ge'Sylvanus Ulanti, that is, D'onne the divinely beautiful daughter of Patriarch Sylvanus of the House Ulanti. The very name brought back bad memories and a surprisingly hot flush of anger. That name was not commonly known in the Underhive. D'onne Ulanti, for sure, but her full name hadn't even been used on the bounty flyers. That, more than anything else, pointed to the genuine involvement of another noble, quite possibly even a family member.

Donna approached the edge of the tier, where it was unfenced and ragged before the yawning drop. It was quiet in this section, far from the nearest toll-lift. She picked out a sturdy looking cable and carefully wrapped her legs around it before sliding herself over the edge. A cool, foetid breeze blew up from the depths and ruffled her long hair with ghostly fingers as she swarmed down the cable. The floodlit warehouses of the next tier looked doll-sized and distant below, further down than she had thought. The indirect approach of sneaking down onto the third tier without being seen had seemed the smart thing to do. Dangling above a dizzying drop on a rusted old cable made it seem a lot less smart.

'Nobledam,' she hissed to herself. 'Ge'Sylvanus,' she spat. Gripping the cable suddenly seemed a lot easier when she could envisage it as her father's throat.

Strakan's warehouse had the trappings of a typical guilder place: three-metre fence rigged with booby traps, a main gate that could stop a tank, guard towers, wall guns. Donna squatted on a nearby roof and contemplated her options. She counted two armed pit slaves making the rounds inside the compound and three more in the towers. Jumping the fence was just about possible if she got it right. She had thought about just going up to the gate and demanding to see Relli but even Mad Donna wasn't that crazy.

It started to rain, a fine drizzle of condensation falling from the upper layers and bringing a smell of wet ash sharpened by a tang of ammonia. The two slaves in the compound hurried for cover, obviously frightened of acid rain. Stupid green hivers, Donna thought to herself as she dropped from the roof. The kind of effluvia from above which could strip flesh from bones smelled of rotten fruit. This rain produced only a mild prickling burn and was actually good for getting rid of lice and other parasites.

She ran, fast and limber, towards the fence with its ominous hanging fruit of booby trap frag grenades and scatter shells. At the last instant she leapt forward and up, kicking her legs high and arching her body to clear the top of the fence. Wildsnake and the wet surface conspired to screw up her landing, so she turned it into a shoulder roll and came up next to a pile of crates.

No alarms sounded from the slaves in their little towers. All good. A sort of covered veranda ran around the outside of the warehouse, cloaked with invitingly deep shadows. She moved cautiously towards it, resisting the urge to run and staying in cover. The two pit slaves on patrol rounded the corner and she froze as they went by. They were tough-looking characters for all their obvious inexperience. Like most pit slaves, their owner had modified them with crude bionics to suit their function better. One's arm ended in a circular buzz-saw blade and his legs in metal claw feet that rang on the veranda as he approached. The other sported a piston-powered set of shears on one forearm and a half-skull of metal. Both were carrying big bore stub pistols and a bandolier of cartridges.

The modified pair was making more noise than a Goliath gang at a line dance and passed Donna obliviously. As they rounded the corner out of sight she got up and started across the few metres of open space to the veranda. Then it happened.

A door opened and Donna made out a figure emerging. She was then blinded by a row of floodlights kicking on along the edge of the building, bathed in a harsh sea of light totally unfamiliar to someone used to the natural gloom of the Underhive. As she tensed to spring back, a hotshot las-blast scored the plates at her feet in a glowing, spitting question mark. Avignon had been right. It was a trap and Donna was well and truly friked.

'D'onne Ulanti aka Mad Donna, by the authority of Lord Helmawr I arrest you on warrants outstanding in the Spire.' She recognised the harsh, whispering voice. It was Shallej Bak, an ex-Delaque gang fighter turned bounty hunter. If he was here, the puke with the hotshot was probably his cousin, Kell Bak. Like so much else in the Underhive, bounty hunting was a family business.

'Drop your weapons.'

'Come and get them, Shallej, if you've got enough fingers left to try.'

Another hotshot sizzled into the plating close enough to make her involuntarily skip sidewise.

This was hopeless. She could hear the two pit slaves coming back but she could barely make out either them or Shallej in the glare. She raised her hands and closed her bright blue eye.

One thing most people forgot when it came to bionics was that good ones could have distinct advantages over the fleshy original. Donna's artificial eye was a top-range Van Saar model. Among several useful quirks it featured an automatic photosensitive glare filter.

Shallej, a bald, bulky figure in a long flak coat, was standing a little to the left of the door, covering Donna with the red dot of a bolt pistol targeter.

Buzz-saw and Shears were approaching from the right. Shears had his pistol holstered and was carrying a jangling set of manacles. Donna reckoned Kell was in a tower also off to the right.

Shears grinned confidently and stepped forward to toss the manacles to her. As he did so, he momentarily blocked Shallej's line of fire. That moment was all Donna needed. She bounded forward and grabbed Shears in an arm lock. Buzz-saw's stub pistol boomed off a round but fired wide and Kell's shot was a fraction of a second slow as the hotshot's power pack struggled to build up a fresh charge. Shears howled when Donna bit off his remaining ear and spat it in his face. Shallej cursed.

Blinded by the hot, sticky blood covering his bionic thermal sensor and reeling off balance, Shears was in trouble and he knew it. He panicked and tried to use his piston-enhanced strength to throw the snarling, laughing woman off, but Donna spun him by the elbow and rammed his cumbersome bionic blades into Buzz-saw's guts. It was unfortunate for the bloody pit slave that Shallej's bolt round caught Shears just above the eye at that same moment. The .75 mass reactive gyro-jet pulped his head like a ripe melon being hit by a truck. His death-reflex jerked his shears shut and messily eviscerated Buzz-saw into the bargain.

Donna was still moving while the pit slaves swayed in their gore-slicked embrace of death. Shallej expected her to run for cover, diving left or right, but she came straight at him instead, ripping out Seventy-one and thumbing the chainblade to life. Her shoulder blades itched with the expectation of a hotshot at any moment but Kell was obviously off-form and no shot came.

Shallej didn't raise his pistol to shoot at Donna since that had cost him three fingers last time they met and he'd learned from the experience. Instead he ducked out into the yard where he could count on support from his cousin. Donna's screeching chain-blade tore at Shallej's coat as she made a backhanded slash but she kept going, diving through the open door and into the warehouse.

Donna rolled to her feet and kicked the door shut, pumping a couple of las-shots through it at chest and groin height to dissuade pursuers. She turned and sprinted off between the rows of crates and bales, sword and pistol ready.

Nothing rose to bar her path. She could hear shouting outside, and then a volley of shots before the door banged open behind her. By that time she had already found what she was looking for: two heavy trapdoors in the floor with a girder-work, a frame and winch assembly over them. No guilder would pay the lift-tolls to have their goods brought up Glory Hole, so each warehouse had their own hoist to the tier below. It was the ideal escape route out of the bounty hunter's trap, or it would have been if the trapdoors weren't secured by heavyweight tungsten mag-locks.

The bounty hunters became stalking shapes behind the rows of chipped plastic crates and overstuffed bales. The distinctive rising whine of Donna's plasma pistol about to discharge sent them ducking back like jackals before a lion. The warehouse was sharply lit by an actinic blaze as the pistol fired, a thunderclap report and wash of ozone sending hard black shadows leaping to the corners.

Bounty hunters knew their guns and a plasma weapon took precious seconds to recharge. They moved quickly to encircle their cornered prize, emerging at the skeletal A-frame hoist in a coordinated rush.

They found the trapdoors melted through, their edges still glowing cherry red from the fearsome heat of a plasma blast. Of Mad Donna there was no sign.

DONNA SWORE LONG and loud as she applied a stinger mould poultice to her burned shoulder. A drip of molten steel had caught her as she clung to the bracing beneath Strakan's warehouse, listening to the Bak brothers bitching and planning their next move. They hadn't mentioned Relli so it didn't sound like he was in Glory Hole. She'd almost bitten through her lip but hadn't uttered a sound.

She was 'holed up', as Underhivers say, in a broken pipe halfway up the wall of the dome below Glory Hole. She had a dew-sheet stretched out and a small fire going with a couple of cat-sized rats roasting on spits, the dribbling grease hissing and popping in the flames. She kept an eye out in case any other scavengers were drawn to the smell, but most Underhive creatures instinctively steered clear of fire and smoke, except those on two legs of course. Looking out into the gloom Donna could see white ash dunes and mesas of fallen rockrete topped with twisted forests of girders. The only thing moving was a distant string of lights, probably the lanterns of some guilder caravan. It wasn't safe here but it was quiet and it gave her some time to think.

No matter how far she ran or how deep she buried herself she could never outdistance her past. The Underhive was a haven for criminals and renegades of all sorts, and for hivers desperate enough to gamble everything on starting a new life at the very fringes of civilisation. Most were running from something, but most were safely forgotten and ignored once they were in the Underhive – it received both outcasts and hopefuls to its dark bosom with equanimity. Not so for D'onne Ulanti.

Being a feared and hunted outlaw sounded exciting and romantic but the reality was a grim, sometimes desperate, existence dogged by the ghosts of the past. Donna's previous life in the Spire was a half-remembered dream which at moments like this her mind would treacherously patch together as a mosaic of her best memories, pushing her further down the spiral road of regret and despair. Donna occasionally convinced herself it had all happened to someone else. In truth she had become someone else now – Mad Donna had replaced D'onne Ulanti even though she wore her stolen flesh. She had fallen so far and lost so much of the comfort and security guaranteed by life in the Spire. Sometimes she wondered why she kept going at all; it would be so much easier just to put a pistol to her head and end it for good.

To end up in the Underhive was the worst thing that could happen to someone from the Spire. Suspicion was the best you could hope for, since half of those you meet would be happy to kill you just for having an uphiver accent. If the Underhivers didn't kill you, then there were a hundred other hideous deathmongers close at hand: spiders, scorpions, snakes, rats, millasaurs, carrion bats, ripper jacks, face-eaters, sludge jellies, lash whips, wire weed, brain leaves, gas spores, zombies, cannibals, mutants. The list went on and on, and there were plenty of other things even the Underhivers didn't have names for. There were also the toxic spills, the sludge pits, the acid rain, the gas pockets, the carcinogens in the dust, the food, the water, the air, the hive quakes, flash floods, electrical discharges or the simple expedient of a long drop onto something unforgiving. It was not a gentle land.

And now Donna must walk that land and find some answers, find out *how* Relli had found her and, more importantly, why. In the Underhive, notoriety was like body odour – everyone had it. Actually finding someone specific instead of a bunch of rumours took persistence and no little skill. If she was going to avoid being caught, Mad Donna needed to know a lot more about her hunters. She knew that the best places to find news on guilders were the settlements of Dust Falls and Two Tunnels, both of which see more guilder caravans than anywhere else because of their locations. The only alternative would be to keep running in the Badzones between settlements until the hunters caught up with her again, and next time she might not be so lucky. And why not simply end it all, simply stop running and lie down to die? Because then it would all have been for nothing, and she would have given in to to her innermost daemons, the ones with her father's voice that said it would have been better if she had never been born at all.

Trekking to Dust Falls from Glory Hole usually meant a roundabout journey across the White Wastes up to the rusting gantries over Cliff Wall. From there the commonest paths went through the Looming Halls and down the interweaving tunnels of The Lesser Trunk. There were other ways, quicker ones even, but that was the easiest and safest one. Because of that there was always a good chance that gangers, outlaws or both (and it's often hard to tell the difference) would be roving in parts of the Looming Halls, taxing or murdering travellers as took their fancy. Enterprising gangs often put up toll-blocks on Cliff Wall too, or fought vicious battles for possession of them.

The alternative was to strike out straight across the wastes to the foot of Cliff Wall, go across the rotting pipes at its base and into a confusing tangle of ancient turbine chambers. If you then could find a way through the sludge pits and collapsed areas you would emerge, perhaps, into the generatoria dome at the bottom of The Lesser Trunk, and would only be a march away from Dust Falls and the edge of The Abyss.

Going the roundabout route was simply not an option. There was too much of a chance of being recognised on the way and word getting back to the bounty hunters. They would have thrown out a web of informers around Glory Hole within an hour of losing her, hundreds of ears sharp for any news. Time was also an issue. If she kept ahead of any reports reaching Relli she would have an edge. She desperately needed one.

Flexing her shoulder experimentally, Donna found it surprisingly free of pain. The poultice was doing its work. She realised that her injury would not hinder her and she was pleased since the lower route was sure to be physically demanding. She checked her weapons too, as the sludge pits were supposed to be rife with vermin.

Seventy-one was as close to full charge as it could be, its ceramite teeth sharp and moving freely. She found some torn scraps of Shallej's coat caught between the teeth and braided them amid the other trinkets in her unkempt hair as a memento. Her laspistol was an exquisitely made spyer pattern that she had carried for as long as she had been in the Underhive. In all that time she had never had to replace the power cell or even recharge it, nor once clean the muzzle lens, yet it remained ever ready to inflict harm. She loved and hated the elegant pistol, and had almost thrown it away or sold it dozens of times over the years. The gun didn't care and continued to serve her as faithfully as a hunting hound.

Her plasma pistol was a different story; a heavy, crudely made and pug-ugly looking Underhive piece. She had cut it out of the dead, nerveless hand of an outlaw called Kapo Barra after a fight outside Two Tunnels. Kapo and his gang had ceased to exist when Mad Donna and Tessera's Escher had caught them in an ambush. The bounty fee from the grateful hivers of Two Tunnels had not been as great as promised, but the loot was excellent.

Donna had kept the cumbersome plasma pistol because it was such a great equaliser. No matter how tough an opponent was, a blast of incandescent plasma would seriously wound or kill them and they knew it. Even the sound of it about to discharge would make most foes duck for cover, and as the escape from the warehouse had proven, its ability to annihilate obstacles was more useful still. It was on a three-quarter charge, the power-hungry pig that it was, and firing it would have to remain a last resort until she was near a viable power source. Finding a replacement plasma flask for it would be harder still where she was going.

Smoked rat meat plus water from the dew-sheet and filter can would be her food and drink for the journey. What she needed to do now was rest and save her strength for a few hours before setting out. She settled herself into the pipe and flipped her bionic eye to its alarm mode. If anything bigger than a fly approached her hiding place, a motion-sensor would instantly wake her. She slept fitfully.

THE FIRING STUTTERED *and died away into echoes.*

D'onne stuck her head out to see what was going on and a stub round smacked into the pillar right beside her the instant her head was visible. Tola pulled her back in sharply. 'Don't be stupid, Donna. They knows we're still here.'

Another shot and a ricochet whined past as if to underline the point.

'So what do we do now, Tola?' *D'onne tried to sound sarcastic instead of frightened while pushing her blonde plaits out of her eyes. She felt unable to quite believe that she was being lectured by an Underhive brat, five years her junior, who couldn't even get her name right. Tola didn't even seem to notice her fantastically withering glare.*

'Well, if we waits a while they'll start a-sneakin' and a creeeepin' up here,' *she sang quietly, eyes wild with the rush of the firefight.* 'We could pop out then. Pow! Pow! Mebbe take a couple, but then they'd shoot us down like rats.' *She scowled dramatically.* 'Not good.'

Having a child talk to you as if you were another, younger child is, D'onne concluded, one of the most excruciating things that can ever happen to a person. She was just glad there was no one else around to hear it. If Tola kept this up she'd rather get shot than stay behind the pillar with her.

'And then...' *she prompted.*

'Then we could try'n a-sneakin' away ourselves, find a spot and wait for them to come nosin' around our old post and then Pumph!' D'onne clapped her hand over Tola's mouth to stifle her from saying 'Pow! Pow!' again. Her eyes were bright with fearful intensity.

'Shut it, Tola. I hear them!' D'onne hissed.

And here they came, the jingle and squeak of gun harnesses a chilling counterpoint to the heavy clump of running boots. It was an incredibly menacing sound: the sound of people running to kill you.

D'onne and Tola were in some kind of manufactoria, and it was as dry and dusty as old bones. Most of it seemed to be filled with rusting iron-plated tubs three times the height of a man, and D'onne surmised that they were big silos or mixing vats of some sort.

D'onne had given up trying to tell what the places used to do where the gang went. What was important is what they did now, and that was serve as a battle ground for the gangs.

D'onne was trying to learn but it was hard to look at things in a different way than you had been taught for your whole life, to look at a scene for the tactical instead of the aesthetic. But she was learning.

Once she would have looked around the old building and appreciated the fractal chaos of its disintegrating roof panels, and the coy glimpses they offered of the gantry-garlanded ceiling of the city dome the building stood inside. She would have enjoyed the subtle irony of factories growing old and having to retire and going to pieces just like the workers inside, but how this happened simply over a longer span of time. She might have written a poem about it, or painted a picture in charcoal to get those shadows right.

Now D'onne looked for cover, and for somewhere she could run to before an enemy could draw a bead. She looked for what would stop a bullet or a las-blast, and what would only hide you, where the shadows lay, where the sniper nests might be. She was learning, oh yes.

D'onne let Tola go and the little brat just sprinted off without a word. D'onne followed a second later, skipping backwards for a couple of steps to cover their backs. Then she turned and ran after Tola as if a pack of murderers were on her heels.

Which they were.

Tola jumped down a rubble embankment, slithering down broken chunks of rockrete and kicking off a cascade of smaller bits and pieces that rattled and clattered explosively. It made enough noise to attract the attention of their pursuers and shots boomed out. D'onne stifled a little shriek as rounds cracked past her. She weaved and ran in a different direction, diving behind a fallen beam and dropping flat.

Tola was out of sight and D'onne was suddenly very much alone. She lay as quietly as she could and tried not to pant loudly. After a breathless moment she crawled on her belly towards the other end of the beam and stopped to listen.

The running noises had stopped. Everything had gone quiet again. D'onne hated it: the fear, the feeling of impotence while everyone around her fought out a deadly battle, the fact that she hadn't had the faintest clue what was going on, where her side was, where the bad guys were or what they were trying to achieve. Juves like her and Tola were a liability in a gang battle, D'onne knew, because the experienced gangers told her so loudly and so often. No one wanted to risk a juve getting in their way or drawing attention to them in a firefight. So Juves were abandoned in a fight to sink or swim on their own. It was a form of Underhive natural selection that was brutally efficient at creating live, competent Underhive gang fighters or very dead wannabes.

In some ways it was no different to the Spire; it was all about looking out for number one.

Gunfire cut through the silence, flashes lit the shadows and made them jump, and a man screamed. D'onne smiled at that since her gang – *the* gang – was all female, like all those from House Escher. The other gang was all male, like all gangs from House Goliath. Whoever had just screamed was an enemy.

Back in her other life (hazy and distant now, but was it only a few weeks ago she had still been living it?), she had learned about the Industrial Houses of Hive City: the Goliaths, the Escher, the Delaque, the Van Saar, the Orlocks, the Cawdor. They weren't like the noble houses of the Spire; there was no pair-bonding or guardianship of the bloodlines. Her tutors had taught her that they were mongrel partitions of the proletariat with little more integrity than common labour guilds. Reality, of course, was very different.

These Industrial Houses occupied well-defended enclaves within the city and dealt with one another only in conditions of utmost suspicion and secrecy. Each jealously guarded its own traditions and attitudes and old enmities like rival nations. The noble houses frowned on anarchy and disorder in Hive City, so members of the Industrial Houses descended beneath Hive City to fight over the hundreds of square miles of abandoned hab domes, transitways and other crumbling strata of previous industrious generations.

The Escher told her they came to get more resources for their sisters in Hive City, where every mouthful of food or cup of recycled water was treasured. D'onne had a strong feeling they did it because they were sick of Hive City and just wanted to fight. She couldn't blame them. Just a few hours in Hive City had made her understand the desire to give violent release to the unbearable tension she'd felt. To live every day cheek by jowl with a billion angry people in a *polluted maze shut away from the skies... D'onne was amazed they didn't all go mad, or perhaps they did and that was how they could stand it.*

So the mad ones, or the sane ones, depending on which way you looked at it, came below to fight.

The Goliaths were the diametric opposite of the Escher – a bunch of steroid-fed half-wits who relied on brute force and ignorance to get the job done. This was what the Escher had told her. These Goliaths were outlaws, gang scum who couldn't abide by the coarse rules of the Underhive and had earned a bounty on their heads. The Escher gang's leader, Tessera, had cut a deal with a nearby settlement called Two Tunnels to wipe out the Goliath gang or at least drive them far enough from the settlement to stop harassing anyone who travelled there.

There were only supposed to be half a dozen outlaw Goliaths holed up in the manufactoria, and the Escher were to outnumber them almost two to one. It didn't feel like that at all at the moment. D'onne was alone with the enemy all about her, as evinced by the occasional rattle of stone or clink of metal in the shadows. She had also stayed in the comforting but illusory shelter of the beam for too long – whole stale seconds too long in the midst of a minutes-long firefight.

She started to move. A hail of bullets sprayed across the beam, kicking up tiny explosions of dust all around her as she hastily ducked back out of sight. The bullets kept coming, angrily buzz-sawing chunks out of the beam in a seemingly endless stream. When the fusillade stopped, the momentary silence seemed unreal and disorientating to D'onne after the chaos of being under such heavy fire. In the distance she heard the click of a magazine being ejected and that familiar drum-drum-drum of running boots.

Something about Tola's words earlier came back to her and she knelt suddenly upright with her pistol in hand.

Pow! Pow!

A Goliath stood not five metres away from her. He was tall, but massive pectorals and biceps made him seem squat and troll-like. Chrome spikes and rings prominently pierced his nipples, face, arms, and crotch. He had a heavy cylinder-fed slug gun in one hand and a steel bar in the other. The Goliath was looking down, dumbly surprised at the two smoking holes D'onne had put through his meaty chest. He looked about as old as Tola.

D'onne saw the second Goliath right behind him, and amazingly he was even bigger and definitely more ugly and scarred than the other one. He was grinning nastily at D'onne while slapping a fresh clip into his autopistol. As he did so, the corpse of his fellow ganger dropped neatly out of his line of fire. She gaped in astonishment at the realisation that he had used the younger Goliath to draw her out, how he had callously sent him to an almost certain death to get her to come of out of cover. He saw the shocked expression on her face and laughed out loud, a deep booming sound like rocks falling down a shaft.

'Nevuhr mind girly-girl,' he said, levelling the autopistol at her. 'If yer quick yer'll catch 'im.'

Donna's eyes were already closed and she flinched as shots hammered out, her body tensing involuntarily at the last instant before giving up her life. After a second she opened them to find she still lived, and instead the Goliath was sprawled in a bloody heap. He seemed shrunken now that hot lead had torn through muscles, organs and bones. D'onne couldn't get the confused idea out of her head that somehow the autopistol had misfired and he hit himself, lots of times, or something.

'That's the last of them,' Tessera's firm voice called out.

Footsteps scrunched all around D'onne as the Escher appeared from the shadows one by one. Big Faer with her heavy stubber still smoking from the deadly burst which had killed the last Goliath. Little Tola smeared with dirt and covered in bruises, looking like the child she was. Avignon and Sirce were up in the roof supports with their rifles. Jen, Alli and Sara were on the ground with pistols. Crazy Kristi had cuts all over her body and a lot of blood on her long, slender sword that wasn't her own. They carried out the other juve, Veshla, who had a gut wound that probably wouldn't heal before it killed her.

D'onne realised that she had never been alone and that there had always been allies within reach of her. She also realised that Tessera had used her and Tola as bait, just like the Goliath but with a bit more sophistication. That simply reinforced a lesson she already knew, one she had learned at bitter cost in the Spire.

Number one always comes first.

Tola came up to her afterwards and said, loud enough for the whole gang to hear, 'Watcha go a-runnin' off on your own like that for? You're mad, Donna!'

2: CLIFF WALL

MAD DONNA STARED up at a vast, curving cloud approaching her as she tramped across the White Wastes. Twinkling stars strung its upper reaches and hung down like looping garlands across black lightning bolts frozen in the act of splitting the smooth face asunder.

Cliff Wall. Her mouth felt dry at the prospect. Or maybe it was the dehydrating salts of the White Wastes, it was hard to be sure.

The route from Glory Hole was high up to the left from this perspective, climbing a succession of ruined buildings and fallen roadways along the dome wall to come up level with the cliff top. The right hand end of the cliff top road led out of the White Wastes and into the ominous Looming Halls. A ratskin had once told her there were evil spirits there, and truly the rows of towering machinery rusted into solid heaps but not yet completely quiescent were disturbing.

The chalk-white dust of the wastes gave way grudgingly to cracked slabs in a pipe-choked channel near the base of the cliff. Donna went cautiously, testing each step before advancing. The finest dust from the White Wastes could flow like water and would often pool in pits or crevices on its periphery. Usually this was just inconvenient and meant stumbling in unseen potholes, but the base of Cliff Wall was rife with cracks deep enough to swallow a man, or woman, whole. Even a solid-looking slab or pipe might be resting at the edge of an unseen precipice and just waiting to tumble an unwary traveller to their doom.

She stopped, squinting between the pipes and trying to see what had caught her attention. There, a scatter of small bones and chitin. She reappraised the thick tangle of fallen wires hanging above the spot. Tiny, subtle movements made it look like the wires were swaying in a breeze, but there was no breeze to be felt. Wire weed. Doubtless a chunk had fallen from a toll-block at the top and survived down here by catching rats and spiders. Donna counted herself lucky. Larger thickets would have hidden the evidence of their kills better. The first inkling she might have had about the weed would be when it was looping tendrils around her pretty neck. She had heard stories of wire weed that had learned to lurk under dust or sand, or even behind walls, and burst out on its prey from hiding. Suddenly the floor of the channel seemed a less safe place to be.

She went up, climbing creaking pipes and corroded stanchions, steering well clear of the weed she had spotted. Now that she was alert to it, she spotted a few other clumps dotted around. Nasty as it was, wire weed was a lurker, and as such it was a fair bet that it would be lurking near well-used trails. The weed patches seemed to be spread evenly around a bank of six-metre high outflow pipes, and that would make it likely that they connected to the turbine chambers beneath Cliff Wall.

By the time she got level with the outflow she was dripping with sweat, and the jagged metal she'd climbed had torn her gloves. She clung to a section of gantry and eyed the rockrete apron in front of the pipes dubiously as she caught her breath. There was no sign of what she'd expected to find – the fine grey sensor hairs sticking out of cracks and crevices that denoted the presence of lashworms. It was easy to see why. Every crack or crevice around the outflow pipes had been meticulously broken open and there was obscene rat-graffiti everywhere. Looked like rats had eaten all the lashworms.

Donna hated rats. She started contemplating other directions to try instead of the outflow. A las-bolt whipped past her face without warning, close enough for her to feel the furnace breath of its passage. The bolt struck sparks of molten steel from the metal gantry and the whole thing suddenly shifted beneath her.

Most people get shot in situations like this because their immediate response is to stop and look around for who's shooting at them. If they were really lucky they'd get to see their attacker just in time to get themselves killed dead, dead, dead. Gang fighters, especially ones of Donna's calibre, knew better. Cover first, then worry about who's shooting. The decision isn't a decision at all, its an instant response in a world where death is only ever a trigger-pull away.

Donna pitched herself over onto the rockrete apron. A second bolt clipped shards off the edge as she wiggled over it. The gantry swayed alarmingly as her weight left it for firmer ground. Donna lay flat for a moment and glared around wildly. No shapes moved in the outflow tunnels, and no more shots came from above. Whoever was shooting at her was below at the base of the cliff.

The practical solution would be to get going before they decided to start lobbing frag grenades up at her, but Donna was consumed with curiosity. She slithered along the edge for a few metres and slipped out a specially polished throwing blade she kept in her boot top. Easing it over the edge allowed her to see a view down the wall with the blade's mirrored surface, which her assailants were unlikely to spot in the dim light. Donna had often considered getting some kind of remote for her bionic eye for times like this but Tessera, her old mentor, had been derisive. 'A gadget will always fail you,' she had sneered. 'Only rely on things that can't go wrong!' She had accepted only grudgingly that Donna needed to replace her eye at all.

There. A figure with a shouldered rifle. It was scanning around the outflow area. She shrank back in case the figure had a scope sight. He had been standing on a slab close to where Donna had started to climb, with another figure just behind it, a darker blur in the gloom. She edged along a little further and put her little blade over the edge to see if there were more of them.

She caught sight of movement and turned the blade to catch a small group of maybe three or four marching up to the slab, obviously allies of the sniper. The figure at the head of the group looked to be dressed in white clothes or armour, and the rest were shadowy blobs that looked like they were cloaked and hooded. The figure in white dashed the rifle out of the sniper's hands and some kind of argument broke out, fragments of angry imprecations floating up the wall from below. Donna smiled nastily. They wanted her alive, so they *were* bounty hunters. Not Shallej and Kell Bak, but some other posse, fresh out of Glory Hole no doubt.

All attention was being drawn to the argument so Donna risked poking her head over for a better look.

The figure in white (armour she realised, a full-body suit of shaped ceramite pieces by the look of it) stood with his legs spread pointing down imperiously at the fallen lasrifle. Skulking just in front of it was an Underhive gun-scummer, the kind of trash for hire you can find buzzing like flies around any of the settlements. It looked like he had a gun-scum buddy hovering between backing him up and slinking away.

The two remaining members of the group looked rather, well, weird. They were heavily cloaked in dark robes but that couldn't disguise the fact that one was short and round, the other tall and rail thin. The tall one scarcely moved at all, and the short one seemed to be constantly swaying as if in time to unheard music. Neither carried any visible weapons.

Things were hotting up on the slab. The scummer was shaking his head and White Armour kept jabbing his finger at the lasrifle again and again. The scummer looked surly, his hand flexing closer to his holster. Just when it looked like violence would erupt at any moment, another figure moved fluidly into view. It was low and lean like a hunting hound, all polished chrome and brushed steel. It was in fact an enforcer hound; a standard enforcer cyborg occasionally seen in the Underhive indentured to guilders, watchmen or bounty hunters.

The fire went out of the scummer as soon as he saw the mastiff and he hastily picked up the rifle. Donna cursed inwardly and wished she had a few frag grenades to drop on them. It was too far for a decent pistol shot, and trying would get her in a gun battle with men with rifles – a definably bad idea.

The thought gave her another idea, however, and after some searching she found a hands-breadth section of pipe that would serve her purpose. Coming to a crouch at the edge, she popped up for a second fully exposed to those below. One of the cloaked figures, the short one, seemed to sense her first and pointed. The others were caught flat-footed, clumsily swinging around to look for their forgotten prey.

'Eat frag, you scummers!' Donna yelled and threw the pipe into their midst before ducking out of sight. Alarmed yells could be heard, and Donna imagined them all diving for cover from the so-called frag grenade she had thrown.

As she entered the outflow pipe she heard the first screams floating up from below as the wire weed feasted on its unexpected bounty. She smiled a full, cruel smile.

THE FIRST COUPLE of hundred metres of pipe ran straight, and then it went through a slow left corkscrew and rose perhaps ten metres before debouching into a large chamber. That was where Donna found the rats.

Two-dozen pairs of glinting, narrowed eyes were studying her as she exited the pipe. As four sets of eyes moved closer, her bionic saw their long sinuous forms sidling insouciantly to surround her, their worm-tails dragging in the dirt. She stood her ground; running or even backing off now would most likely bring the whole pack down on her in an instant.

Necromundan giant rats were the stuff of nightmares, over a metre long with scabrous, oily pelts, naked wormlike tails, taloned claws, piercing, red eyes that glitter with malign intelligence and a jaw full of jagged, disease-ridden fangs. Mutations are so common it's unusual to see a rat without bloated tumours, or two heads, or poisonous spines, or drooling acidic green foam. They'd long since learned not to fear humans and there are many parts of the Underhive that belong more to rats than men.

Donna thumbed Seventy-one to life and menaced them with it, the malicious whine of its whirling teeth oscillating as she swung it in a casual figure-of-eight.

'You want some, boys? Want a little rat *fricassée*? Come on. Donna's waiting and she doesn't have all day.'

The rats stopped when they heard Seventy-one's keening challenge, but hunger or maybe her talking back needled them into advancing again. One skeletal specimen with bony horns on its head hunched its shoulders to jump, but Donna burned it down with her laspistol as it sprang. The distraction gave the other three the opening they wanted, prompting two of them to leap at her face while the third went for her belly.

Her chainblade whipping up in a tight arc, Donna took the head off one rat in a spray of gore and gouged bloody chunks from the other, making it squeal as it was hurled aside. Donna spun with the momentum, twisting desperately to avoid the slavering fangs of the third as its leap carried it past. The wounded one landed near her feet and snapped furiously at her but she kicked it away, levelling her pistol and popping off a shot at the one she'd dodged as it tensed to jump again. The rat skittered away from the las-shot with almost preternatural speed and then started to slowly edge away, chittering and glaring at her menacingly.

Donna stood poised, her heart hammering in her chest. She had passed the test for the present. The other rats began preening disinterestedly or nosed around, pointedly ignoring her. Several of them ambled casually after the wounded one, lapping at the crimson trail it left as it desperately tried to crawl away.

Others trotted over to the rats she had killed and started gnawing on them with shameless cannibalistic gusto.

Donna strode forward through the chamber displaying more confidence than she felt, boot heels scrunching on scattered bones. Two large, square tunnels were visible in the far wall so she headed towards them, trying to cover every angle at once and not run. As she got closer she could see more rats watching her from the left tunnel and steered to the right.

The rats might be trying to trick her by sending her deeper into their nest but it was unlikely. Having tested her mettle they would be content to follow her now, waiting until she was hurt by something else, sleeping, or off-guard before they came for her again. Or, as the burst of agonised squeaking behind her underlined, they would finish off anything else that crossed her path but limped away from the encounter. Rats were nothing if not supreme opportunists. For now her only hope was to push on and stay ahead of the bounty hunters. They were the real peril.

The tunnel was streaked with crusted patches of old slime and little puddles of moisture winked up at her from the floor. These were good signs that the route connected to the dank turbine chambers. Sure enough, after twenty metres the tunnel ended at a set of corroded, gap-toothed rungs set into the wall. Looking up Donna could see a tangle of rusted metal partially blocking the lip of a shaft perhaps three metres above.

There was an old Underhive adage that said, 'Never trust a rung when you can make the jump,' but then another stated, 'Never make a jump when you can make the climb.' Donna opted for the former this time. She backed up a couple of paces, turned to blow a kiss to the glittering rat-eyes in the shadows behind, sheathed her weapons, and leapt. She caught at the lip of the shaft with both hands but her torn gloves made her hands slip and one skidded off. Flailing around she caught the topmost rung and it tore straight out of the crumbling ferrocrete. Disgusted, she tossed it away and made another grab at the lip. This time her grip held and with some unladylike grunts and scrabbling she hauled herself over the edge.

As she did so the pile of rusting scrap creaked ominously. A twisted turbine blade was dislodged and spun lazily down the shaft with a horrendous clattering noise. She gingerly wormed out from under the mass of machinery as it teetered further and settled towards the edge. Donna held her breath.

An instant later the rest of the scrap avalanched down the shaft with a drawn out screeching and crashing fit to wake the dead. Donna got up and ran from the spot before anything turned up to find out what all the noise was about.

Perhaps a hundred metres away, Mad Donna ducked down beside the rusting carcass of another turbine mounting and caught her breath. She was in a broad court studded with the things, and wide archways in all directions gave way onto similar chambers. It had once been an orderly place with the machines set out in precise rows like soldiers on parade. The ranks were now all but obliterated by chunks of masonry that had fallen from the ceiling and the floor was scattered with unidentifiable machine-guts. Stray slivers of light illuminated chambers far into the distance, indicating to her just how deep the giant cracks in the surface of Cliff Wall truly went.

Donna set her back to the direction the tunnel had taken into the shaft below. She hoped that would at least take her vaguely in the direction she needed to go. She started to pick her way through the rows of machines, noting that she had picked up another pair of rats for company. Or was it the same ones from before? It was hard to be sure. She kept her ears sharp for the flutter of carrion bats or ripper jacks as she moved, but all was quiet. Perhaps the noise had frightened them off for the time being.

Hours later it had become apparent to Donna that the biggest threats in the turbine chambers were hunger and thirst. She had come down several dead end rows and had to backtrack so many times that she was afraid of getting hopelessly lost. But when she used a thermal view to check her own trail it confirmed she was moving ever deeper in. Apart from the rats she had seen nothing living in all that time and the chambers seemed to stretch for miles.

A few hours more and Donna was starting to get seriously worried. Even if she could find a way out of there, at this rate she would arrive in Dust Falls to find the bounty hunters already waiting for her. No, she told herself as she strove to quell her frustration, that was just paranoia. Plodding through the endless ranks was getting to her. There had to be some better way to find a clear path, some clue she had missed before now. She gazed intently around her, willing a solution to appear.

Looking down, she saw a telltale gleam of reflected moisture beneath some scrap. She bent closer. Greyblack sludge was seeping out of a crack in the floor. She followed the crack back several rows until it disappeared under a machine and from there she could see a glistening rivulet of the stuff wending its way between rubble piles. Donna followed it and after only a couple hundred metres came out from between two crushed rows of machines into a relatively open space where the floor sloped up at an abrupt angle.

Mad Donna breathed out a gusty sigh of relief and almost choked when she breathed in again. A bitter, noxious stench was wafting down the slope and warring with her nose and throat, threatening to make her cough or puke, or both. She quickly looped a scarf around her face and trusted its carbon-impregnated weave (well, soot-smeared anyway) to filter out the worst of it. It helped a lot and she scrambled up the slope on her hands and knees without any trouble, scuttling crabwise to avoid several cracks dribbling thick sludge on the way.

The top of the slope opened out onto the wide, ugly vista of the sludge pits. Narrow rockrete piers stretched out in a grid pattern delineating dozens of steep sided cisterns. Some of the cisterns were cracked and dry, others were full to the bubbling brim and slopping obscenely over the sides. Patches of slime, algae and fungus dabbed spots of lurid colour here and there, casting sickly, dim phosphorescence over the scene.

Many of the piers were shattered or at least slick, treacherous and crumbling, and by now Donna expected nothing less. One slip could mean either a bone-breaking fall into a dry cistern, or a slow drowning in a full one. Depending on how corrosive the sludge was, the latter could be infinitely more agonising. Donna looked back down the slope; rat-eyes glittered up at her from between the rusting machines at the bottom. Donna cursed at them dispassionately. She was tired and could use some rest before tackling the pits. But staying up here would mean slowly choking to death, and going down among the machines would mean no rest at all.

With a weary sigh she wandered along the edge to find a row of intact-looking piers she might traverse. Rumour had it that the far end of the sludge pits led to the bottom of the Lesser Trunk and thence to Dust Falls. She turned and stepped out onto the piers. Having come this far she had to believe that rumour was true.

A route avoiding the most cracked piers perforce took her beside or between the fuller cisterns. As she made her way further out she found very few of the cisterns were actually empty except along the edge. Most had at least three metres of foul smelling glop in the bottom, usually bubbling flatulently or swirling in slow, rancid eddies. She steered well away from anywhere the sludge was seeping over and crossed no crack that was bigger than a long step. While looking back to see how far she had come, Donna caught sight of low, lean shapes slinking along the piers after her. At least the rats still had their hopes up.

Donna slogged on through the dizzying stench and concentrated on keeping her feet from straying. Her knees were starting to feel uncomfortably weak when she reached yet another intersection between the piers with four especially full and eye-wateringly foul pits. Donna looked around at her choices and glanced back to check on her rodent companions, noting interestedly that they were nowhere to be seen.

That was her first warning.

She heard a soft plop behind her like a particularly large bubble rising to the surface of the sludge.

That was her second warning.

Something gelatinous writhed around her ankle. She whipped her foot away in revulsion and whirled about. A nest of translucent, questing tendrils was reaching blindly out of the sludge at her. She almost backed right off the pier, her arms flailing and heels skittering on nothing at its edge. Another plop announced the emergence of a similar horror behind her. Crouching to regain her balance, Donna whipped out Seventy-one and slashed around her desperately, shuddering every time the spinning teeth tore through soft, yielding flesh. A severed tendril flopped against her arm, and its very contact raised welts on the skin and instantly made the limb go numb. Donna threw caution to the wind and ran along the pier to escape, and in doing so she missed seeing the third attacker until it was too late.

Tendrils lashed at her face, catching in her hair as she ducked away. She was brutally dragged down to the pier and almost over the edge, her face numbing as tendrils brushed against it. She couldn't see, her sword arm felt like a solid lump of ceramite, and the grip on her long dreadlocks tenaciously dragged her towards the viscid sludge. In desperation she ripped out her plasma pistol, pointed it over the edge and pulled the trigger. There was a heart-stopping fraction of a second delay, and then a tiny part of the sun touched the sludge pits. Raw sludge flashed into geysers of superheated steam where it struck and flames raced away over the surface. In seconds the flames had reached the limits of the cistern and lapped hungrily at its edges. Whatever had a hold of Donna let go and she crawled away along the pier with her sight dimming from the potent toxins in her face and arm.

She could sense light and heat from the burning cistern. She could also feel it becoming more intense as the fire spread. Thick, choking smoke billowed around her, filling her lungs until it felt like they were coated with black soot. She crawled on, dragging her paralysed arm with Seventy-One dangling uselessly from it. For a terrifying eternity her world shrank to encompass only the rough surface of the pier and her inching painfully along it. About a couple of millennia later she felt herself tumbling over an incline. By that time all Donna could do was flail feebly as she rolled over. She hit bottom and blacked out.

THE RATS, THEIR patience rewarded at last, trotted down to the supine form at the bottom of the slope. Jaws twitched and drooled at the prospect of sinking fangs into firm white flesh. Donna lay paralysed and could do nothing as the pack closed in around her. They were led by a scorched and blackened skeletal horror with bony horns on its head. With malicious deliberation, they started gnawing on her arm and face.

Rats! Donna's first conscious thought brought her sharply awake. She started up violently and fell back down coughing and retching. A burning sensation like pins and needles times a million coursed through her arm and face. She cursed and slapped at them to get the circulation going while she glared around for her tormentors. Outside of her fever-dream there were no rats to be seen, just a bare incline behind her that led up to the sludge pits. She must have crawled to the edge and rolled down before losing consciousness.

Donna had no way to know how long she had been out but the air was acrid with smoke and she could make out wavering patches of orange illumination smearing the clouds at the top of the slope. That indicated some of the pits were still burning, presumably not too much time had passed. She picked herself up more cautiously this time and bent slowly to scoop up Seventy-one and her plasma pistol from where they had fallen. The Pig was down to a quarter change; she must have pulled back on the trigger way too hard back there. She was lucky it hadn't overheated and taken her hand off.

Whatever horror was in the sludge had either burned on the surface or had been driven to the bottom.

Donna would wager good credit on the fact it couldn't come after her or she would already be dead. She limped slowly away from the pits, her arm and face burning, every part of her body feeling scraped and bruised. She wanted nothing more than to lie down and rest, but instead she kept going and made a mental note to shoot the next rat she saw for all the trouble the little frikkers were causing.

There had been no revenge killings on her part by the time she reached the back wall. The air was a little cleaner here, but not much as the fires were still burning. Blinking through the smoky haze, Donna felt a moment of heart-crushing defeat as she saw the wall was unbroken along its entire length. There was no way through. The stories were wrong and she was as good as dead. She shook her head to get a grip on the gibbering panic that was rising inside her and looked again, paying more attention to the smoke. It was definitely swirling away from the wall in some places. The fires were drawing air into the pits from an adjacent space, and if air could move there was presumably a way through.

She found an old service crawlway after a dozen steps but it was mostly blocked off by debris so she kept looking. She found an identical crawl space ten steps further along and hauled herself into it. It was a tight squeeze, making her wonder just how big maintenance workers had been back then. Donna didn't really care as the cleaner air was sweet and, most important of all, a way out of the thrice-damned sludge pits.

DONNA DROPPED OUT of the crawlway and into the generatoria dome. Her legs were shaking with exhaustion but she was so far from being in a safe place to rest it wasn't even funny. After the pits, the generatoria dome seemed majestic and cathedral-like. Building-sized reactor stacks reached upward before splitting into branched conduits like so many giant candelabra, their sweeping ironwork arches lit by beams of sodium-yellow light as they ran off out of sight hundreds of metres above. Dark specks floated through the saffron shafts like so many dust motes, probably flocks of carrion bats out looking for a meal. At least some of the generators were still working; Donna could feel vibration through the floor and see the occasional jewel-like blinking among the branches. It was frustrating to be in the presence of so much coursing energy and be unable to use it, but Donna stuck to the dome wall for good reason.

In ages past there had been a time of crisis above as desperate power shortages plagued the ever-growing Hive City. Desperate decisions had been made and some heroic team of engineers had descended to the old generatoria dome to reactivate as many generators as possible. It was a Herculean effort marred by frequent accidents and Underhiver scav-raids making off with equipment, tools and materials at any opportunity. At the end of it all, the techs had left an enduring gesture to their hosts by rigging the casings of the reactors (and just about anything else nearby) so that they ran with live power. Donna could see that each stack was surrounded by its own drift of burned scraps and blackened bones left by over-ambitious power tappers, incautious vermin and ignorant green hivers.

She tried to stay off any areas of metal, whether it be grill-like floor plates, protruding supports or even just where cracked rockrete exposed its reinforcing internal mesh of rods. When there was metal unavoidably in her path she threw bits of scrap at it to see if they raised a spark. She was paying such close attention to her feet that she didn't even notice the little holestead in the dome wall until she was almost parallel with it.

A narrow door had been crammed into a crack in the wall; a crude thing of scavenged plates welded together. The rubble floor in front of it was beaten flat and devoid of cover for several metres, and there were a couple of slime-trenches close to the entry. She was cautious, despite her bone-weariness, since holesteaders were an ornery bunch. They had to be to try and make a living beyond the comparative safety of the settlements. As such they were as likely to shoot at strangers as welcome them, which was not surprising given most gangers viewed any holestead as a potential source of income in exchange for their dubious brand of 'protection'.

Donna warily approached the door. She drew her laspistol but held it loosely at her side – it was good manners and good sense to show that you were armed and prepared to shoot in the Underhive, if only to show that at least you weren't a liability. Close up she could see the door was hanging slightly ajar and dark handprints marked the jamb. Not a good sign. She raised her pistol and drew Seventy-one with her other hand (still tingling, dammit!), hooking the door fully open with it.

A short entryway led straight into the living area. The holesteaders had widened this part of the crack and dug out sleeping niches but it was still barely more than a corridor. Plastic sheeting hung down separating the living area from another half-dug chamber at the back. There was blood everywhere. There were drag-stains on the floor, handprints on the wall, and arterial spray patterns looped chaotically about the room. Furniture and belongings had been scattered around in some kind of struggle: broken plates, a shattered pict, a child's rag doll that made Donna shudder internally for its owner. Judging by the sleeping niches at least four people had lived here, but there was no sign of any of them.

Some horrible tragedy had occurred at this holestead, and it was all the more mysterious as the door could only be opened from the inside and hadn't been forced as Donna had first assumed. On the bright side their fuel rod was still burning; the wan yellow lights glimmered as she moved through the hole, and there was a humming power outlet near the door. Without hesitation she snapped out the Pig's power pack and slotted it into the outlet. Grisly as the place was, it was the closest to safety Donna had seen in a while. She closed the door and locked it before selecting a sleeping niche and dropping into fitful slumber, her pistol at the ready and internal alarms set on a hair trigger.

DONNA WAS HOURS from the holestead and almost out of the generatoria dome when she noticed she was being followed. She was watching yet another flock of carrion bats circling over one of the stacks, indicating that they were waiting for something to die. She suddenly sensed movement on the ground. A small group – three of four figures – moved together and slowly followed the route she had taken. Even at this distance she could tell they were not gang fighters; they shuffled along too hesitantly and bunched up all the time.

The exit from the generatoria dome was up a series of switchback ramps of compacted rubble. The group trailing her would have her in a tight spot on the ramps. There was no cover and nowhere to go except up or down. Donna decided to hide and get a look at whoever they were from closer up, and then she would decide whether to just let them pass or deal with them.

She hunched behind a tumble of fallen rockrete and waited… And waited. An interminable time later she heard feet scrunching through the dirt, drawing gradually closer. Donna's patience was already shot, and impulsively she decided to confront them and have done with it. She bounded out behind them, sword and pistol at the ready, and hissed, 'Freeze or you're dead.'

The words had barely left her lips before she realised she had made a mistake. They were already dead.

Two men, a woman, and a little girl stood raggedly before her. Donna immediately reckoned that they were the missing holesteaders. Horrible wounds marked all of them: torn throats, hanging intestines, flapping skin, glistening bone, missing eyes. They were plague zombies.

Even in the Spire Donna had heard stories of the fearful neuron plague that periodically swept the hives of Necromunda with a liberal dose of anarchy and chaos. It destroyed the victim's higher mental functions while leaving intact, or even intensifying, activity in the hindbrain. The result was a creature always hungry for flesh and incapable of feeling pain.

Every time the afflicted pulled down another victim they infected it and added a new member to their ranks. At their peak the zombie plagues touched even the Spire, choking the promenades and boulevards with heaving crowds of restless, ravening dead. Once in the Underhive, Donna had learned that the plague had never really gone away at all, it just lay dormant in the darkness below and contented itself with taking odd victims here and there until it rose again in full force.

Donna felt sick with fear. She had slept in the plague-struck holestead so she might be infected already. Failing that, the zombies could inflict it with so much as a scratch of their ragged, filth-encrusted claws. She caught sight of the little girl's face, miraculously intact but with slack, drooling lips and cloudy eyes. Something snapped inside Donna's mind, an old familiar break that came when some part of her own hindbrain said 'no more'. She saw red and the fight that followed became a stop-motion flick book of carnage from her perspective.

Two shots as she charged, one body down with limbs flailing. A backhand cut from Seventy-one sliced through the top of a skull like a knife through an egg. Another cut lopped off a reaching claw. A point-blank las-shot fired into an empty eye socket. A zombie tripped on its own entrails. A decapitation. Hacking, hacking, hacking at the dead little girl until she finally stopped writhing.

Mad Donna came to herself sitting, weeping, with her weapons dangling in her hands. The dismembered bodies of the holesteaders lay nearby in a pathetic heap. They had barely even had a chance to move from the spot where she had confronted them. Donna drew a shaky hand over her face to wipe away hot tears and stood abruptly. She would check herself for wounds later; right now she had to get out of this place. The least she could do was return the holesteaders the favour of her use of their power outlet and sleeping niche. Sheathing her other weapons and pulling out the Pig, she lavished the power she had looted from them on their funeral pyre.

'Among the noble houses of the hive spires of Necromunda the bond of blood is everything. Powerful, avaricious men have schemed and fought quiet but vicious battles on Necromunda for a hundred centuries and more to gain ascension to noble status. They know no bond of deed or word will pass the test of generations among themselves – naked ambition will always prevail. They know no riches can secure men's loyalty either – for what has been bought once can always be bought again. And most of all they know that nothing can supplant the power of the family, the age-old genetic bond of blood. The responsibility of an offspring to house and to family is taught from the cradle, even from the womb. Maintaining the bloodline means careful breeding, so the ever-spiralling politics of necessity weave a delicate dance through balls, banquets and engagements to the lofty bedchambers of the noble houses.

'The myriad social niceties of the Spire serve to disguise a sharp-toothed survival instinct.'

Excerpt from: *Xonariarius the Younger's Nobilite Pax Imperator – The Triumph of Aristocracy over Democracy*.

* * *

SHE REMEMBERED HER *mother best of all: breathtakingly beautiful despite two centuries of anti-agathics and restorative surgery, willowy and graceful despite bearing over two-dozen noble offspring of House Ulanti. She had been a proud and distant goddess, seen only occasionally by D'onne and her sisters when they were young, but beloved by all. Each of them aspired to have her stunning looks and queenly presence when they grew up. They all vied for her attention with the pictures, songs, acrobatics, dancing and recitals they worked feverishly to perfect as her visiting day came closer. As the youngest and the prettiest, D'onne had always known that her mother liked her the best.*

She remembered her and her eleven sisters having their portrait painted by a famed artist with a strange, off-world accent – Bruphoros? Burfis? She couldn't recall the name now, and had been too young to pronounce it properly then. They had spent interminable hours sitting primly in elegant chairs in the great gallery, chafing in their formal gowns while the artist moved them fractionally back and forth and fussed endlessly over ambient light or composition. It was an especially good memory because it was the last time she remembered all of her sisters being together at the same time.

She had complained precociously to the artist that spending hours painting was stupid if you could take a pict in an instant. Instead of being angry, he had stopped fussing for a while to explain to her that the true value of something was in direct proportion to the effort put into it. A pict might have sufficed for any normal hiver, but the Noble House of Ulanti deserved better than that. Indeed, it deserved only the best even if it took a little longer. The artist had made her feel very special and from then on she had made an effort not to fidget and to give him her prettiest smile.

Then there was the time an Ulanti hunt had returned in triumph from Hive Bottom. At the time, the Underhive was a home to the worst bogeymen and monsters for D'onne. Its name was invoked only in spooky stories and dreadful admonishments from harried nursemaids. The very idea that someone would descend from the Spire to fight the hideous mutants and outlaws below seemed fantastic to her. The hunters had come up from The Wall in procession, showered with blossoms and heralded by clarions every step of the way. D'onne had squeezed herself to the front of the crowd of well-wishers that met them on the steps of the grand manse to get a good look at the conquering heroes.

There were three men and a woman, all lesser cousins but now lionised by the household for their bravery in the face of the semi-mythical perils of Underhive. Their off-world hunting rigs were darkly magnificent suits of baroque armour, each one entirely different to the others. The hulking silvered form of an Orrus-rig contrasted completely with the spindly obsidian insect-limbs of a Malcadon. Another wore a Yeld-rig with its glittering bladed wings proudly swept back like a cloak of knives.

But the one that had caught her attention the most had been the woman in Jakara armour with her mirror shield and molecular blade. She was small and lithe, stepping lightly with the easy grace of a predatory cat. She had caught little D'onne's wide-eyed gaze as she mounted the steps and winked at her, and it seemed as if she was saying, 'See, noble daughters can be just as strong as noble sons.' They had played spyrers and scavvies for weeks after the hunt returned, and D'onne had always held out to be the Jakara.

Her most favourite place in the Spire had always been the arboretum. It was a marvel of a much earlier time, beyond the skill of anyone to recreate in this day and age. The first time she had been taken there it felt like she was stepping into another world. All her life had been spent among the sterile, high-arched halls of the Ulanti district where living things were confined in beds and borders, planters and terrace gardens. Many of the plants she had seen were cunning artifices of metal spun to take their form, some so finely made that they grew, blossomed brazen flowers, and then withered away again to rust.

The arboretum was different. Everything there was organic and the very air itself seemed vibrant because of it. There were towering trees and meadows of long grass, and bushes and thickets of heady-scented blossoms with colourful insects and birds fluttering between them. Semi-wild animals had grazed shyly among the shadowed trunks, and bright-eyed simians leapt joyously between the overhanging boughs.

Better than that, the arboretum formed a great torus over multiple levels of the Inner Spire. By some great cunning artifice, each quadrant of the torus was at a different point of growth. In one quadrant the trees had bare, leafless branches, and the ground was covered in white powder like ash, but made up (so she was told) of frozen water vapour. In another, the growth was fresh and green with new shoots unfolding and baby animals everywhere. In the next all was ripened and fulsome, lazily dreaming beneath warm sunlight from the skylights above. In the last the leaves were withering in a fantastic display of reds, oranges and browns, the fallen ones forming a scrunching carpet everywhere. This changing landscape slowly rotated through the year; each part of the arboretum undergoing the cycle of death and rebirth.

Her tutors had told her that this incredible ecosystem was the way of it on many worlds. There were often seasons which changed the environment completely through the year. Not so in the great hives of Mankind, they had said. Here man had brought nature to heel entirely and was troubled by the seasons not at all. It seemed a great *shame to her at the time, and as she was to find out later, it was not entirely true.*

3: DUST FALLS

IN AGES PAST a trickle of waste seeped down from Hive City into an abandoned dome. In time the trickle grew to become a torrent and collapsed the roof, burying the floor below in sediment. Eventually, further erosion of the dome's floor caused it to collapse as well, and the accumulated debris plunged into another, older dome beneath.

Year after year the flow of effluent grew, carrying detritus further down and wearing away a whole series of domes. At its height there were roaring falls of multi-hued effluent that disappeared down a gaping chasm into the deepest levels of the hive.

By Donna's day the flow had dried up but for a thin trickle of dust cascading from above. In its place, there was the shaft itself, plunging through the Underhive to the darkness of the Hive Bottom. This was the Abyss; a mile-deep hole that pierces dome after dome in the path of the old effluent falls.

Perched on the edge of the Abyss was Dust Falls, a large settlement from which ambitious gangs took the steep path down into the depths of the hive. The trail led to the Hive Bottom itself, and to the lake of pollutants and chemical slime at its base. And at the bottom, Down Town, the furthest reach of what could be called civilization. The toxic crush zones of the Abyss held great riches for those strong and brave enough to win them: spider mares, stinger mould, veins of precious alloy, archeotech, spook, the rare pelts of elusive mutant breeds. They held death too – death in abundance.

Donna watched Dust Falls for a long time before even thinking about making her move. She wanted to know which gangs were in town, whether any guilder caravans were passing through, whether any Redemptionists were haranguing the locals; anything that might make a difference to her plans. She had hoisted herself into the crumbling upper floors of a half-ruined hab that slouched at the edge of the dome. She had felt no onset of fever from the plague, nor found any injuries caused in the fight with the plague zombies. Still, every twinge or ache seemed like a death spasm when viewed through the lens of a potential onset of plague.

She had a pretty good view of Dust Falls half a kilometre away with the yawning pit of the Abyss seemingly poised to swallow it beyond. Buildings tumbled by the floods centuries ago dotted the edge of the dome, getting lower and finally petering out to rounded-off heaps around the Abyss. The settlement was surrounded by a high stockade with narrow, twisting streets between shanty buildings visible inside. There was only one building that stood out among the others: a three-storey, worn-looking oblong of plasteel that stood at the centre. That was Donna's target.

Everything seemed quiet enough. If anything, it was too quiet. There was hardly anyone on the streets but many up on the gates and stamping along the stockades in between. Lots of lights too, everything from fuel-drum fires to halogen floods. Donna waited and watched, and eventually she saw what she was looking for; a flicker of movement in the rubble beyond the light. Donna didn't try to look for the source, she just watched the area and waited for her eye to pick up movement again. There, two more shapes moving. They looked like tumbling scraps of cloth but the distance was deceptive. Donna upped the magnification in her bionic eye a notch and the blurs sprang into sharp focus.

Donna's full lip curled unconsciously. Scavvies – the very dregs of humanity. No, scratch that; scavvies were so devolved and twisted that they didn't even qualify as human any more. Their sallow flesh and ugly appearance showed all too clearly despite the filth-encrusted rags swathed around them. The ones she could see were armed with a crude assortment of flintlocks, hooks and rusty axes. Now that she was looking in the right area, Donna could see at least a dozen of them crawling like grey lice towards one of the settlement's gates. She watched events unfold with interest.

They were spotted maybe fifty metres out, las-shots suddenly spurting around them like bright rain. Some of the scavvies raised their long muskets and started firing back, but most jumped up and ran (or limped, or hobbled in many cases) towards the gate. Donna was taken aback to see there were more than twenty rushing to attack, they popped up so suddenly it seemed like a magician's trick.

She saw them windmilling their arms and it took her a second to realise they were throwing bombs at the gate. A couple exploded but most burst into clouds of noxious-looking vapour. Several scavvies were down and writhing by this time, or deathly still, but the gate defenders were driven back by the vapour and their firing slackened appreciably.

The fiery stab of autoguns among the scattered flintlock volleys momentarily distracted Donna. When she focused back on the gate, the scavvies were smashing at it with hammers and axes. A heavy stub gun fired from the parapet off to one side of the gate, its angry stutter ripping a bloody tear through the packed mass. It was followed by the vicious crump of a frag grenade going off. Rags and bits of scav flew in all directions. The survivors broke away before the smoke cleared. Las-rounds plugged a few more scavvies as they limped for cover, leaving perhaps a dozen torn bodies strewn around the gate in mute testimony to the ferocity of the brief skirmish.

Checking carefully around the other gates and parts of the stockade, Donna spotted at least a dozen more scavvy bodies alone or in clusters. For scavvies that showed almost unthinkable determination, or else they were present in disturbingly large numbers. Scavvies ambushed, raided holesteads, set toll-blocks or, if they felt especially brave and numerous, camped outside a settlement and demanded a 'tax' of anything going in and out until they were driven off or left of their own accord. There was a standing bounty on scavvies, although it was so paltry only the most hard luck cases went out looking for them. If scavvies had got it into their heads to start rushing a well-armed settlement like Dust Falls, something was seriously awry.

The situation posed a completely different set of problems to those Donna had anticipated. It was going to be ten times harder to get past the stockade while it was so heavily manned, so she decided that slipping through the streets without being recognised would be a lot easier. Also, bright lights were all well and good, but men with their eyes adjusted to watching lit areas often missed what was in the shadows. The scavvies were a double-edged sword: they might catch her outside the settlement, then cook and eat her, or they might provide the ideal distraction for getting inside.

Donna picked out a route to a hollow in the rubble midway between two of the gates and about sixty metres from the stockade on a section covered by floodlights. Fixing it in her mind's eye, she slid down from her eerie and set off quickly through the ruins feeling unaccountably optimistic. As the cover got lower she had to crouch and then slither on her belly through gravel and rounded-off pebbles that lay thick on the floor of the dome. She kept a sharp lookout for scavvies, using her nose as well as her eyes and ears. The rank stench of scavvies was unmistakeable, and there was a stiff breeze swirling up from the Abyss.

After crawling for a while she came across a slight depression scooped out just deep enough so that a prone body inside it would be invisible from the stockade. The shallow trench wound away through the rubble in the direction of the settlement. She wriggled along the little rat run and found it branched and then branched again. She was grateful for the cover from the stockade but the thought of crawling into some pack of scavvies lying in wait made her nape hairs rise. She reckoned it was still five or six metres to the hollow when she almost tumbled into it, kicking free a scatter of gravel as she swung herself precipitously over its lip and into shelter. She quickly discovered she was not alone.

A rag-wrapped form was turning towards her, close enough to touch and possessed of a stench that made Donna's eye water. She caught sight of its lumpen face, one eye closed by sprouting tumours, the other comically bulging in surprise as it saw she wasn't a fellow scavvy. Its slack-lipped mouth dropped open to show black, rotted teeth as it drew breath to yell for help.

Donna rammed her fist into the wet orifice, muffling its cry with some extra broken teeth and slamming its head against the rubble for good measure. It made a grab for a knife but she pinned its arms with her knees before smashing it in the head with a handy rock. The scrawny form bucked violently and almost threw her off. An adrenalin surge made her muscles bunch furiously as she silently smashed the rock into its head again and again. It cracked open with a wet splotching sound and the scavvy spasmed feebly once more before lying still.

Donna looked up and listened intently, trying to determine if the struggle had been overheard. Gravel scraped nearby – something was crawling closer! She rolled the hot, foetid corpse of the scavvy on top of her, pulling its rags over the crushed head that was now leaking a slow ooze of blood and brains across her cheek and shoulder. She saw the dim blur of a face poking over the edge of the hollow.

'Shh't K'pidahn stooped,' a hoarse voice whispered. 'U gedersal' kilt.'

The voice stopped in mid-whine and Donna heard it snuffle a couple of times – the sound of mucus rattling in its nostrils. 'Thass blut,' it muttered incredulously. She was equally amazed it could smell anything over the foul stench, but apparently it could. She clutched for a throwing blade at her waist but the dead weight of the corpse impeded her. The scavvy must have seen movement because it raised itself up at the lip for a better look and was momentarily silhouetted by the floodlights on the stockade. It was a stockier creature than the last one and it had a crude but functional-looking autopistol clutched in its fist.

Donna froze and watched in fascination as a bright little bead of red light suddenly appeared on the scavvie's head. The red bead wobbled there for a moment steadied. There was a flash and the head exploded sideways in a crimson spray. A split-second later the hiss-crack sound of a long las-shot came from the direction of the stockade. The overly inquisitive mutant throwback dropped as if it had been pole-axed. Donna muttered a little prayer of thanks to her unknown and unknowing guardian. She carefully moved as far as possible down the hollow from the two stinking carcasses and settled to wait, keeping her head down out of respect for the unseen sharpshooter.

DONNA CAME ALERT to the sound of the first shot. How long had it been? An hour maybe? She had rested and now listened to the rattles and scrapes of the scavvies creeping towards the gates again. It sounded like they were mostly massing to her right, between her and the Abyss. Evidently the sight of a sniper-shot body lying in the open had persuaded the others to try different routes. At any rate she was undisturbed in her hiding place. Hoarse shouts and more shots sounded out but she waited until she heard the returning hiss-crack of las-fire before poking her head up.

Same story, different angle. A hoard of the stupider, lesser-armed scavvies charged at the gate to draw fire while the smarter ones hung back and sniped. Now Donna had to work fast. She turned her attention to the floodlights nearest her on the stockade and shot out a couple rounds before ducking back down. She crawled along a little from the spot where she'd fired and then scrambled over the lip into a half crouch. All attention was on the gate and shots buzzed angrily back and forth punctuated by screams. Her little contribution had gone unnoticed. Donna was up and running towards the patch of darkness she'd created even as the first grenades exploding by the gate indicated the fight was getting serious.

Now it was all down to luck. Luck that some gun-scum on the stockade didn't send a barrage of shots her way. Luck that she didn't hit some booby trap or deadfall. Luck that the scavvies didn't spot her and shoot her in the back.

But she had loaded the dice. Darkness and chaos were on her side. Even if anyone saw her she was just one running figure; a waste of ammo when there was a fire-fight going on. Her bionic's thermal vision didn't pick out any tripwires or pressure plates, but then she saw a trench at the base of the stockade at the last second. Wire weed confined inside it thrashed ineffectually as she leapt across. She caught a support girder and flipped an effortless somersault onto the rampart above. She didn't register anyone close by but she didn't stop to look. Mad Donna's boot heels had barely rung on the grille of the walkway before she darted off into Dust Falls.

Dust Falls was usually one the liveliest settlements in the Underhive, full of the very best readying themselves for a trip into the Abyss and survivors who have come back to celebrate their success and new-found wealth. Not many came back at all, of course, but that made the plaudits all the louder for those who did – everyone loved a winner.

Now the streets were quiet. Throughout the jigsaw puzzle of sheet-built huts and plastic shelters that made up Dust Falls, doorways were shuttered and window meshes were down. Stray chinks of light showed here and there but otherwise the only illumination was from the stockade, the lurid lanterns of a couple of slop shops and the cold, bright floods surrounding the Dust Falls Administratia. Calling it a civic office was a bit grandiose; in truth it was an old bulk-shipping container that had been swept down from frik-knows-where during the floods. But, with some floors welded into it, and some doors and windows cut in the sides with a generator installed, it was a veritable mansion by Underhive standards. It served as city hall, courthouse, jail, armoury, safe storage and citadel for all that passed as authority at the top of the Abyss.

Normally the area around the old container would be thick with buyers, beggars, traders, hawkers and gawkers, but the scavvy problem had pushed them all indoors. There were a couple of bored-looking guards on a gantry around the second storey and that was it. Donna waited until they had paced out of sight before gliding over to a little-used hatchway in one corner. The hatch was one of the originals and gave access to an internal crawlspace intended for checking cargo distribution levels inside the container. A single-minded machine spirit still faithfully kept the hatch sealed, the one purpose in its long half-life was to deny access to anyone who didn't input the right clearance code.

What few in the Underhive would appreciate was that once, before its long plunge below, the container had belonged to House Orlock. House Orlock was famed for many things in Hive Primus; primarily it was known as the House of Iron whose miners supplied much of the other Houses' ferrous metal requirements. Only slightly less well known was their bold and aggressive seizure of the fantastically lucrative Ulanti contract from House Delaque, an action which started a bitter vendetta between the two houses that raged on to this day.

Donna removed her glove and pressed her thumb against the reader. Scanning for a geneprint, the machine spirit correctly matched it against one of the many potential overrides to its encryption protocols. It was an Ulanti privilege. An icon flashed green and the hatch obligingly popped open. If it had been given a voice, the machine spirit would have simpered. With a cynical chuckle on her full lips, Donna slipped inside.

Inside, the container's remodelling had turned the crawlspace into a narrow stair running up all three levels. The internal volume of the container was blocked off with walls, floors and ceilings of a variety of materials. Many areas were simple cages to cut down on their weight, others were more substantial office-like blocks of flak-board and cement.

As she crept up the stairway, Donna could see shadows moving and caught snatches of conversations that indicated a number of people were around and involved in eating, sleeping, tending the injured or repairing weapons. She stopped bothering to sneak; it was only going to make her stand out more. She walked blithely into the second storey entry of an ugly looking block with bars on the windows, acting as if she had every right to be there.

Once inside she travelled down a short corridor with two doors off it before coming to a stairwell at the end. She tried the door on the left and found it open. Slipping inside, she found a darkened office with worn furniture covered in teetering piles of parchment. A brass-framed baseline cogitator burbled quietly in one corner, its bone keys ticking out a slow rhythm. Hearing footsteps coming up the stairs and voices in the corridor, Donna stepped smartly behind the door as they stopped outside.

'Yes, and the fact remains that there's nothing that can be done while we're besieged, warrant or not. She's not going to show up here anyway.' This in a tired-sounding baritone.

'You can at least post warrant fliers, Hanno. As chief watchman I'd have thought that was your job,' a sneering whisper replied.

The first voice turned cold. 'I'll not dance to your tune, Bak. I've got bigger fish to fry as you well know. If you want some help, go down to the slop shops. There's plenty enough gun-scum there too precious of their hides to risk them on the rampart. Go form a purge if you want. You can start right outside the gate.'

'Shallej will hear of this!'

'Well, tell him he can come right down and we'll discuss it man to man if you like. No? Then you better get going. I'd offer you a drink but I don't really like you, so get lost.'

Footsteps retreated, the door opened and a man came in, dropping a heavy-framed pump shotgun on the desk. He rubbed a hand over close-shaved grey hair and massaged his thickly muscled neck before reaching for a bottle on the desk. The hand had a blocky, black Aquila tattoo on the back of it, and a number.

'Same old sins, Hanno? I'm disappointed in you,' Donna said in her most seductive tones.

Hanno dropped the bottle and half-whirled around, grabbed for the bottle in mid-air, caught it, juggled it and finally caught it again after slopping some. He glared at her.

'Damn it, harlot, you almost cost me the last liquor this side of Slag Town.'

Mad Donna laughed out loud for the first time in days. 'I need your help, and it sounds like Kell has rather nicely just filled you in on the details of why.'

His hand was on the butt of his well-oiled bolt pistol. 'You've got some nerve coming here.' Hanno sounded angry. 'It's my sworn duty to protect Dust Falls from people like you and Bak: outlaws, bounty hunters and anyone else who thinks they can shoot the place up or settle a score here and breach the peace. Well, not on my watch.'

A bolt pistol was great for a fire-fight but was a liability in a fast draw where its heavy magazine made it difficult to pull cleanly in a hurry. Really slick operators learned to overcome this by hip firing – simply angling the pistol in its holster to let off a first round before drawing the gun. You could spot practitioners by the way they strapped their gun high on the hip with an open-toed holster. Well, practitioners and posers anyway. Hanno strapped his bolt pistol high on the hip, and he wasn't a poser.

'Hanno, if you point that hand cannon at me, I'll have to take it off you. You know you wouldn't like that.' Donna shifted slightly and there was an almost palpable aura of menace in the movement.

Hanno froze and then relaxed his grip slightly. 'I can't have you running around in Dust Falls right now,' he said, his voice calming to stern disapproval. 'Not now.'

'Yes, I met the new neighbours on the way in. I can't say I like them much.'

'If you were sneaking around on your own out there you're lucky to be alive. So far we've had to listen to them skinning and cooking four men who thought they were savvy enough to sneak out.' Hanno shook his head and took a pull at the amasec. 'Some people are born stupid and they die stupid.'

'I can look after myself.'

Hanno put the bottle down, realising it gave away the fact that his hands were shaking. He asked her bluntly, 'What will it take to get you out of here? You know that by rights I have to report your presence to the bounty hunters, unless you're prepared to kill me to keep quiet.'

'Don't think I haven't considered it, especially 'cause I heard you talking to Kell Bak. When the hell did that bastard show up anyway? I nearly broke a nail myself getting here this fast.'

'Just over two shifts ago he came in with a couple of ratskin scouts. The word is they set out from Glory Hole with two pack slaves as well, but they didn't make it through. Knowing Kell he probably sold them to the scavvies.'

'They didn't try to stop him getting in?'

'They let any extra warm bodies in – more mouths to feed, see. They just don't let anybody out.' He looked at Donna, seeing her as if for the first time. 'Throne, you're a mess. You look like you've been dipped in the sump. Is that blood?'

'Some of it, not mine. And brains, also not mine. And a lot of stings too, which are mine and I wish they weren't.' She tilted her head coquettishly. 'Forgive me for not bathing acceptably before presenting myself, noblesir Hanno, but I was breathless to be by your side.'

Hanno pulled a sour face and was about to retort but he refused to be baited. 'Why are you here, Donna?'

'I need to take a quick peek at your guilder manifests.'

Incredulity cracked Hanno's shaky self-control like breaking glass. 'I knew it. Like there isn't enough trouble here, you want me to make more by letting you assault the guilders.'

'Look Hanno, all I know is that a guilder contacted me in Glory Hole and arranged a meet. When I got there I found Kell and Shallej waiting to jump me.' A slight distortion of the truth, but it would have to do. 'I hightailed it over here as fast as I could because, after Two Tunnels, this is the best place in the Underhive for checking up on guilders.'

Two Tunnels was a sprawling settlement at the bottom of the most well-trodden paths down from Hive City. At some point the wares of most guilders passed through there on their way up or down. Dust Falls occupied a similar position in relation to the Abyss; any guilder caravans moving up or down it came through there. Sump Lake and its surrounding strata of compacted scrap held some of the richest prizes to be found in the Hive Bottom, so much so that even though it remained almost completely uncharted and extremely dangerous (even by Underhive standards), no guilder could stay away from it for long.

'You're an outlaw D'onne. You chose to walk that path. Bounty hunters will come after you wherever you go.' Hanno was consciously trying to reassert his control of the situation. He obviously didn't like this talk of guilders one bit.

'Frik you, Hanno. That pompous crap isn't true and you know it. You're just hiding behind a watchman's badge. Even when daddy dearest had the whole of the Underhive posted with my name and face the guilders stayed out of it. They never get involved in family feuds. It's like a rule to them.'

Hanno was looking stubbornly determined. He laid his hand back on the butt of his pistol. 'No dice, Donna. I'm taking you in this time. Your personal vendettas will just have to wait.'

THE OUTER GATE rolled back smoothly, and warm, foetid air washed in. D'onne almost fainted. It was like the worst body odour she had ever smelled multiplied by a million, but also suffused with streaks of sulphur, machine oil, faeces, smoke, plus a hundred other obnoxious taints.

She remembered the filter plugs Lars had given her and suffered the indignity of shoving the soft little cylinders into her nostrils. The discomfort of wearing them was definitely worth it. At least D'onne now felt she could breathe in without gagging, as long as she kept her mouth closed.

Outside the gate it was hazy, and a dull mist crawled over an iron walkway leading to a road lit by the yellow glow of overhead lamps. It was hard to focus her eyes with the flashes of memory that kept replaying in her mind: the sprawled bodies, the Count...

She swayed and almost fell. A figure stepped out onto the walkway, the sinister black silhouette seeming to tower above D'onne.

'Nobledam, are you all right?' A voice crackled from a vox-speaker mounted in the figure's armoured chest. Its helmeted head turned suspiciously from side to side as if looking for an assailant.

'No, I-I am perfectly well,' she hazarded a guess, 'enforcer.' Opening her mouth to speak allowed the foul vapours to rush in once more and she stifled a cough at the noxious taste.

'You have no entourage, nobledam?' The flat effect of the vox rendered the speaker emotionless, but to D'onne's etiquette-trained ears, the cadence of the words relayed a level of surprise verging on incredulity.

She shook her head. 'KindlydirectmetoHouseEscher,' she rushed out in one breath before clamping her mouth shut again.

The figure stopped and regarded her for a moment, as if truly seeing her for the first time.

'House Escher?'

She nodded imperiously in response, determined not to let any more of the stench into her mouth.

'Please wait one moment.'

The figure stepped back out of view and she heard a clipped snarl of comm-link vox chatter go back and forth. The seeds of doubt in D'onne's guts started to take root in earnest. She was never going to get away with this. Imagine that she could just walk out of the Spire and no one would stop her! After what she had done every enforcer in Hive Primus was probably looking for her by now.

The enforcer reappeared carrying quite the biggest gun D'onne had ever seen. Her shoulders slumped in defeat as she looked at the man blocking her way to freedom. He was alert, armed, and just about fully armoured head to foot with smooth black plates of ceramite, including a full helmet. D'onne fancied she could just about see his chin and make out where his eyes should be beneath the tinted visor. The pistol tucked into the small of her back felt icy cold against her flesh.

The enforcer turned his back to D'onne and started clumping along the walkway.

'This way, nobledam. I have permission to accompany you as far as House Escher territory.'

D'onne blinked as the mists tried to swallow up the figure of the enforcer and then after a moment's indecision she hurried after him. For whatever reason the enforcers weren't all over Hive Primus looking for her. Obviously daddy dearest was hushing things up. Not too surprising given that the enforcers amounted to being Lord Helmawr's official policing force and private army within the hive.

The planetary governor was known as a keen proponent of humbling noble houses on any possible pretext; 'cleaning house' as he had famously described it. It stemmed from an ancient political creed that the noble houses showed weakness by failing to keep order among themselves. The creed stated that the most powerful faction – that of Lord Helmawr – could and should take the opportunity to demonstrate dominance over the other bloodlines while coincidentally ensuring the matter was not resolved to anyone's lasting satisfaction.

How scandalous. It was a classic lever for keeping the houses off-balance, squabbling among themselves and seeking favour from the governor like lap dogs. That was something that Patriarch Sylvanus of House Ulanti would find unbearable. Centuries of his life's work could be swept away within a decade by one wayward child. His child, that was. D'onne Ulanti.

She reached the roadway thinking of the enforcer as protection instead of a threat. Enforcer armour was sculpted to make its wearer look threatening and impersonal, from the wide shoulder plates to the heavy boots. But as D'onne stood looking at the man, she also realised that it was subtly designed to show there was a man within it. The lower face was visible and, although he had heavy gauntlets threaded in his weapon belt, the enforcer's hands were bare and stark against the black metal of the gun. He had a tattoo on the back of his hand that showed an abstract, triangular eagle gripping a number in its talons.

The enforcer seemed to catch her looking and either assumed, or pretended to assume, that she was looking at the gun.

'It's a new model eighty-nine shot cannon, nobledam,' the vox crackled flatly. 'Personally, I hold best with the old seventy-fives. They were fine pieces in their day.'

There was a pause as if the enforcer was thinking that he had forgotten himself and had spoken out of turn.

'Sadly necessary around swing shift, nobledam,' he continued gruffly. 'The proles are apt to get a little antsy as they come off the lines. I've summoned a felucca for you. It should be along presently.'

With that he obviously decided to shut the hell up. D'onne considered for a moment. He must be burning with curiosity as to why a noble woman, a mere girl really, would be going into Hive City alone. Such things were almost unprecedented. But he was constrained by the laws of obeisance not to enquire after a noble's affairs without due cause and empowerment. He was probably sticking with her to spy for Helmawr, but had a quite legitimate claim to be protecting her in Hive City, which was perfectly within his jurisprudence.

D'onne decided to use the arrival of the transportation vehicle (she presumed that was what a felucca was) as the opportunity to politely but firmly send the enforcer back to his post. Then they would see whether the man in the big armour had the balls to argue with a noble, no matter how young she looked. She decided to start laying groundwork now to better assert her dominance later.

'Whatisyourname?' she managed.

'Enforcer Hanno, nobledam.'

Ah, that was interesting. He didn't just reply 'Hanno'. He reasserted his office at the same time, as well as acknowledging and downplaying hers. It left the none-too-subtle implication in her shapely ears that no one, not even nobility, was above the law. She smiled inwardly as she imagined him practising saying it in front of a mirror every morning.

Enforcer Hanno, noblesir.

Enforcer Hanno, nobledam.

Enforcer Hanno, citizen.

Enforcer Hanno, scum.

He certainly had the timbre just right to communicate the full force of the law at his command. Still, she knew his name now and he didn't know hers. And she knew he was clever.

Oh, and she knew he was vain.

4: UNWELCOMINN

MAD DONNA AND chief watchman Hanno were facing off, eyes narrowed, hands over their guns, both ready to draw and fire in an eye blink. They were poised like statues, knowing the slightest twitch could be a prelude to an explosive gun battle at all of two metres range. With two fighters this deadly, it was guaranteed neither of them would be walking away from it.

Mad Donna spoke first, saying quietly, 'You're forgetting, Hanno, I know who really pulls your strings.'

'That's not–'

'Fair? True? Perhaps, but if the folks around here even dreamed you were in the Cult of the Redemption, you'd be as dead as Hagen.'

'The path of the Redemption is the path of salvation for us all, D'onne,' growled Hanno.

'Don't waste your dogma on me. You know I'm as irredeemable as the rest of the scum in here or out there.' Donna nodded towards the stockade outside, implying the whole of the Underhive. 'You also need every fighter you've got, otherwise those scavvies are going to be here to stay.'

Hanno's eyes flickered uncertainly at the mention of the scavvies, which was weird because someone like him shouldn't be frightened of them. Donna suddenly began to understand what was really going on in Dust Falls.

The Redemptionists were an extremist cult that believed in redemption through fire and penitence, that only through the mortal purging of sin in all its forms could man be pure enough to meet his maker. Sin took many forms, including drinking, gambling, fornication, shooting people – all the fun stuff basically. But it was the heretics, mutants and psykers that really brought out the mobs and whipped them into a fever pitch.

The Cult of the Redemption was a force to be reckoned with in Hive City. They had devotees and converts in every house, and virtually ran House Cawdor in its entirety. But in the Underhive, they were far less powerful, and their sympathisers were few and far between.

The Redemptionists came into the Underhive for only two reasons. Most settled in their own heavily armed and tight-lipped little communities to be away from the sinful temptations of Hive City or any other settlements. The others were the worst psychos, bullies and fanatics in the cult; men whose views and methods had become too extreme even for the ruthless Redemptionist hierarchs. These hardened few were sent below on 'Crusade', or given a holy mission to enter the den of corruption that is the Underhive to scourge and purge every sinner that crossed their path. Redemption crusaders persecuted mutants unmercifully, especially scavvies.

'You've been using Dust Falls as a front to arm the Crusaders, haven't you, Hanno?' He looked shocked at that. Bullseye! Donna sensed weakness and pushed harder. She held up an elegant finger and ticked items off an imaginary ledger. 'Caches of weapons buried in the Badzones, a little promethium for the flamers, some food at sympathetic holesteads, and all of it nice and handy to pick up before going down into the Abyss. I'll bet you've made their purges a lot more successful of late.'

Donna shook her head sadly.

'Scavvies aren't all that smart, but they can work out when their enemies are getting more ammo and weapons. And if they can work that out, they'll figure that you're getting them before going down the Abyss – that you're getting them from the settlement at the top!'

Hanno was defensive. 'It isn't that simple. King Redwart's been stirring up the clans, and those from outside have been yelling that he was coming with an army to burn the place. That devil Valois has been at work too. Plague zombies have been seen all the way up in the Looming Halls before the siege even started. These are evil times, D'onne.'

'Yes, there's a world of sin out there, Hanno, but you're ready to draw down on me because I've come by with an inconvenient request? Shame on you.' She was hammering unmercifully at his one big weakness – an overdeveloped sense of justice – and she knew it. Hanno was looking doubtful, which was a definite improvement over his stupidly determined face.

'Look, Hanno, just let me see the register and I'll be gone. No one needs to know I came here. When I get out of Dust Falls, and you know that I will, I'll tell the Watchmen – Throne! I'll even tell the guilders – what's going on so they can send help. You're not alone, you know. There's over five billion people just a few sewers away.'

Hanno smiled a little at the wan joke and some of the weight seemed to lift from his shoulders. 'You're right, of course. I'm acting like some medieval Baron and seeing Dust Falls as a tiny light amidst the encroaching darkness. Others will come to our aid.'

Donna laughed cynically. 'They'll come all right, if only to stop the scavvies before they get a success under their belts and become ten times as nasty.' She reached out and snagged the bottle of amasec and swigged some, savouring the slow release of tension as the stiff liquor tickled her palette. Hanno had, more than likely, left the idea of locking her up far behind and now she had become a potential ally in a time of need.

'You seem to be creaming them out there,' she observed. 'They're losing a dozen at a time rushing the gates.'

'But two or three dozen more scavvies turn up every shift, and they're chewing through our ammo faster than we can make more. I've had to limit firing to lasguns unless the scavvies are threatening to breach a gate. We've only suffered a few deaths so far, but they're starting to mount up.'

'Do you think King Redwart's coming with an army?'

'No. I think the army is already here.'

'His name is Theodus Relli?'

'That's right.'

Hanno's old cogitator rattled and ticked for a while before lines of lurid green text ghosted into being across its window.

'Here we are. Nothing came this way from him in the last six months.'

'Where does he ship from?'

Hanno spun a small cog at the side of the window and the words retreated up the glass. 'Down Town. He has a manse there registered as his shipment address, and seems to receive shipments of scrap, archeotech, stinger mould and lapweed. He also deals in weapons, ammunition, bionics, survival gear – all the usual stuff.'

'But he's done no trading of any kind up the Abyss in six months? That's weird.'

'There are some additional notes in the registry but they're locked. I'll see what I can do.'

'Want me to try?'

'Please, D'onne, remember who taught you to tickle a cogitator in the first place.' Hanno's gnarly fingers flew with surprising delicacy across the dirty bone keys of the cogitator, the eagle tattoo on his hand swooping and diving like its living counterpart.

'Isn't doing this for me a sin, too?'

'Technically, it's a sinful theft, but the guilders are self-serving agents of corruption and hence it is permissible to use any means against them, so sayeth the lore.'

'I never knew Redemptionists considered guilders the enemy. They are purveyors of moral turpitude perhaps, but not really on a level with mutants and Wyrds.'

'There were some... incidents a while back that led to the guilders outlawing all Redemptionist Crusaders. They've even posted bounties on the Arch Zealot, The Redeemer and Father Kaminski. They're complete fools. The worst fanatics now have no restraints at all and those genuinely trying to protect us are hunted men. The guilders made a mistake aligning themselves against the righteous.' Hanno's brow furrowed and the tapping of the bone keys doubled in speed. 'Now be quiet a moment. I need to concentrate.'

Donna wandered across to the small barred window in the office and peered out. She could see the halo of light from the stockade, and fancied she heard the distant snap of weapons fire. The chalybeate roofs of Dust Falls seemed to huddle close below. Among them she caught sight of a lit sign of a slop shop in the next street. Originally, it had read 'Come In!' but some wag had climbed up there with a can of paint and sprayed it to read 'UnWeLcoMinN'. Donna wondered if that was where Kell Bak had crept off to after leaving here. She craned to see another slop shop nearby but couldn't tell which was the closest.

'What are you so interested in?' Hanno asked from behind her. Donna quelled an urge to flinch.

'Just trying to see the stockade perimeter,' she lied.

'Well, I'm through the locks on Relli's register entry and there's something odd here.'

Donna came back to where Hanno was sitting and peered over his shoulder. After a moment she gave up and shrugged in disgust. 'I don't even know what I'm looking at.'

'Guilders don't make their records easy to understand, it's true. Otherwise, any scum could break in and find manifests, route plans and all kinds of useful information.' Hanno was warming to his subject. He obviously spent a lot of time thinking about how to screw over guilders. 'But most of this is just simple acronyms, contractions and code numbers. See, look at this here.' Hanno pointed to a specific line on the screen and Donna looked obediently.

<<.350.98/Ex./DMH@4.83x5.37x1.21/mbr.7/E.V.1293GC//F2R// Rclm.>>
<<.622.98/Ex./DMH@4.83x5.37x1.21/mbr.14/E.V.3571GC//F2R//Rclm pen.>>

'You are seriously ticking me off, Hanno. What the hell's all that supposed to mean?'

'It's what Relli's been up to in the last six months, and it tells us that he's in a lot of trouble.'

'Do tell.'

'Well, this first part is a date stamp. The next is what Relli financed on that date, and these are normally caravans or partnerships or investments. "Ex" is for expedition, which is usually sending a pack of gangers out into the Badzones looking for something.'

'Oh really? Like what?' Donna was getting impatient with the whole back to school act. Hanno blathered on obliviously.

'Could be after anything: scav, stinger mould, or even taking some Spire noble on a hunting expedition to bag spider mares.' Hanno cocked an eyebrow at Donna and her obvious impatience but she refused to rise to the bait.

'So what you're telling me is, it doesn't say,' she retorted.

'No, but the rest of the entry gives us more clues. The next part is a location index, and it's one I'm not familiar with so that tells us it's well out of the way. I can tell you that it's pretty deep down, almost at Hive Bottom. Also, both expeditions were heading to the same place, and the little "at" mark means they didn't have a precise fix on the location.'

'Now that's intriguing.'

'Oh, it gets better. The next two parts are about the expedition itself: the first one had seven members, and the second one had fourteen. The EV-number-GC part is the equipment value of the expedition in guilder credits. The first was pretty well-equipped, and the second even more so.'

'So what does F2R mean?'

'Failed to return.'

Donna felt a chill down her spine. Relli had sent twenty-one people to an untimely grave in some corner of the Badzones. What could possibly mean so much to him? And more importantly, why had he sent a message to her? She wished she knew who had been on those expeditions, whether any of them she might have counted a friend. She hoped not.

'So is that why you said Relli's in trouble, because of all those people lost?'

'Oh, Donna. You still don't understand what hivers are really like, do you? Especially guilders. People count for nothing. The reason Relli is in trouble is because the two expeditions have put him almost five grand in the hole with no return on his investments. "Rclm" means he reclaimed the cost of the first expedition from the central guild funds, as guilders are entitled to do when they take a loss. But the second claim is pending and the other guilders are likely to ask a lot more questions about sending two expeditions to the same place and losing both of them. Once, you can put down to misfortune, twice will be read as incompetence.'

'So why's he gunning for me?'

Hanno rolled his stool back from the cogitator. It sighed contentedly as it closed its window, safely forgotten and free to pursue its matriculations again. The watchman went to his desk and pulled out two dirty glasses. He frowned at them and gave them a guilty rub before deciding that alcohol would kill off any germs, far more so than his sleeve anyway. He poured a measure of amasec for each of them and sat back down.

'I don't know, D'onne. Have you considered he might not be gunning for you at all? Shallej and Kell are smart, and they might just have intercepted the message and decided to be opportunistic with it.'

'And croatalids might fly out of my butt. Coincidences like this don't happen in my life.'

'It's true that everything happens for a reason, like when we met for the first time. Meeting you began a chain of events that convinced me to give up everything I had in Hive City and come below, because I discovered that I was needed down here more than up there.

'All I'm saying is that Relli may not be out to get you,' Hanno continued. 'It's more likely he wants something from you. You may not know it, but you could have information about those lost expedition members, or where they went. It's well-known you frequent the Badzones more than most.'

Donna pondered this. Had Relli sent the hunters to catch her for interrogation? Had he sent the hunters after her at all? Since Glory Hole, she'd not had long enough to think things through, and information on Relli had been next to non-existent. He'd proven only to be a successful behind-the-scenes villain with the Baks as his brutish henchmen up front. Hanno was right. It could be, and most likely was, far more complicated than that. Relli had his own concerns, otherwise, no matter what his underlying motives, he never would have been desperate enough to contact Donna in the first place. There was only one sure way to find out.

'All right then, I'm going to find him in Down Town. He can tell me himself.'

Hanno's eyes bugged out slightly and he said, 'You never did take long making your mind up about things, did you?'

'Oh, I take forever when it comes to what to have for dinner or which lip gloss to wear, sweetheart.'

Hanno laughed in spite of himself, shaking his head again. 'You may be a raging psychopath at heart,

D'onne, but you always knew how to put people at ease and get them on your side. If you could just be responsible about it you would make a great leader.'

Donna's tone was instantly scathing. '"Saint D'onne of the Redemption?" I don't think so.'

'You know you could do a lot of good. You could turn your past into something positive for a change, instead of hiding from it down here.'

Donna threw back the last of her amasec and favoured Hanno with a withering glare that sent his gaze skating elsewhere. She got up and headed for the door. Hanno started to rise and said, 'Wait, D'onne–'

Donna turned on him and cut him off furiously, her words coming in a rush. 'No, Hanno, you wait. I cut you a lot of slack because of what you did for me. But…' She fought for calm, trying not to scream at him. 'I am not going to have this argument with you. You're stubborn and I'm mean and I like you too much to want to end up shooting you again.'

She pushed him back down onto his stool and kissed him on the cheek, turning away quickly so he wouldn't see her tears. She was pleased with herself for not slamming the door on the way out.

BEFORE STEPPING OUTSIDE, Donna took a deep breath to calm herself. She shook out her dew sheet and wrapped the plastic fabric around her head and shoulders. With the filter can dangling down at the hip, a dew sheet made a decently improvised burnous, and it was common to see them worn in the Underhive. They also hid your face and hands pretty well, so they were popular for other reasons, too.

Donna made her way to the UnWeLcoMinN to start looking for Kell. What she hadn't pointed out to Hanno was that the easiest way to find out more about

Relli was to track down one of the bounty hunters. With suitable encouragement, like a gouged eye and a few lost toes, Kell would be willing to spill his guts figuratively because he wouldn't want to do it literally.

Hanging lanterns and crackling neon tubes lit the front of the slop shop. It was a low, shed-like building that ran between two alleys with an entrance at each end. Pushing open the door, Donna was met by a wall of smoke, body stink and noise from inside. The place was full to capacity and the atmosphere was plain ugly.

Donna moved through the crowd cautiously, trying to get a feel for who was there without obviously staring. Most of the patrons were gang fighters or juves from different houses. She saw hulking, muscle-bound Goliaths with shaved heads and industrial piercings, hooded Cawdor in pseudo-medieval sackcloth, and long haired, leather-clad Orlocks. Different gangs had staked out various parts of the bar for themselves and were spending most of their time eyeing each other murderously. The slop shop's barkeep and his flesh-girls looked harried. They were constantly moving between the different groups, trying to keep everyone happy and not provoke any jealousies.

There was a barely suppressed undercurrent of violence. Evidently, the siege was wearing on everyone's nerves. These were all members of successful gangs; they were tough, well armed and experienced. They had come to Dust Falls to go down the Abyss and seek their fortune, but instead they found themselves bottled up with the very gun-scum they should be competing with (which is to say shooting at) in the Badzones.

It was a testament to Hanno's ability as watchman that they weren't already at each other's throats. It was also worthy of note that gangers from the most antagonistic houses – the Goliaths and the Escher, the Orlocks and the Delaque – had evidently been separated between the two slop shops in Dust Falls to keep tensions down. Donna couldn't see a Van Saar, a Delaque, or an Escher in the whole place.

That was with one obvious exception. With his long, black coat and pallid, shaven head, Kell Bak stood out like a stick of charcoal in a box of crayons. Donna spotted him in the far corner talking to a disinterested-looking bunch of Goliaths. Two ratskin scouts were lounging nearby at the bar and drinking heavily. Donna edged in closer so she could overhear what was being said.

'It's easy money,' Kell was saying in a scratchy whisper. 'We link up, blast a way clear, find the bitch again and take her down. Suddenly you're a hundred credits richer and you're out of Dust Falls.'

The Goliath leader was a huge brute of a man with steel bolts threaded through his bulging biceps and pectorals. He talked in a slow, bass rumble like tectonic plates grinding together. 'Yur gonna need more guns than uz, and no skank's gonna fire up alla dese boys for a hunnerd stinkin' creds.'

'You're not confident of beating a ragtag bunch of scavvies?' Kell was trying not to offend the Goliath but it still came out as a sneer.

The big Goliath grinned nastily before continuing on as if Kell hadn't spoken. 'Ye see yur scavvies're no good when yur can chase 'im down and kick 'im, but inna open they'll jest run and keep shootin' yur ass from the dark. Needs a hole buncha guns ter keep lookin' every which way. Nobodie's riskin' that run out when da uvvers are stayin' behind nice an' safe.' The leader swung a meaty fist around at the bar expansively before swigging back his stein. 'Everywun goes or everywun stays, no crap bounties gonna be worth gettin' messed up fer on yur own.' He banged the stein back down, indicating that his final words of wisdom on the matter had been dispensed.

Donna caught one of the ratskins looking at her strangely and then none-too-subtly whispering something in his neighbour's ear. She tensed up, ready for action, expecting the two to alert Kell of her presence. To her surprise they both got up and trotted out of the bar without a backward glance. Kell didn't seem to notice.

'But Mad Donna is easy meat; all rep and no action,' Kell wheezed, still trying to elicit some interest. 'Just Shallej and me was all it took last time and she had help getting away. Didn't she skin a member of your gang once? Don't you want payback on that?'

That seemed to rekindle the Goliath's interest. His jaw stuck out menacingly. 'You sayin' Goliat's is weak? Izzat watcha sayin? That Donaz badass, man. Mean as they cum. Couldn'a taken one of uz otherwise.'

'Badass? She's just a spoilt little uphive bitch that's been whipped once already.'

There are times in life when looking back at your actions, you find them hard to fathom, or indeed even believe. Donna's plan was to trail Kell until she could get him alone. But hearing him crow about running her out of Glory Hole made her blood boil, and she couldn't let it go unchallenged. The plan went out the window. She flung back her cloak, stood up straight and magnificently with hands on hips for all to see.

'Hey Kell!' she challenged in a loud, clear voice. 'Want to try whipping me again? Or should I wait here until you fetch your big cousin and half a dozen pit slaves?'

The unmistakable timbre of her uphive accent cut across the packed bar like a knife, grabbing everyone's attention. The gangers nearby hooted appreciatively and shouted crude encouragement. Kell spun around, shock written all over his toad-like face, his hand darting for his pistol.

'No guns!' the barkeep shouted desperately. 'Order of the watch!'

Kell froze, his eyes flickering to the giant Goliath for support. The gang leader spat and then grinned again, showing off steel-fang incisors as he rumbled, 'Thass right, boy. First one shoots a gun gets stripped an' thrown to the scavvies. We's all swore uselves to it.'

Suddenly the brute stood up, towering over the bounty hunter. He turned to the gathering crowd and raised his voice in a stentorian bellow. 'We seddle ur fights like men!' There was an answering roar of approval from the assembled gangers, all their enmities temporarily forgotten (apparently along with the fact that Donna wasn't a man) at the prospect of some bloodletting.

'Face-ter-face,' he shouted before pausing dramatically and peering down at the faces of Donna and Kell.

'Hand-ter-hand,' the giant bellowed once more, turning away with arms spread impossibly wide. That got another, louder cheer.

'To the death!' That nearly raised the slop shop's roof. Bets were already being laid and credits changing hands. Even thinking about backing out now would mean being lynched.

So much for the plan.

IN SITUATIONS LIKE this, keeping your poise was everything. Showing fear or uncertainty in front of a bar full of bored, restless gangers was like swimming among ripper fish with an open wound. Donna's opponent was strutting back and forth full of false bravado, assuring anyone that would listen that he was a deadly hand-to-hand fighter. She simply rolled her dew sheet back into its can, drew out Seventy-one, and waited silently while the tables were dragged aside and the crowd drew in to form a rough, jostling circle around the pair.

The giant Goliath, who someone called Krug whilst betting, had taken it upon himself to be master of ceremonies. He announced both of the combatants with mock formality, raising a lusty cheer for Donna and a lot of pantomime booing and hissing for Kell. He then proceeded to announce the rules.

'There's no rules!' he bellowed triumphantly. He stopped as one of the other Goliaths muttered something in his ear. 'Oh yeah. There's no rules 'cept no guns!' That got another half-hearted cheer but the crowd was getting bored of the showmanship now – they wanted action. Correctly reading the mood, Krug surrendered the impromptu ring of sweaty, yelling gangers to the two contenders with a final theatrical bow.

Kell stepped forward and took a few experimental cuts in the air with his blade. It was an unusual weapon, a short but heavy looking chainsword formed like an espadon with two cutting edges and a needle-sharp serrated blade at its tip. Most chainswords had a single cutting edge with the return edge of the blade inset for around two thirds of their length. This was because fighting with one chain weapon against another was nasty, dangerous work; the contra-rotating teeth could bind and spit each other back with surprising force. It was all too easy to have a chain-blade rebound into you after a messed-up cut or parry;

hence the protective cowling. The bounty hunter had to be supremely confident of his skills to wield a weapon like that.

Donna thumbed Seventy-one into life and darted forward, intending to distract Kell by edging him back into the crowd. Kell held his ground and thrust at her as she closed in, his blade licking out like a serpent's tongue. Donna caught his attack expertly with Seventy-one and flung it aside with a flick of her wrist. The standard circular parry almost cost Donna her life, as Kell whipped his shorter weapon back across to make a left-right slash at her before she recovered to a guard position. She skipped backward to avoid more slashing attacks, but received a long scratch on her forearm from the serrated point. The pack of gangers cheered, groaned, leered and whistled all at once with every single attack and counter-attack.

The bounty hunter was grinning like the fight was already won, which was disconcerting. Donna circled more cautiously and tried out a few exploratory feints to see how Kell would react. She learned quickly that he wouldn't be drawn to attack. He was seemingly happy to bide his time and, like all members of House Delaque, Kell wore dark goggles to protect his eyes (due to a photophobic bloodline disorder which just made the Delaque all the more creepy). Because Donna couldn't see his eyes, she couldn't predict his moves very well and had to fall back on the less successful technique of reading his body movements instead.

The gangers weren't interested in a display of fancy swordplay, they wanted flesh hacked off in bloody chunks. Boos and catcalls followed every dodge or parry. The circle of gangers started pressing inward, forcing the duellers toe-to-toe. Jumping back to avoid a blow, Donna found herself being jostled and pushed forward.

'Frik this,' Donna mumbled to herself and swung Seventy-one in a wide figure eight. It was aimed vaguely at Kell but meant really to shoo the gangers back and get some elbow room. Sure enough, Seventy-one screaming past their faces worked like a charm and the space around her cleared as if by magic. The downside was that the bounty hunter had a ready opening to exploit and Donna knew it.

She was ready for his rush but it was oddly half-hearted when it came and she beat him back easily. It dawned on Donna that Kell was what her old dancing mistress would have called a 'lead foot', or someone who couldn't shake the habit of always stepping off on the same foot.

She tried a couple of looping attacks, one overhead and one uppercut. Each time Kell's footwork was poor. He still seemed supremely confident though, as if he didn't need to strike at Donna again. Amidst their circling and sparring her brain churned out the answer with sickening certainty – Kell's blade must be poisoned!

The shock must have shown through on her face because it made Kell crow, 'Feel it now? Just a little scratch or less and this sludgejelly venom can paralyse you.' Donna could indeed feel a tingling sensation spreading up her sword arm from her small wound. Kell laughed and pressed on with his attack.

She fell back, Seventy-one wavering in her hands as if it suddenly weighed twice as much. The gangers scattered as she lashed out drunkenly to keep from being cornered. Kell came forward, his heavier blade snarling and darting at Donna's weakening guard. He didn't try anything fancy, just battered away and forced her to parry again and again. Presently Donna felt the hard plastic of the bar against her back and slumped against it, struggling to keep her blade up. Kell paused to gloat.

'Shallej is going to be pissed that I got you first,' he said. 'Of all the dumb luck, catching you here.'

'Wherezeeat?' Donna managed to slur.

'He went to Two Tunnels. He swore you'd run there. Guess I was right and he was wrong.' He leered at Donna's inviting curves. 'I don't mind telling you, it's going to be a fun trip back.'

'Oi!' bellowed Krug from the sidelines, 'No pansy stuff. Kill 'er or we kills yer both!' Angry-sounding gangers assented. Most of them had bet on Donna and were not at all pleased by the performance so far. It was questionable whether they would let Kell get out alive after robbing them of their sport.

Kell seemed oblivious. He shrugged, pulling back his sword. 'Dead or alive makes no odds to me,' he whispered. 'Still plenty of fun to be had later.'

With that, Kell unleashed a killing thrust aimed at Donna's heart.

Falling. No hiver was really afraid of heights; they lived their lives as much on the vertical as the horizontal. Sheer drops and dizzying ledges were part of their daily environment, no more remarkable to them than giant rats and toxic pools were to the people of the Underhive. Nonetheless, hivers do have a peculiar horror of falling. For them it's one thing to have your life in your hands in battle, but it's quite another to lose your grip on a ledge and fall. Perhaps it's because 'impact trauma' remained one of the most common causes of death among the notoriously short-lived denizens of Hive Primus. According to the hive census, it accounted for thirty-eight-point-two percent of reported fatalities, putting it ahead of gang violence, carcinogens and industrial accidents on a daily death toll that counted in the millions. Of course, that bland statistic covered a multitude of causes ranging from suicide through to carelessness and neglect to outright murder.

House Ulanti possessed a sweeping esplanade around its outer quadrant on the Spire that was actually open to the skies. It was one of the many fantastic indulgences that D'onne always took for granted whilst she still lived up above. In fact, D'onne didn't like the esplanade much at all. It was a bright, harsh place beneath stratospheric clouds by day and limpid, hazy stars by night. What made it worse was the power field that enclosed it, creating a constant stink and an accompanying faint buzzing sound that was enough to set your teeth on edge.

D'onne's sisters had made up a game to play on the esplanade long before she came on the scene, and it remained a firm favourite of all ages. It was very simple; the girls would line up along the baroquely carved guardrail and hang over it to gaze down at the flank of the hive below. It was perhaps the only time D'onne ever saw Hive Primus from the outside, from that buzzing esplanade.

What they could see was a craggy metal mountainside that disappeared into roiling clouds miles below them. The hive surface was etched with dishes, platforms, landing areas, antennae, hoists, towers, exhaust ports, pylons and a million other oddities. There was constant activity across the surface of the hive, making the name seem very appropriate. Day or night there were streams of sub-orbital traffic etching their contrails up and down in lazy spirals or straight ascent burns. The inter-hive carriers with fat wings flew lower and slower, and a multitude of lifters and shuttles buzzed around the hive constantly like bees vainly looking for pollen. The traffic never stopped.

The eldest sister present would act as judge. She would secretly pick a colour and a number and the rest of them would vie to see who could guess the right number of craft of the specified colour first, shrilly shouting out: 'Gold: five!' or 'Red: twenty-two!' At a nod of approval from the judge, the delighted victor would then take her prize by shoving the other observers one by one so that they flailed at the edge of the balustrade over miles of sheer drop. That delicious sensation of terror before being caught and held by the warm embrace of the power field caused the sisters to scream at the top of their lungs. If the sister judging believed that the cry had gone up too soon, she would shake her head and all the other players would shove the would-be victor.

Because she was the youngest, it took D'onne a long time to understand what the game was really about. She eventually realised it was actually all about authority and favouritism and had very little to do with spotting flying vehicles. The elder sisters used it as a way to test their subtly shifting allegiances with each other and establish their authority over the youngsters, and the youngsters used it to establish a pecking order among themselves. It was also a test of nerves. To wimp out and jump down from the balustrade was to give in to a social death which lasted several days. It was a vicious little children's game they innocently played that trained them in the skills they would need so much in later life: ruthlessness and domination.

One night soon after the artist completed their potrait, D'onne had caught three of her elder sisters – Corundra, J'ustene and Loqui – sneaking off to the esplanade. She had been looking for someone to comfort her because she was frightened by a storm raging outside; one of those statistically irrelevant seasonal variations man had supposedly mastered on Necromunda. She saw them stealing along a hallway, their white gowns glowing eerily as lightning bathed the scene. Not knowing what else to do, she followed them.

They had almost reached the esplanade before Loqui noticed D'onne tagging along behind. Loqui looked angry when she saw her and said something to Corundra, the eldest of the trio. Corundra was dark-haired and statuesque, almost old enough to marry. J'ustene and Loqui were both willowy and blonde, and indeed sometimes they were hard to tell apart even though Loqui was the elder by almost a year.

Corundra looked at D'onne and favoured her with a strange smile before saying, 'Let her come. She may actually learn something useful.'

Outside, the esplanade felt surreal. Thanks to the power field, lightning flickered harmlessly only metres away from them and storm-force winds seeped through only as scant breezes. Crackling static showed where the edge of the field started a hand-span from the railing, and it was the first time D'onne had ever seen the field defined. Beyond it, clouds churned and roiled with fast-forward motion, twisters writhing between the layers and the constant flare of lightning arcing against the hive.

J'ustene and Loqui went to the edge, J'ustene reluctantly it seemed and Loqui confident. D'onne took a few trembling paces forward but as lightning skewered the skies again before her she gave a yelp and fell to her knees, the wind blasting icy fingers across her body. She wanted to run back inside, convinced they would all be killed if they stayed, but her legs had turned to jelly. She could only kneel there helpless with terror and watch what happened next.

Corundra calmly announced over the crash of thunder and sighing winds that she had chosen a colour and a number. D'onne couldn't see how they could spot anything in the storm. Long seconds dragged past as her sisters at the balustrade counted ships.

'Red: twenty-two!' Loqui shouted. It was a common choice, so common that the game was often called 'Red: twenty-two', or simply just 'Red'.

Both J'ustene and Loqui looked at Corundra, and another actinic flare of lightning etched out her impassive features like an alabaster mask beneath the dark foam of her hair.

Corundra shook her head. Loqui screamed as J'ustene tipped her over the edge.

Afterwards they told her it was an accident; a childish game that got out of hand and ended in tragedy. How could a child understand that lightning could make the power field fluctuate for an instant? And how could a child know that the air outside was so thin it was almost a vacuum and *could suck things through? But D'onne was there, and D'onne saw and knew that the timing of the push was deliberate.*

The horrible thing was that Loqui flew upwards at first, arms and legs flailing, the open pit of her screaming mouth made silent in the winds. Then she was swept outwards and away, shrinking into a spinning speck in the distance that fell forever towards the distant cloud base.

J'ustene watched her fall. Corundra turned towards D'onne and laid one perfectly manicured index finger against her lips to warn her to silence. At that moment, D'onne's world had spun and turned black.

When she awoke she was in the tower.

5: PENUMBRA

A depth, a breadth,
A place so steep, a hole so deep.
Beyond edge of sight, tipped into night.
Down.
Down.
To velvet lake of phosphor shrouds,
Of twisting heat, of burning clouds.
To where the spider mares abound,
Down to where my dreams are found.

Excerpt from *Abyssa Obscura and Other Visions*, the collected works of Scelerus Greim, the spyrer artist, poet and anarchist.

IN THE LAST frozen heartbeat between life and death, Kell's snarling blade was narrowing towards Donna's breast.

Seventy-one was a blur in Donna's hand as it came smashing down on the thrusting blade with stunning force. Both chainswords shrieked defiantly as their spinning teeth struck, binding together for a fraction of a second before being flung violently apart. Donna recovered her guard position with a practiced flick of the wrist. Kell's heavier blade swung wildly and gouged a bloody furrow across his thigh. The bounty hunter shrieked a curse and staggered backwards. The crowd roared its approval at the unexpected comeback.

Donna straightened up from the bar and let Seventy-one idle quietly for a moment. The watching gangers all fell silent, enrapt by the unfolding drama.

'Y'know, Kell,' she spat through gritted teeth. 'Poisons are funny things. Not four shifts ago, I was stung by sludge jellies, in the sword arm no less, and it feels just fine now. I guess it's been poisoned enough already.'

That was a lie. Donna's forearm felt afire as if it had been dipped in bowl of biting insects, but it certainly wasn't paralysed.

Kell was trying to clamp the flow of blood from his thigh with one hand while keeping his blade up with the other. The more he bled out the weaker he would get, so now it was Donna's turn to gloat and let the shock set in for a moment. Besides, Donna had a lot of frustrations to exorcise and she wanted to savour the moment. She stalked towards the bounty hunter with a murderous gleam in her beautiful blue eye.

'I've had bounty scum like you on my ass ever since I came down here.'

'And what a great ass!' some wag shouted from the audience. Normally she would have maimed whoever said that on principle, but right now she barely even noticed it.

'And if there's one thing I hate about all of you,' she continued, 'it's that you're not in it for money, like you claim, or for justice or protecting hivers'.

She fired up Seventy-one again, its low snarl accentuating her words.

'No, you do it for the glory. You do it so you can strut around and pretend you're better than the scum you're hunting. You do it so you can hurt people and claim you had to do it, that you had no choice. Well, we all get to make choices. You made yours, and now I'm going to show you mine.'

Donna advanced with her sword held loosely at a low guard.

'I'm going to leave your arms and face until last, Kell, so you can keep fighting for as long as you feel like,' she told him, and took a lazy cut that forced him to limp backwards. She circled like a merciless predator.

'Trying to ambush me in Glory Hole was enough reason to kill you on its own, but the crap you've been spouting tonight...' She shook her head and her long dreadlocks swayed with the motion. Her voice became a husky tocsin of utter menace. 'For that I'm going to carve you up first.'

Donna leapt into the fray, bellowing a murderous shriek and whirling Seventy-one like a dervish. Kell presented a parry but Donna's first move was only a feint. She whirled around him at the last instant, making a straight-armed cut at his backside.

Her chainblade struck home, ripping through the heavy material of Kell's flak coat and its lining of mesh armour like paper. The bounty hunter howled as the relentless teeth chewed off a meaty slice of haunch and upper thigh before glancing off his hipbone. The blade splattered crimson rain across the bar and the spectators cheered again with bloodlust. Kell slid awkwardly onto one knee in a spreading pool of his own gore.

Donna was still moving, slamming Seventy-one down like a guillotine on Kell's exposed foot. The chainsword Donna called Seventy-one became Seventy-Six in that instant, tearing through boot, tarsi and metatarsi to send Kell's five toes rolling away like fat, wriggling maggots.

Donna spun away with a pretty dancing step she had been taught when she was six. She pirouetted around her prey, forcing Kell to drag his mangled foot over hard-packed dirt and broken glass to keep facing her.

Kell alternated between blubbering incoherently and screeching as Donna dodged in with her blade biting again and again. He tried to lunge at her, so she took an ear and left it dangling by a scrap of scalp.

Donna laid open her opponent's shoulder so that the glistening bone of his scapula could be seen peeking out. She carved through ribs and into a lung to make a wound that blew out pink froth in time with Kell's ragged breathing. A dozen other nicks and gouges marked his quivering body as she teased and caressed it lovingly with Seventy-six.

She was making Kell into her fetish doll, venting her pent-up anger and frustration on his wretched form. She spun round faster, wilder. Even hardened gangers blanched and turned away as she stripped Kell's flesh from his bones. He could barely stay upright now, swaying and gurgling as his life-blood leaked out of torn flesh. The blade clattered from his nerveless hand.

Somewhere in Kell's wrecked body a spark of defiance still burned. He clawed at his holster, painstakingly dragging out his bolt pistol.

Donna laughed. 'Come on Kell, last chance!' She stopped and posed for a moment, letting him raise a shaking arm to take aim. Gangers scattered from the line of fire behind her. Kell pulled the trigger and sent a bolt round roaring off to explode against the bar. Naturally, Donna was no longer there.

A flesh girl started screaming shrilly. Donna leapt behind Kell and jammed her own gun against the back of his bald skull. Another bolt round roared off from his pistol, this time exploding in flesh with an obscene smacking sound.

Donna felt an almost orgasmic sense of release as she pulled the trigger, spreading Kell's brains out across the dirt floor of the UnWeLcoMinN. The shot was a shout of ecstasy in her ears; the bolt was her incandescent euphoria as it burned his hated skull to ash.

In the momentary warm afterglow, Donna looked down and found to her surprise that she had shot him with the Pig. There wasn't much of Kell left that wasn't charred and smoking.

The whole bar erupted with gunfire. For a split second Donna thought they were saluting her somehow. Bullets came zipping past close enough for her to feel. No. They were shooting at each other. As she dived out of the firing line she found that they were shooting at her, too. Autopistol rounds tracked holes in the bar next to her as she ran, and a shotgun blast kicked up an eruption of dirt at her feet. Bodies were dropping everywhere, arms jerking and flailing as they were hit.

Donna ran for an exit amidst scenes of unmitigated mayhem. Gangers flipped tables into barricades and went at it even as their friends and enemies got blasted into meat puppets around their ears. Vicious hand-to-hand brawling and point-blank shooting was quickly defining three groups – the Orlocks were congregating at one end of the bar, the Cawdor at the other, the Goliaths (and Donna) in the middle and a lot of twitching corpses in between.

Donna had no hesitation running for cover with the leather-clad Orlocks. They whooped and waved her on, putting down a creditable covering fire. It was an easy choice for her to make, since the Goliaths would have skinned her in an instant and the Cawdor would no doubt burn her for being a she-harlot or something. Orlocks, on the other hand, hated Delaque like Kell with a passion, and also they just liked to have a good time. She cracked a Goliath's shaven skull as she ran towards them to return the compliment.

'Thanks, boys!' she cried, bounding behind a table.

It was quite intimate in there, with about twenty Orlocks wedged in behind five tables. They were grinning happily and blazing away. Hot, jingling shell-casings rained everywhere. The mad release of tension Donna had felt seemed to be contagious; the Orlocks were working out their frustrations with firepower too. The Orlock nearest her turned and shouted something but Donna couldn't hear a word of it over the constant rattle of auto-fire. He nodded at the door. Donna saw that the Orlocks were moving off, dragging their wounded out the exit first.

Donna checked the Pig. It was out of juice just as she'd feared. Holstering it, she unsheathed her laspistol and stood, snapping off a couple of shots. She only half aimed since the shots were meant to keep the Orlocks sweet than actually do any damage. The first shot, however, took a Cawdor smack in the forehead, putting a smoking third eye through his penitent hood and straight into his brain. The second hit was equally miraculous, taking down a Goliath with a solid body hit at the other end of the bar. The Orlocks whooped and yelled even louder, battering her with comradely punches as she ducked back down.

A frag grenade went off in the bar as Donna was crawling for the door, and the indiscriminately scything shrapnel signalled a general exodus for all parties. The Cawdor poured out of the other exit and the Goliaths forced their own way out through a wall in typically brutal fashion. The pitched battle inside turned into a running battle through the twisting alleyways outside. Every door and corner seemed to be lit with gunflashes. Gangers darted everywhere, loosing off shots at half-seen shapes in the darkness, and smoke and flames billowing out of the bar gave the scene a ruddy, hellish quality. Anarchy was running naked through the streets of Dust Falls with all guns blazing.

Donna and a pack of maybe a dozen Orlocks from different gangs rallied in a nearby street. The Orlocks seemed to have latched onto Donna as a lucky charm in the confusion. Her height and swinging mass of stained, blonde dreadlocks made her nice and easy to spot in the dark too, she thought ruefully. She was still wondering how to get rid of the Orlocks when Hanno arrived on the scene.

Even in the dark, and from the other end of the street, Donna could see that Hanno was about ready to burst a blood vessel. He had a gang of watchmen with him, all armed to the teeth, and a trailing crowd of Escher, Van Saar and Delaque from the other slop shop. Hanno spotted Donna and started striding forward with a face like thunder.

At that moment a group of Goliaths appeared out of another alley and let fly at the Orlocks, who retaliated in kind. The watchmen intervened, loosing off scatter rounds at both gangs. All sides went diving for cover and another gun battle erupted in earnest. More gangers were drawn to the noise and the fight soon crackled up in intensity like a flash fire.

Donna saw Hanno leading the watchmen forward by bounds, determinedly trying to force apart the warring factions with shotgun blasts and gun butts. She certainly didn't want to be around by the time he reached her vicinity.

'Time to go, boys. It's been real fun,' Donna called to the Orlocks, and then ran off down the street.

To her dismay, the Orlocks took this as a piece of sage tactical advice and ran straight after her. The Goliaths chased the Orlocks, the watchmen chased both groups, and the gangers followed the watchmen. Donna had no clue where the Cawdor had gone until she reached the stockade and found the gate was wide open.

The zealous bigots of House Cawdor had decided to go out and start their own ugly little war with the scavvies. They hadn't gotten far. The rubble outside was littered with Cawdor and scavvy bodies. A knot of die-hard hood-heads was making a last stand in the lee of a large slab out in the waste zone. They were surrounded by at least ten times their number of scavvies and going down fast. It sounded like they were singing psalms.

Donna, the Orlocks, the Goliaths, the watchmen, and then everybody else careered out of the gate and into the fight with all the subtlety and tactical acumen of a blinded milliasaur. They hit the back of the scavvies and killed a score of them before the ragged horde realised it was being attacked from two sides at once. The Cawdor immediately rallied and started forging a path through the scavvies with fanatical fervour. The anarchic battle that had started inside Dust Falls now engulfed the waste zone outside, and shots flew like hail.

Donna was never sure how she survived the encounter. The scavvies were a threat to all but beyond that it was every gang for themselves. There were over two hundred fighters around her, duking it out with everything from sharp rocks to plasma cannons. It became one of the larger gunfights in Underhive history, and it certainly was the biggest, most chaotic brawl Donna had ever seen.

She weaved through the fight, loosing off shots at the scavvies and slashing at them in her path. She needed a way out – any way out – but all around her were brawling gangers and darting mutants. Bullets whined about her and las-rounds hissed back and forth in a deadly crescendo underscored by the throaty bark of bolter rounds and the wild rattling of autoguns. There was no shelter. Every rubble pile or shallow trench was fiercely fought over with its own knot of besiegers and besieged.

It was a measure of Donna's desperation that she found the safest place to be was actually fighting the scavvies in hand-to-hand combat. If she was being shot at, the scavvies were just as likely to hit her opponents as herself. She kept ducking and diving, trying to work her way towards the Abyss through the seething ebb and flow of battle.

That was working fine until she ran up against the scavvy giant.

Who knows what Badzone rad-hole spawned that monstrosity, or what random mix of chemicals and poisons conspired to throw up a chance mutation like that? But life always found a way to survive and thrive, no matter how ugly the results were.

This was the stuff of childhood nightmares. Its bullet-shaped head and slab-muscled shoulders towered above Mad Donna. Spade-like claws and a thickly scaled hide completed its inhuman appearance. Incongruously human-looking mismatched eyes, one green and one blue, were the only things betraying its true parentage.

It looked far from human when it tossed aside the broken body of a ganger and lumbered towards Donna, its slit mouth bellowing a wordless challenge. Ducking under a reaching claw, she slashed at a wrist thicker than her thigh, but Seventy-six skidded off its iron-hard scales. The giant chuckled as it sent her reeling with a casual backhand.

Donna's ears were left ringing by the glancing blow. The giant was slow but one hit was all it needed to snap her bones and incapacitate her. She could see more scavvies closing in out of the corner of her eye, taking confidence from the fearsome presence of their bigger brother. Donna desperately needed an edge to even the odds, but the Pig was already out of juice and it was her only weapon capable of taking down something so big.

Scurrying backward over the treacherous rubble, she saw that she was being forced closer to the edge of the Abyss. She made a snap decision and ran straight for a spar jutting over the dizzying gulf with the scaly giant lumbering right at her heels.

Flakes of rust and chunks of rubble fell from the rotting spar as she ran out onto it, and the whole thing vibrated alarmingly in time with her footsteps. Donna sheathed Seventy-six, turned, and faced her foe with the inky void at her feet.

The gigantic mutant hesitated at the brink with almost comic uncertainty written on its bestial face. Donna felt a brief flash of hope that it might just give up and go find someone else to eviscerate. No such luck. It carefully placed one broad foot on the spar and stretched out to seize her with its ape-like arms. The metal creaked in protest under its weight.

Donna ducked beneath its scaly arms and desperately fired her laspistol into its face. The shot only singed, but that was enough to make the giant rear back, its arms wind-milling for balance. She hung on for dear life as the rusting beam shook wildly, and then aimed a vicious kick at the creature's ankle.

Her thick boot heel struck bone with a satisfying crunch. The giant grunted in surprise and teetered past the fatal point of no return, gathering speed like a falling pillar as it pitched sidewise into the Abyss with a disconsolate wail. Donna almost fell off, too, trying to watch him disappear into the darkness below.

Scavvies were skulking on nearby heaps of rubble. They had long muskets and bullets zinged off metal and rocks near Donna but nothing came even close to hitting her. Generally speaking, scavvies were the most appalling shots and had poor weaponry to go with it, but they compensated by making sure numbers were most definitely on their side. There was no going back that way, not for a while at least. Donna holstered her laspistol and hung off the spar with both hands so she could swing along beneath it and get some cover. As she did so, she spotted a cracked half-pipe jutting out below the edge of the dome floor nearby. It was hard to ignore the vast, hungry gulf at her back as she clambered over to the pipe, but Donna didn't freeze and made it across before her strength gave out.

A rank stench and an ooze of old slurry flowing from the pipe told her it was for waste disposal, but she wasn't fussy. It was this or go back into battle, and Donna reckoned she had seen her fill of fighting for this shift. She decided that she definitely would rather crawl away down a pipe full of effluent.

A CRACKLING SOUND and a shower of sparks over on the roadway caught her attention and distracted her from the earnest Enforcer Hanno. At first she thought there had been some kind of accident among the lines of moving vehicles, but then she looked more closely at the roadway and realised she was mistaken. It wasn't a solid road at all. It was a wide, grid-like mesh of thick rails that fizzled and spluttered with vagrant electricity in the cloying mist. A vehicle breaking away from the steadily moving traffic stream had caused the sparks. It had jumped onto different rails that curved over to the walkway where she and Hanno stood.

As the vehicle drew closer, Donna saw a blank-eyed servitor at the controls. It was severed at the waist and attached to a turntable at the prow. A long, narrow hull covered by a grimy plastiglas cabin stretched back behind it, large enough to carry perhaps twelve. At the rear of the felucca, a larger turntable bore what looked like a huge crab claw, but instead of gripping the rails it only touched them with its two points, seeming to stick there and carry the whole weight of the craft. The arcane sciences of electromagnetism were at work.

D'onne waited for Hanno to open the door for her before going onboard first, intending to turn at the threshold and send him away. She was so shocked at what she saw inside, however, she completely forgot about him for a moment. The narrow bench seats inside the felucca showed that it was intended for transporting at least forty or fifty people, with overhead rails for others to steady themselves while standing. D'onne was mortified at the idea of so many people crushing themselves into the filthy vehicle and was glad that the nose plugs kept out the stink of the unwashed. Although the felucca was only half full at most, D'onne stood and gripped a rail; she couldn't face sitting on one of the hard plastic benches amid the filth.

Hanno stepped neatly aboard behind her and slid the door shut. Without further delay the felucca swung on its turntable and started picking up speed in the direction of the main traffic flows.

D'onne suddenly saw that the streams of vehicles hung both above and below the rails. Weaving, splitting and rejoining, their head and tail lamps made knotwork traceries in the mist. Buildings swirled past: great slabs like tombstones pierced by roads at different levels, skeletal towers covered in lights, squat-looking steely ziggurats. All different, all ugly.

Enforcer Hanno took off his helmet and regarded her levelly as if about to say something. He had cropped hair that was greying at the temples and a craggy, not displeasing countenance D'onne would have labelled 'honest' if it weren't for his eyes. They were pale grey and all-too-sharp, glittering from his otherwise impassive face like stab-lights, probing, examining, weighing and measuring.

D'onne was frankly offended and responded with a look that was withering enough to send Enforcer Hanno's gaze skating off elsewhere. She pointedly turned back to watching Hive City slide past. They were descending between two towering blocks inter-connected by a multitude of bridges, or it might have been a single block cloven through by the road. It was hard to be sure.

Without warning, the felucca juddered to a halt, almost throwing D'onne off her feet. She looked up, expecting to see the blocks sliding past vertically as they fell to their deaths, but saw they were stationary aside from a slight swaying that may have been her own unsteadiness. Without thought she sat down on one of the benches with a bump. Near-death experiences were coming way too thick and fast at present and she was feeling distinctly weak at the knees.

Hanno creaked uncomfortably in his armour and tried to sound formal and comforting at the same time. 'Swing shift, nobledam. There's always a power drop so they clamp off the road net temporarily to avoid accidents. Here they come now.'

He was looking out of the grimy plastiglas window at the bridges, D'onne realised, and all the other vehicles had stopped too, just as he had said. She looked down in horrid fascination. Where the bridges had been all but empty before, they were now filling with the tiny dots of moving people. Thousands, tens of thousands thronged the bridges within sight alone. There were two streams on each bridge crossing in opposite directions. One stream was swift and disciplined, almost martial. The other was sluggish and meandering. One shift of proles were coming off the lines and returning to their habs, and another shift was coming from their habs and going to the lines.

On occasion the two flows intersected in violent little swirls. At one bridge in the distance D'onne saw black-armoured enforcers wading in to separate them. In another place several tiny figures fell from one bridge onto another, the tiny ripples of their impact conveying none of the carnage they must have wrought on those below. Hanno called in something on his vox at that and D'onne turned away from the sight. It was too reminiscent of a murder less fresh than the one presently in her mind, but more painful.

'Stupid.'

D'onne realised immediately that Hanno wasn't addressing her, he was watching the ritual anarchy of swing shift and talking to himself. Caught up in the moment, he had voiced his inner thoughts, forgetting she was even there. He thought swing shift was stupid. Interesting – a bit of a reformist at heart too, this Hanno – she could work with that.

A moment later they jolted forward as the traffic started moving again. D'onne felt a tiny stab of guilt as they swept past platforms crammed with proles. No doubt they were waiting for feluccas like this one to take them back so they could begin their downtime: ten precious hours in their habs before they were on the lines again.

'OFFICER HANNO, WHY do they fight?' D'onne discovered the taint wasn't as bad as she'd feared when she opened her mouth, and besides she was going to have to get used to it.

'Every reason you can come up with, nobledam. Anger, frustration, revenge, jealousy, prestige, spite, self-gratification, goods, money, men, women, drugs, even pets. There are antagonistic work-gangs on different shifts that elevate quota-rivalries to the level of house warfare. That's all without any real inter-house conflict to contend with.' Hanno's voice was weary and edged with contempt.

'You haven't answered my question, Hanno. I asked why they fought, not what reasons they give you for it.'

Hanno looked at her shrewdly. She recognised the look of someone wanting to say something they felt was controversial and bursting to share their view with someone else.

'Because they have no hope of salvation.'

D'onne decided to dig a little deeper. 'Really? Not shortages or austerity measures or the eighty-hour work cycle?' These were all things her tutors had cited as causes of unrest.

Hanno shook his head. 'It's my belief that all these can be borne, have been borne in the past, when men have hope of a better future.'

He looked back at the city outside. They were still descending, the blocks rising higher above them all the time and the felucca passing through more and more tunnels as they wormed deeper into Hive City's guts.

'Did you know that some logistician has calculated that if someone fell from those bridges every time we took a breath, then newborns in the city would replace them a hundredfold before we took another? We have made a place that makes and breaks men faster than we can breathe.'

D'onne was thrilled that Hanno was so easy to draw out and now she couldn't resist going further. No doubt he had harboured feelings of disquiet for a long time and had been unable to voice them to anyone. The truth is that everyone liked the sound of their own voice. The speaker just had to believe that the listener was interested in what they had to say.

'And how can it be made right? What would give them hope?'

Hanno spread his hands out helplessly. 'I... I don't know.'

Stupid! She had pushed too soon. Now Hanno had reverted back to his introverted manner instead of remaining extroverted and expansive. Her tutors would have scolded her for such an elementary blunder. To speak any more on this topic would only serve to make him sullen. It was time for a subject change.

'Is it much further?' D'onne asked in a dignified yet vulnerable voice, hoping to draw him back to his protector role.

'No, nobledam. We are almost at the border of Escher territory now, proceeding to a main interchange to seek access.' Predictably, Hanno put his helmet back on. Doubtless it made him feel more comfortable after the moment of vulnerability he had shown. Encouragingly, he left his vox unconnected for the time being so he spoke normally.

'Do you have a preferred point of entry, nobledam?'

'The closest.'

'Very good, nobledam.'

The roadway was converging with many others, plunging into a conical well where the traffic's controlled procession broke up into a maelstrom of turnoffs, docks and lay-bys. The felucca came to rest at the bottom of the well beside a broad pavement of white stone. A great portcullis of glittering chrome reared above them, so baroque and heavy-looking that it had to be ornamental.

Members of House Escher were scattered everywhere but Hanno and D'onne were quickly singled out and approached by armed House Escher guards in combat fatigues. They approached the enforcer warily, but not at all deferentially. Just as the stories had claimed, every member of House Escher was female. Many were craning an ear to find out what was happening. Strangers here were obviously rare.

'What is your business here, enforcer? Why were we not informed of your arrival?' The house guards were brusque and edgy with Hanno, and they barely even seemed to notice D'onne. She stepped between them and Hanno before he could reply, ready to deliver the lines she had been rehearsing ever since she exited the Spire.

'This enforcer has been good enough to accompany me here for my safekeeping,' she said in her best Spire accent. 'I am D'onne Astride Ge'Sylvanus Ulanti, and I formally seek sanctuary with House Escher.'

6: THE ABYSS

'Are you not men?' Mad D'onne challenged, her magnificent bosom heaving with scarcely controlled passion. 'Wouldst you let your poor women and babes be slaughtered and Dust Falls burn about your ears while you sit here drinking and gambling and hiding from the fight?'

The gangers had hung their heads in shame at that. To be scorned for want of bravery was bad enough, but to be impugned by a lady of the Spire, one who had shared the many hardships and adventures of the Underhive at their side, that was almost too much to borne. One fierce fellow, a mighty Goliath named Krug Hammerhand, spoke up for all. 'Pray tell us nobledam, how can we save the settlement? Is it too late?'

She drew her slender duelling sword and brandished it high. 'A woman I may be, but this I learned at my father's knee. It is never too late for cold steel and the fierce resolution of true men to win the hour. Come with me now to the gate and we shall see what can be done.'

And such was her beauty and such was the virtue of her words that the fighters readied their arms and came willingly, where not even Lord Helmawr could have commanded them to go before.

They marched to the walls and set about the foe with the awesome fury of true men. The battle raged ceaselessly for *hours. On the one hand stood teeming multitudes of foul, tainted abominations hungering for human flesh, on the other stood the stalwart folk of Dust Falls, resolute in their faith.*

Shoulder to shoulder they fought, Delaque beside Orlock, Goliath beside Escher, Van Saar beside Cawdor and always D'onne at the fore. Wave upon wave of horrors were forced back into the abyss from whence they came. D'onne's mad bravery inflamed them all to ever greater efforts. Wherever the battle-line bent, she held them. Wherever the enemy retreated, she attacked, but a dire tragedy struck the gallant defenders with their victory all but won. Brave D'onne was seen battling at the brink of the abyss with a mutant giant of tremendous stature and scales of grey iron. After a titanic struggle she laid it low with a mighty blow to its brow, yet even as it fell the beast carried her over the edge and into the pit. Hearts were broken and men wept openly to see the noble lady lost so.

Excerpt from Tales of Terror and Adventure **Chapter XXIV – How Mad D'onne Saved Dust Falls, Free Salvation Press.**

DONNA WAS SPLASHING along a sewer pipe somewhere beneath Dust Falls. A scarf across her face was failing to keep out the eye-watering stench and she was in a mood to match the stink. Every few minutes she stopped, listened and shook her head before moving on again. She was lost in the labyrinth of pipes and had been for hours since escaping the battle. Now she thought she could hear something else moving down there. Every time she halted, the sound of splashing carried on for a second or two before stopping. At first she had convinced herself it was just weird echoes of her own progress, but that didn't explain why the sound kept getting closer.

Splash-splash-splash.

The Pig was out of juice, Seventy-six was down to a half charge. Her arm was still tingling with the after-effects of Kell's poisoned blade. If it came to a fight she would be at a serious disadvantage.

Splash-splash-splash.

Every hundred steps or so there was an alloy inspection ladder hanging down from a vertical shaft in the top of the pipe. She had tried climbing up the first half dozen ladders she found but every one had ended at a cover that felt suspiciously like it was sealed shut by tonnes of compacted rubble on the other side. After that she had given up and had tried to navigate the confusing branches and turns of the sewers instead. She had considered marking her progress with scratches on the wall to help find her way, but now she didn't want to leave a handy trail for whatever was following her.

She consoled herself with the fact that her noble laspistol was still as brim full of power as it would be had it never been fired. She was far from defenceless.

Splash-splash. Stop.

In the distance: *Splish-splash-splish-splash.* Then nothing. The sound died away abruptly as if something else had stopped to listen. Donna wet her lips beneath the scarf. This was not good.

She went up the next ladder she came to and found it blocked like all the others. Instead of climbing back down, she wedged herself in the narrow shaft with her feet pushing her back into the opposite wall. She pried a few small chunks out of the cracked rockrete and dropped them into the sewage below to simulate the sound of her jumping back down into the main pipe.

Splash.

She waited. Minutes dragged by and her calves started to cramp up. She tried to ignore the nagging sensation and focus on the dark instead. When Donna had first come to the Underhive it had seemed a realm of inky midnight to her. The Spire is a place of sunlight and open, airy chambers where filterglass and silvered armourplas is as common as steel and iron is below. When access to open skies becomes a statement of power and influence, every artifice and architecture is used to put it on display. Even in the inner hub of the Spire there were countless balconies, promenades and vista windows overlooking the open spaces of the arboreta.

Nothing had prepared her for the impenetrable gloom she had encountered, nor for how the yellow sodium, lurid neon and bright halogen of the settlement lights could only push it back for a space but could never defeat it. Eventually Donna made friends with the dark and began to appreciate it like all Underhivers do. Once your eyes become adjusted you start to understand that what people mean when they say 'pitch-dark' usually means little more than 'there's less light than I'm used to.'

The truth was the slightest scatter of photons would be picked up and processed by those hungry little cones and rods inside your eyes. In normal light your brain had plenty to handle without trying to utilise every tiny shred of information – it just kind of fudges it like a pict journalist does. If there was a hive quake they wouldn't show you every fallen stone and broken bone, you just got a few picts of fires and mortuary wagons and your imagination would fill in the rest. The point being, when they know there's been a hive quake anyway, human beings are curious and want to know more, but not every last detail. That's what human brains are like. As long as it thinks its got the big picture, it's not too bothered about the details.

But when your brain gets starved of its normal levels of info it pays more attention to what it has got available. After an hour or two in the dark, a human brain would start to realise it's not really 'pitch-dark' anywhere in the Underhive. A faint backwash of light from settlements and even caravans carries remarkably, reflecting off rockrete here and getting absorbed by shadow there to give a grey, grainy illumination for kilometres around, not unlike moonlight.

The hive was full microscopic fungi and lichens everywhere, giving off a faint phosphorescence that could be used to navigate through pipes and tunnels. Most old structures and machines had lamps and telltales shining out like beacons even though their long-dead masters would say that they were but dim ghosts of their former selves.

With the help of her bionic eye, Donna had found that the dark was the greatest ally a lone fighter could have in the Underhive. It became your both her cloak of invisibility and her sanctuary in one.

Peering down into the darkness, Donna saw it getting lighter in the pipe at the bottom of the ladder and thought somehow that her hunter had crept up silently enough that she hadn't heard anything. Nothing appeared in sight and she waited, fretting about how exposed she would be if whatever it was chose to just look up. Still nothing. She was about to climb down and look when she heard a whisper of sound.

Splish-splash-splish-splash.

It sounded like a group. The sewage threw what light there was into thin pearly ropes on its surface as it rippled in response to the not-too-distant disturbance. Donna caught the faint clink of metal on stone, and the murmur of breath rasping from unhealthy-sounding lungs.

Splish-splash-splish-splash.

The light grew stronger and gained an amber colouration. There was a group coming. Donna froze, willing her calves to stop trembling for a moment. A shape appeared at the bottom of the shaft, weirdly underlit by something casting a diffuse fountain of light that was caught and reflected by the slurry. Donna mentally flipped her bionic eye to a passive thermal scan. Ethereal blooms of heat from the skin of the weird figure below betrayed its shape to Donna's enhanced vision as it glanced up the shaft towards where she was hiding.

It looked like a Delaque.

Donna held her breath as the Delauqe seemed to look straight at her. Part of her mind registered that the light beneath his upturned face was the tiny glow from a power readout on the ganger's laspistol.

After an endless moment, the black-goggled face turned away and the figure moved further along the pipe. Donna willed herself to breathe in slowly without gasping.

'Crap,' the Delaque whispered. He made a low whistle.

Others moved down the pipe: six, maybe seven in all, it was hard to be sure. It was also hard to hear their voices when they spoke. The sibilance characteristic of this particular Delaque gang was always dancing at the edge of perception. There was something about 'Ulanti bitch,' and 'bounty.' It sounded like there was a disagreement going on. She heard 'back' – which could have been about going back or a reference to the dead bounty hunter Kell Bak, or to his live cousin, Shallej. Once again she wished for a frag-grenade but knew it would probably kill her as well with the shockwave in such tight confines.

One voice was raised above the whispers, and it held the tones of command.

'We split up and keeping looking,' it rasped. 'The bitch can't get to Relli. Those are Bak's orders.'

And that, apparently, was that. The group waded off along the pipe without another word and would no doubt start splitting up at each junction they came to. That left Donna in a prime position to descend and go in entirely the opposite direction. Or it would have done if they hadn't left one of their number behind to watch out for her in case she doubled back. The lookout was out of sight from Donna, but by the amber light she could guess it was the same ganger they had sent to scout ahead. 'Ganger' was a misnomer. He was evidently a fresh-meat juve and jittery as hell.

It was typical of these particular Delaque to send in an expendable first, one with a half-empty laspistol, and then to leave the kid behind as a back marker. All he had to do was scream or fire his weapon and the rest of the gangers would be back in an instant. Hell, he could even be bait for a trap.

The sad fact was that Donna couldn't stay hidden in the shaft indefinitely, as sooner or later the juve would get bored and start poking his nose into things he shouldn't. Juves were always doing dumb stuff – it seemed to be a rule.

Donna started to ease herself down the ladder. She planned to hook her feet over the rungs so she could swing down head first into the pipe and break the kid's neck, assuming he was obliging enough to venture into neck snapping range.

The juve was most obliging, even a little too much so. As Donna's feet reached the lowest rungs, she looked down to see the moon-faced juve was below her with one foot on the bottom of the ladder. He looked up and his mouth opened in a wide 'O' of alarm.

Donna's boot heel scrunched into his face, snapping his head back and sending broken teeth pin-wheeling into the sludge. She followed up instantly, swinging gracefully from the ladder and double-kicking his chest. His ribs were splintered into dull knives that skewered heart and lungs as her powerful legs pistoned into him with the full weight of her body behind them.

The juve flopped against the side of the pipe and slithered into the sludge vomiting, red froth from his shattered mouth. Donna nimbly dropped off the ladder and onto his sagging chest to push him fully under the surface. He died with barely a ripple. Donna glared about her, expecting a barrage of gunfire, but all was quiet. In the distance she could occasionally hear the other Delaque splashing around through the sewers. Time to go.

She started wading back along the pipe, trying to keep quiet and look in all directions at once. She was perhaps half way back to the next junction when she heard a low whistle echoing back eerily from the direction the Delaque had taken. After a few more steps it was repeated, and a heartbeat after that Donna heard the unmistakable splashes of many men running.

Ploughing through the stinking sewage was like a waking nightmare, bent over and almost-running but moving so agonisingly slowly that she expected each step to be her last. There was a deafening rattle of shots behind her and autogun rounds whipped past as she breasted the corner. A las-bolt flashed into a hissing cloud of steam as it struck the surface of the liquid, scalding her as she dived sideways into the junction. Just as the situation seemed like it couldn't get any worse, Donna heard a distant *basso profundo* roar cut across the thunderous weapons fire. The natives were getting restless.

The firing stuttered and died away into echoes. An illusion of peace settled for a moment, but it was only an illusion. Right now, Donna knew, the Delaque would be slinking forward silently and fanning out to catch her in a net, covering the spot where she had disappeared from sight with guns alert for the first glimpse of movement.

Well screw that, Donna thought, and she kept wading until she could duck down a narrower branch in the pipes than she had tried before. Whatever monstrosity had started roaming around sounded so big, hopefully it wouldn't fit down there.

The narrow pipe gave way to a tunnel the size of a boulevard within twenty wallowing steps – so much for that plan. Donna mounted crumbling steps onto one of the walkways that ranged down either side. Now that her ears weren't filled by the sound of her own progress, she could hear all kinds of distorted echoes in the pipes around her: continuous splashings, occasional shots or crackling salvos, more blood chilling roars, babbling or gibbering voices. Nothing was in sight; the slurry in the wide channel was serene and undisturbed, but the echoes made it sound as if the end of the world was occurring just a few steps away.

Donna was paralysed by indecision. Staying here left her exposed with no cover if anyone came out of the half dozen tributary pipes that entered the tunnel from either side. To keep moving was to risk blundering into a Delaque in the confusion, or worse still she might run into whatever they were shooting at – because it certainly wasn't her any more.

As she was standing there, her dark-adjusted eyes (real and artificial) picked up light flowing from one of the tributary pipes on the opposite side of the channel like moonlight. It was a cold phosphorescence, pallid and diffuse but it seemed unfeasibly bright in the gloom. Donna watched in horrified fascination as the light brightened perceptibly; whatever was making it was moving closer. She could hear a slithering, splashing sound coming with it that could only be made by something really, really big moving through the pipes. Little wavelets raced away from slurry pushed down the pipeway by its displacement.

The glow died away in one pipe and then started to grow in the next one. Donna heard chuffing breath and a low, throaty rumble like an engine ticking over. Was the thing was moving along parallel to the tunnel, casting about for more victims? Probably. The next pipe dimmed as it moved on. Two more pipes and it would be opposite Donna.

She had a brief internal struggle between curiosity and common sense before discovering she had no real desire to find out what it was. She selected the nearest pipe on her side and made for it, intending to put as much distance between her and the thing as possible.

Donna saw the Delaque illuminated in the tunnel mouth as he fired a single manstopper round from his shot cannon aimed straight at her head.

A scatter round would have smeared the contents of her skull across the tunnel, but the manstopper trades spread for hitting power. She was already turning and a preternaturally fast flinch meant the solid lump of lead tore a smoking hole through her dreads instead of her brain. The shock of it made Donna fall prone instantly, as though her brain was so scared by the close call that the only thing it could come up with was to drop her like a puppet with its strings cut.

Donna wildly loosed off shots with her las – none of them even vaguely close to where the Delaque had been standing. He span away with his long coat-tails fluttering like bird's wings. He was out of sight before she recovered her aim enough to shoot accurately.

She heard him rack the slide on his shot cannon and the plop-hiss of a spent cartridge being ejected into the slurry. That sent her rolling to one side so that if he came out for a snap shot she wouldn't be right where he expected her to be. It was a standoff now with both fighters alerted, close enough to touch and with only a single corner between them. She hoped he didn't have any frag bombs.

'Ulanti bitch! You should have stayed out of the Underhive. You were a fool to come down here.' The Delaque's venomous hiss echoed from the pipe.

'What, and miss all the marvelous ambience? And the fine company?' Donna was silently shifting into a crouch by the wall and inwardly bewailing the smell of her burning hair. It was a safe guess by now that he didn't have any frags.

'Stay out of Relli's affairs or it'll be the death of you.'

She wondered what the Delaque was trying to pull, probably just covering the pipe and waiting for his buddies to arrive.

Donna caught a flicker of pallid light across her; the dim shadow she cast on the stained tunnel wall was growing. The monster!

She whipped around to see great, fanged jaws issuing from the pipe on the opposite side of the tunnel. Actually, it was more like the tunnel had grown a circle of teeth, the maw filled it so perfectly. The dull, luminescent flesh was streaked with blood and gore, tatters of skin and cloth hanging from the dagger-like fangs like grisly banners. Donna heard the Delaque snickering as he backed away to safety.

'Bon appetit, nobledam.' His whispered taunt was barely audible over the rumbling hiss of the newcomer. 'I do hope you find your dinner guest engaging.'

Donna was already running.

She didn't look back. When running for your life that only makes you trip over and lose it; your life that is. She sprinted along the walkway past the pipe where the Delaque had been hiding. The dull boom of his shot cannon came on her heels a split second after. He was way off, and he must have been a good distance away by now, and putting in still more distance had probably become a bigger priority than covering the end of the pipe.

The analysis of the Delaque's intentions flipped through one part of her mind while another watched for broken sections of walkway or slippery patches as she ran. A third monitored the hissing, splashing progress of the thing behind her. In the corner of her eye she could see a bow wave surging along the channel after her. Whatever it was, it was big and it was fast.

Ahead the walkway and channel apparently stopped in empty air as the tunnel opened out into an inky gulf. She was cornered.

She kept running for the edge anyway. Perhaps the monster would be as dumb as the giant and just run right off it? Failing that, Donna decided she might just want to jump rather than get eaten.

As she got closer, Donna's enhanced eye could pick out that it wasn't a sheer drop, rather the channel became a sluiceway, a sheer slope at an angle of about forty-five degrees. She couldn't see if there was a walkway or steps along the side of it. Peachy.

Her ears told her that the monster was slowing down. It was smart enough to know she was trapped and it wasn't about to go charging off a concealed edge. Donna had a second to stop and take in the sluiceway before turning to confront her pursuer.

The sluiceway converged with three others into a wide vertical shaft maybe twenty metres in diameter. The mouth of the shaft was covered by a grid work of thick bars which had caught all kinds of detritus despite their wide spacing and corroded condition. Donna glimpsed fallen spars, rubble, bones, even the wreck of an old utility vehicle. It was like a huge, sagging web spun by industrial strength spiders, an image she tried put out of her mind as she span around.

The monster was regarding her with reptilian eyes from twenty metres back along the channel. From blunt snout to bladed tail tip it must have topped ten metres long, its jaws fully a third of that. Four stubby legs barely lifted its heavy body out of the slurry, but its thick, powerful tail meant it could belly-surf through the muck with surprising speed for something that weighed a good few tonnes.

Thick plates and scales covered its upper surface. Its eyes were relatively small and widely spaced, hard to hit, and as for brains – who knew? They were probably small and hard to find too. Its flesh glowed with a ashen corpse-candle light from encrusted slime or fungus, probably parasitic since it didn't look like the monster hunted primarily by using its eyes, although using taste or smell down here didn't bear thinking about.

It rumbled a challenge and scissored open its three-metre jaws to reveal rows of gleaming teeth. It definitely had the edge at close fighting – Seventy-six was quite outmatched. In fact, Donna decided, one rush and it would all be over. She had fought some big Underhive critters in her time, but never something big enough that she could stand in its open mouth and still have room to stretch her arms above her head.

She jumped down the sluiceway and immediately started sliding away towards the deceptively solid-looking surface below. The monster gave a rumbling cough of annoyance behind her and started slithering forward. She caught sight of the stumps of corroded railings to one side and kicked over towards them, stumbling onto crumbling steps at the side of the sluiceway.

Her momentum carried her forward so fast she had to skip down the rest of the steps to avoid losing her balance and going headlong. She bounded to the bottom of the sluiceway and out onto the grill over the shaft in the space of a few panic strewn seconds. Rubble dropped away treacherously beneath her feet before she had even taken two steps, but she was ready for that and neatly pirouetted to hop up onto a large fallen slab.

The monster was crawling over the edge of the sluice, using the worn old steps to slow itself down as it scraped down the slope. It looked mightily sure of itself. Donna had a sudden inkling this might be the beast's lair.

Donna kept moving, trying to reach the opposite sluiceway, but what had looked like an almost solid surface from above was a patchwork of detritus islands with gaping holes in between them big enough to swallow her whole. She had to pick her way carefully while the monster slithered forward untroubled. It was too big to even notice the metre-wide gaps let alone be impeded by them, and it was gaining on her.

She reached the bottom of the sluiceway and her heart fell. The steps on this side were completely obliterated. Climbing the slope would be too slow – one good rear-and-snap and the monster would have her in its jaws before she got halfway up.

One of the things that had marked Mad Donna as a natural gang fighter was her ability to adapt instantly to changing circumstances. Where others would vainly cling to their plans even in the face of certain failure, she could recognise one course of action as fruitless and change to another without missing a beat. So she did here. With her retreat blocked she didn't waste a breath cursing the vagaries of fate, or attempt to climb anyway in the hope of being lucky. Mad Donna turned and levelled her laspistol defiantly.

The beast might get its kill but it was going to have to fight for it.

It crawled around the last rubble pile and lazily spread its titanic jaws wide to claim her. Donna shot it in the roof of the mouth, hoping to hit its brain. She didn't succeed in that, but she succeeded in seriously pissing it off. It hissed horribly and the jaws slammed shut with a snap loud enough to hurt Donna's ears. It lunged at her then, its four stubby legs driving it forward with shocking speed. She got off another shot aimed at its eyes but they were too small and it was moving too fast. The las-bolt creased the end of its muzzle and made it flinch reflexively back, saving Donna from being crushed against the sluiceway by its bulk. She skipped aside as it lashed its jaws furiously back and forth.

Donna saw a chance and took it, darting past the beast and towards the bottom of another sluiceway. It caught her a glancing blow with its thick tail, a flying lesson of several metres duration that left Donna bruised, breathless and clutching desperately at the open grillwork so she didn't tumble through. She caught a fleeting impression of a deep well beneath her with the glimmer of sludge at the bottom stirred by restless, hungry shapes. Tearing her gaze away, she saw the monster coming for her again.

No mere flinch was going to save her this time. She aimed as carefully as she could – there was only going to be time for one shot. The tiny reptilian eyes gleamed at her with mocking intensity, as if it knew it was an impossible shot. Donna pulled the trigger... and missed. The monster opened its jaws again. There would be no reprieve this time.

Suddenly the staccato rattle of a heavy stubber filled the sluiceways with false thunder. As if the monster wasn't enough, the Delaque had caught up with her too. Sparks flew as high velocity bullets chewed up rubble and ricocheted off the grillwork. The stream of flying lead tracked towards her and then veered into the monster. Bloody impacts stitched across its bleached flesh. Its answering roar was edged with pain for the first time.

The monster shuddered and twisted aside, crawling away through the rubble to escape its tormentor. More bursts of autofire followed its pale bulk into the gloom. A voice called down.

'Grab the line, D'onne, be quick girl!'

It was Tessera.

Formal sanctuary was a piece of law left over from the house wars of millennia ago, before there was a ruling house on Necromunda. Put simply, it meant throwing yourself on the mercy of one house in order not to be given up to another. In theory, a noble seeking sanctuary could not be ransomed off, executed or exchanged, nor held against their will. That was the theory, though it had been found wanting on a number of occasions when put to the test.

D'onne and Hanno were conducted inside the great gate without hindrance. Then they had to stand waiting while the sergeant of the guard (or whatever the Escher equivalent was) had a long, haggling vox call with their supervisor. They relieved Hanno of his shot cannon before letting him go further, although they allowed him to keep his sidearm – which was ironic considering the holstered bolt pistol he wore at his waste was a far deadlier piece than the cannon he carried.

The white paving stones outside also formed the avenue they stood on behind the gate. D'onne mused that it had been a bad choice, showing its age in the millions of scuffs and drag marks on its surface. High arched ceilings and concealed uplighting gave the illusion of space, a poor imitation that left her feeling briefly homesick for the sweeping colonnades of her home.

Eventually, the guards ushered them along the avenue past lumbering cargo servitors and crowds of curious Escher who whispered in hallways as they passed. The avenue twisted and branched crazily, but they clearly took the main route throughout. D'onne realised the whole zone they were passing through was formed as part of the Escher defences in this area. The twisting avenue would disorientate attackers while its many branches made them easy to outmanoeuvre. Doubtlessly the walls also had concealed loopholes and firing slits hidden in the stonework.

They ended their journey heading up a steep switchback ramp into some sort of communications centre that was hidden behind armoured shutters. A great pillar covered in pict screens of all sizes dominated the centre of the chamber. Maybe twenty techs were working feverishly around the pillar, making and breaking connections at its base or riding platforms to get up by the flickering panels. Servitors in the shadows quietly murmured, returning datum streams from slack lips. A raised deck to one side held a holo-globe surrounded by three women, its ruddy cast making them look like witches around a cauldron. They were the only ones paying attention when D'onne and Hanno were escorted in. Judging by their posture and dress, D'onne surmised that they were obviously ranking house members. But were they to be intermediaries or judges?

As they approached, D'onne picked up on little signs, a head turn here, a lip movement there, that all three women were speaking and listening to unseen others. Intermediaries then. It was quite possible they were just meat puppets.

'Nobledam Ulanti, welcome. Forgive the arrangements but we are at a busy time here in House Escher.' It was a formal address, polite but enquiring. The words were well measured so it seemed likely that they were the woman's own, for now at least.

However busy they were, 'the arrangements' spoke volumes about how they felt about her. They wanted to know more and right now, whatever was going on, they didn't want any political powder kegs hanging around in their halls to screw it up for them. D'onne wondered how many other senior house members were listening in. Hundreds probably.

'We understand you have requested sanctuary, nobledam, a law that has not been invoked here for centuries.'

The woman paused as if listening, but it was probably to let that notion settle in for effect. She continued.

'We feel compelled to ask of you what it is you need sanctuary from, and why you feel it cannot be given to you by your own house, one that is ranked among the most powerful of the pureblood noble families.'

They could well guess what would make her seek protection outside her own family and what it portended, but they wanted it spelled out. Fine.

'My story is no easy one to tell, especially in haste. I seek sanctuary from Patriarch Sylvanus, from my father. He…'

Even a lifetime of comportment training hadn't prepared her for this. She felt Hanno's eyes boring into her, and the cool, appraising looks of the Escher were like a dash of ice water to her cluttered mind. The pause stretched out longer as everyone waited for her to continue. Gathering herself, she tried to start again.

'I am the twelfth daughter of the Patriarch Sylvanus, head of the Noble Household of Ulanti. Until age six I was brought up in the bosom of my family, among my sisters and with my mother. That all changed when one of my sisters died. No, that's not right. One of my sisters was murdered.

'We in the Spire are taught from birth that the family will be your first loyalty, now and always, and the family's honour is your next. I was still very young when I saw that revealed as a lie. One of my own sisters pushed another to

her death with the encouragement and approval of a third. Everything I thought I knew came apart at the seams that night.

'I was placed in a narrow tower on the flank of the Spire, an ancient marvel of the lost arts with tutelage engines and exercise regulators, and machine spirits of great age and nobility. At first I believed I was there for my protection but as the weeks passed I came to understand that I had committed some sort of crime against my family. No one came to visit me and the tower would not permit me to leave. I was imprisoned.

'Time became hard to gauge but I think it was a year before I had my first visitor. The spirits had taught me and kept me company so I was happy enough, in my own terribly young way, but for the aching gap in my heart left by the absence of my family. But I began every day honestly believing things would change for the better and that my mother or my sisters would come visiting. So I was not surprised when the spirits told me to prepare myself for a visitor, just excited.

'So imagine my shock when the lock opened to reveal not my mother or my sisters but my father, Patriarch Sylvanus, in all his finery. He berated me for my slipshod appearance and stalked around the tower for an hour, criticising me for living like an animal and being a disgrace to the family. Every time I tried to speak he angrily commanded me to silence. When I started to cry he flew into a towering rage, shouting that weakness and petty blackmail wouldn't gain me the family's forgiveness. When I wouldn't stop crying he almost struck me. Instead he turned and left, stopping at the lock just long enough to express his own disappointment in me, all sadness now that his rage had blown over.

'At the last he bent down to me and whispered as if he were afraid that others would hear (and the tower would, it remembered every word that was said inside it). "You must try harder, D'onne, for all our sakes." And with that he was gone.

'Imagine the child separated from its family who hears those words – how hard does it try? With every iota of its being, with every ounce of the raw, young energy beating in its innocent heart.

'My father did not visit again for a month, but every day I scrubbed and cleansed and preened and prepared in case he might come. When he did visit again I was devastated by his criticism of my appearance once more. But this time I did not cry, and I noticed his displeasure seemed less as he stalked about the tower. He saw I had tried harder.

'This time as he left he said nothing, but as the lock slid shut I saw him give the tiniest nod. It was a token of approval I cherished to ridiculous lengths in the weeks to come.

'Sylvanus's visits were sporadic after that. Sometimes I would see him every week, at other times he would be gone for half a year. In the times between, I applied myself remorselessly to becoming a true daughter of the noble house of Ulanti. I learned how to please him, how to sense every subtle nuance of his likes and dislikes. I danced and sang for his pleasure, apparelled myself suitably for all occasions. I studied the thousand generations of our family history so I might discourse with him on something dear to his heart.

'He would stay longer if I did well, and reward me with gestures of approval and, sometimes, affection. I became the boldest of thieves, stealing a small smile or a happy nod from him with my antics, eluding his towering rages and cynical traps with my wits and cunning. I came to understand this was what he wanted from me, to be bold and clever, to be a true daughter of Ulanti, able to both please men and bend them to my will.

'As I came to womanhood he completed my training as I came to understand it with arts of etiquette and romance, the techniques of wooing and being wooed, being hunter and prey... Our relationship changed through that time as I became increasingly wilful and challenging, I think, to him. I gained the impression that he only valued my opinion when it mirrored his own. He decided the time had come and announced that I was to be married off to another house.'

As she spoke, Donna noticed the pict screens on the pillar were blinking out one by one. There seemed to be some agitation among the techs surrounding it. The Escher facing her remained serene. She mentally shrugged and carried on.

'I'm told the competition among my suitors was fierce. There were many duels and the bride price I commanded was astronomical. House Ko'iron emerged as the victors, and their eldest son was to be married to the youngest daughter of Ulanti.'

'Wait please, nobledam,' one of the Escher said. All three of them wore that distracted look again. Over at the pillar the pict screens were coming back on again one by one.

Each screen showed a new scene of violence: a transporter wrecked and broken open, its cargo strewn across the slabway; a rioting mob hurling themselves at a line of enforcers; a compound being invaded by masked gunmen; a warehouse in flames; explosions blossoming along an overpass. The comm chamber they stood in trembled slightly from distant shocks in sympathy.

'Each screen shows Escher territory,' one of the Escher women said at last. 'Incidents of violence have increased four-hundred per cent in the last twenty minutes. If our estimates bear out it'll be a thousand-fold within the hour.'

Donna felt her mouth go dry.

'We can safely assume none of these incidents can be traced to House Ulanti, but that they all originate there. Soon the other houses will join in to take advantage of our weakness and house war may follow.

'You cannot stay here,' Tessera had told her.

7: DOWNTOWN

'Burn the filthy mutants!'
Sermons of the Arch Zealot

'How the hell did you find me?'

It was Donna's first question after Avignon had hauled her up out of the monster's lair like a fish on a line. Tessera had just looked superior and all knowing at the time so she didn't hear the story properly until she wheedled it out of Tola later. Not that it ever took much wheedling to get Tola talking; it was shutting her up that was the real trick.

It turned out that Tola and Avignon had trailed Donna after she left Hagen's Place in Glory Hole. Both of them knew Donna well enough to understand there wasn't a cat in hell's chance that she wouldn't go to the warehouse to find out more. They had followed her until she climbed down to the third tier, at which point they had to go back and pay a toll-crank to get down since neither of them fancied emulating Donna's high-wire routine.

They had arrived in time to see Donna caught cold by the bounty hunters at Strakan's warehouse. When Donna made a break for it they strafed Kell's sniper's nest in the tower while she ran inside, which went a long way towards explaining why he hadn't shot her in the back at the time – the little toad was pinned down by their fire.

Once Donna had disappeared inside, Tola and Avignon ran off and hid further around the tier. They had waited for a while and when Shallej and Kell came out empty-handed they had known that she had somehow escaped the warehouse. That's when they hightailed it out of there to tell Tessera what was going on. Simple.

Of course that didn't answer Donna's question: how the hell had they found her beneath Dust Falls? She determined to get the rest of the story out of Tessera at the next rest stop. The gang were descending into the Abyss now, heading for Down Town, which suited Donna just fine. In truth, Donna was rather touched that Tessera had gone out of her way to find her in the first place, so she stuck with the gang out of old loyalties, secretly revelling in the chance to relax a little and stop watching her back.

They were moving through layer after layer of ancient hab-domes, access ways and waste pipes, working their way back along the well-worn paths of the Abyss. The deeper they went, the more crushed down the ruins of the old hive became, compacted beneath the weight of successive generations of demolition and construction. More often than not they followed fracture lines between the strata; an old transit rail might give a few hundred metres of useable passageway beneath its rails before giving way to a sagging plaza whose collapsed roof had left enough crawl spaces to reach a semi-intact street.

They paused at a crossroads of sorts. A cracked waste pipe breached the floor, coming in from one side and crossing their path. Tessera seemed uncertain about which way to take and Donna took the opportunity to talk to her away from the others.

To Donna's eyes Tessera was looking old and tired. Her bleach-blonde hair showed grey at the roots and blackened gums marred the smile that she flashed at Donna. Tessera's face was etched with pocks and scars from a lifetime of gang fights and hardship, but the gang leader's eyes were bright and sharp, her narrow shoulders unbowed. She pre-empted Donna's question before she had even opened her mouth.

'You want to know how we found you?'

Donna grinned back. Tessera was undoubtedly one of the smartest people she had ever met, inside the Spire or out of it. She could read people like books, which was no great skill in itself when you know the basics, but Tessera had a way of making you feel glad about it.

'I like to think I'm hard to track, elusive even, but recent events have made me seriously doubt that,' Donna replied. 'In fact, I'm seriously starting to think I'm trailing a flashing sign that says "Donna is here" in letters that you can see from Dust Falls to Two Tunnels.'

'It was easy to guess you would hit up Hanno for info.'

Ah. Yes, it was easy when Donna thought about it, except for one thing.

'You know I've got history with Hanno, but the bounty hunters don't know about it – Hanno's always been rather… circumspect about his relationship with me.'

'Of course he has, he's chief watchman of one of the larger balls of dirt in the Underhive, and he can't afford to have his name linked with Mad Donna too often – no matter how much he would like to.'

Donna nodded, that was obvious too, really, but it was nice to hear it from someone else. At least he didn't hate her.

'How Kell and Shallej knew you'd be in Dust Falls I can't say, but I'd hazard a guess that they knew where to find Relli and they knew that sooner or later you'd show up to have it out with him for dredging up your past.'

Tessera's gaze weighed up Donna carefully. 'That is what you intend, isn't it? A confrontation of some sort.'

'You know me too well. Relli was singularly ill-advised to bring up my past.'

'It's been an effective way of getting your attention.'

'You mean you're not the only one who knows me well enough to know which buttons to press?'

'You were always a clever one, D'onne. So who could it be?'

'There're only two people I know of in the Underhive who know me that well: one is Hanno, the other is you.'

Donna's tone was challenging, but Tessera didn't even favour her with a response. She just smiled and waited while Donna's brain threw up all the million and one reasons why Tessera or Hanno wouldn't want to make trouble for her.

'So that's not it. Someone from the Spire then?'

'And you already knew that; you just didn't want it to be true so you ignored it and ran.'

Donna shot Tessera a rueful look, feeling very young and uncertain again. Oddly, it was a feeling she cherished in a way. Tessera was right, of course. She'd bolted at the first implication that spyrers were involved and subconsciously headed for the deepest, darkest corner of the Underhive she knew of. She was running straight for whatever was waiting for her down there, like an animal being driven into a trap.

'I think there was a noble after me at Cliff Wall but I lost him.'

Tessera raised an eyebrow. 'Who?'

'I'm not sure. I only saw him at a distance and I thought it was another bounty hunter at the time. But thinking back, there was just something about the way he acted with the hired help that only a noble would expect to get away with down here. Hell, it was an obvious Hive City group when I think about it – too many people and not enough combatants.' She paused, remembering the sleek chrome shape of the enforcer hound slinking out of the shadows. 'And plenty of fancy Uphive tech.'

'A noble showing up on your trail is hard to put down to coincidence,' Tessera remarked.

'Sometimes you can't bury yourself deep enough, the past comes back and gets you anywhere. Hell, I never even got out of Hive Primus so I shouldn't be at all surprised when my noble kin coming looking for me.' Donna had meant to sound determined yet carefree, but her voice came out flat and emotionless instead, barely covering her bitter resignation.

Tessera's voice was calm and reassuring in the gloom. 'It'll be all right, Donna. You're quite capable of looking after yourself as I well know, and now you've got a posse of mean-ass bitches to back you up. You're not alone in this any more.'

Donna lifted her living eye to glare at Tessera. 'I didn't ask you to come. You don't normally set foot beyond Two Tunnels, so why have you dragged your girls halfway across the Underhive to find me? What's your stake in this, Tessera?'

'Now what you're really asking is why did I drag you all the way down here in the first place. Both questions have the same answer.'

'Which is?'

'If you haven't figured it out by now, talk to one of the juves, they can put you straight.'

Donna laughed. Tessera had always given her the same response when she asked some particularly dumb-witted question, ever since she had come down to start a life as the Underhive's oldest juve. Tessera had deflected her question, but that was good enough for now. Maybe she would just ask one of the juves.

'You said Kell *and* Shallej were in Dust Falls? But Kell said Shallej had gone to Two Tunnels.'

'He must have lied. I saw Shallej with my own eyes. He was heading down the Abyss with a big gang of Delaque when we arrived at Dust Falls. I stopped just long enough to talk with Hanno and then came looking for you.'

'That makes sense. I heard the Delaque talking about having orders from Bak. He must have sent some of those gangers into the sewers looking for me. But where the hell did he go?'

Tessera shrugged and rolled her eyes downward. She was right again of course. There was only one place to go at the bottom of the Abyss. The same place Relli had his manse.

Down Town.

THE CHAOTIC DEPTHS of the Underhive gave way to collapsed and compacted ruins at Hive Bottom. This was where the hive's ancient foundation layer began, a region long since abandoned and forgotten by Hive City's inhabitants. Hundreds of metres thick, it's a domain of stagnant darkness where poisoned fumes rise from the putrid sump at the Hive Bottom to choke the labyrinth of crude crawl holes and ruinous caverns around it. But Hive Bottom was far from lifeless. Things dwelt in the darkness, spawned in the toxic waste of millennia, ruined creatures hiding from even the lights of the Underhive but still breeding and multiplying in the shadows.

Down Town was the deepest permanent settlement below The Wall. It stood in the lowest portion of the Underhive, at the bottom of the ancient effluent-worn shaft men call the Abyss. Common wisdom held that it was positioned at the deepest habitable point in the Underhive, although the scavvies would doubtless argue about that, if anybody gave a damn about what muties thought. In truth, it lay even beyond the region of domes and tunnels that comprise the Underhive itself, positioned as it was upon the shores of the toxic sump lake that lay at the very bottom of the hive.

Sometimes, things crawled forth from their holes in the foundation layer, slithering up from the blackness to feed, driven by their hunger for soft, untainted flesh and warm blood. They could be glimpsed from the watchtowers of Down Town, moving through the spoil heaps as they hunted the mutant rats that feed on the refuse there. Their luminous eyes could be seen glimmering amongst the ruins as they studied the progress of a slave train, watching for stragglers and wounded. Their whimpering and snarling could be heard throughout Down Town in the dark hours of lights-out, always close by but always unseen, a sound to haunt the sleep of men.

Once in a while a hunter or prospector would bring the pelt of some strange bestial thing to Down Town. Some of them were men, or used to be men, with scabrous rotting skin and talon-like nails, eyes turned to vestigial pits covered by pallid membranes or black and staring with no visible irises. Others had only the sham of human form, scaly and vile things with dripping mouths and long red tongues. Over the far wall of the Down Town Trade Hole were nailed the skins of many such beasts, hundreds and hundreds of them. Some of the hides were rotted and eaten away by time or infestation, whereas others gleamed with green and golden scales or purple and black chitin, miraculously unmarked by chemical fogs or necrotic fungi. A few of the skins were those of savages and outlaws brought in for bounty, but most were of hunters that had become prey, a warning to the rest to stay away. Mostly they did, except when the poison fogs rolled in off the sump and the people of Down Town had to fasten their doors tight.

Few descended as far as Down Town, and fewer still stayed there deliberately to make a living, although plenty end up staying unintentionally and permanently.

The journey down from Dust Falls was long and arduous to say the least, and getting down the more commonly used paths was often a battle in its own right, with rivals, outlaws, scavvies and worse things to contend with en route. The surrounding domes through the hive foundations were crushed and compacted, riddled with narrow crawl holes and infested with evil things ready to feed on the weak and unwary.

But some of the hardiest and most desperate still went, attracted by the sump lake itself and by the things that dwell in it. In the hard land of the Underhive, there was no tougher work than that which could be found in Down Town, but there was also none more likely to get you really wealthy or really dead. Most people that went to Down Town thought they were going to get wealthy, most of them were dead wrong.

The strongest and the quickest gang fighters went to hunt the monstrous, legendary sump-spiders on the toxic lake, the great spider mares and their kin: White Skaters, Black Leviathans, Scarlet Jennies, Orange Knees, Blue Knees, Red Knees, Tippers and Runners.

Beautiful, huge and deadly, Necromundan spiders were renowned across the stars. Their faceted eyes were as hard as diamonds and greatly prized by the jewellers of a thousand worlds for their scintillating iridescence and undying lustre. The blood spilled to gain such prizes only added to their value, with nobles and merchants vying to show how many lost lives they could display in a single trinket or ornament.

With an equal share in a successful spider hunt, a man might win two fist-sized stones or more, enough to live like a prince for a year in the Underhive, if you could avoid getting killed for long enough to enjoy it. The truth was that for every successful hunt three or more failed, and even in a successful hunt motor-skiffs were overturned and men were killed with shocking regularity. Often hunts failed to return at all, and often the skiff pilots questioned just who was hunting whom out on the slick black swells of the sump lake.

Other travellers sensibly set their sights lower and came to feed off the spoils of the hunt, to bid for the carcasses. They would haggle over tough spider pelts and chitin, boil down the beasts' nutritious fat and extract their deadly venom to sell on; no part of the spider was wasted from its fangs to its spinnerets. There were a hundred petty industries thriving upon the spiders and the lesser creatures of the lake: the skimmers, sharks, slime spawn and the other nameless beasts of the deeps. Many things lived in the sump that lived nowhere else in the Underhive, probably nowhere else in the universe, a unique collection of life forms that had somehow adapted to living on the toxic lake surface or beneath it.

Many of the Ratskin colonies believed that the sump itself was the living embodiment of what they called the hive spirits. To them it was heaven, hell and perdition all rolled into one, and it was where their spirits would go when they died before they got reborn; a hell of a lot of them hoped to come back as sump spiders, which tells you something.

The surface of the sump lake constantly roiled with a consistency that could vary from light machine-oil to molasses and back again within a hundred yards. The gases it emitted were often volatile or corrosive and methane fires and sulphur fogs chased each other across its surface.

Falling into the sump itself would be a death sentence – you'd be lucky if the poisons killed you before the corrosives melted the flesh from your bones. Either way, screaming agony for the rest of your doubtlessly short existence would be assured.

In places around the sump, huge stalagmites and stalactites of coagulated industrial waste had formed over millennia, creating organically grown cathedrals of accumulated foulness and squalor. The layers upon layers of waste mingled and accreted into insane chemical ores that were valuable but too highly corrosive or poisonous in their own right to even approach safely without the right protective gear. Many overconfident prospectors died trying to harvest these ores, and their bones were merged into growing piles that spread millimetre by millimetre, year after year, to create macabre frescoes in their curving walls.

Donna knew all of this, all the hoary old tales of Down Town, but as they approached Hive Bottom the thing she was most impressed by was the stink.

THEY WERE HOLED up on a ledge overlooking Down Town. They had to kick some milliasaurs out of the way to get in when they arrived but no one else seemed to have noticed. When Donna and the Escher showed up the creatures stormed out of their holes to bite them without a second's thought. Dumb little friks. Bullets and las-bolts blew them apart before they even got to use their much-feared venom. Rats would at least have waited until the humans' backs were turned, but that's the way in the Underhive – it takes all sorts. Now Donna and the Escher were watching and waiting, getting their first good look at Down Town.

Questing fingers of fog rolled in off the sump to probe down the narrow alleyways below. Yellow lights showed from slit windows in the high watchtowers that seemed to be on every building, and the trading hole was closed up tight. A line of pillars jutted out like broken teeth into the lake, each one a mooring point for a shoal of flat little motor-skiffs for spider hunting. There was also the odd sump drifter nestling here and there among the skiffs, like a fat sow among piglets, an image complimented by the bobbing motion imparted to them by the lake's swells.

One shape sitting on the lake dwarfed both the skiffs and the drifters. It squatted off to the right a little, just outside the walls of Down Town at its own mooring. The roiling mist on the sump made it blurry, but Donna's crystal eye saw all. It was a fat, teardrop-shaped craft almost two-hundred metres in length with an incongruous set of stub-wings projecting out for about a third of the way along its length.

At first she had taken it for some kind of atmospheric shuttle, but it had open decks on top and a definite keel below, so whatever it was, it had been designed to travel through a fluid medium, although probably not the sump lake. It didn't look like this particular example had travelled anywhere in a long time. The wing she could see looked pitted and crumpled, the hull was rust-streaked and peeling and the whole thing was listing over slightly at its mooring. There were skeletons of similarly sized craft dotted about, their oil-streaked ribs protruding from the sump around the moorings like giant fingers. This one looked to be the last of its kind.

It was Relli's manse.

'WATCHA LOOKING AT?' Tola asked.

Donna stretched out a little where she lay on the ledge before replying, but she kept her gaze focussed on Relli's place.

'Wire weed around the mooring piers, a gun tower on the shore, two more guns on deck with at least one more I can't see. I think I'm looking at about twenty guards of which up to six are Goliaths and the rest pit slaves; it's hard to be sure. I think I'm looking at maybe a dozen more people on the boat-thing: guests, staff, flunkies and all, plus one fat merchant who's the only frikkin' person that I actually want to see when I'm onboard. What are you looking at?'

'Carrion bats eating half a rat while its front half tries to crawl away. Ooh, they spotted him! Go Halfsie! Awww, they got him after all.'

Donna looked around at Tola. The girl had borrowed (probably stolen) a scope sight from one of the other gangers and was avidly watching the life and death struggles taking place all over the refuse heaps below. The rats had taken advantage of Halfsie's distraction to pull down an incautious carrion bat in return. Behold the circle of frikkin' life, Donna thought.

'Ask one of the juves,' Tessera had said. Tola wasn't a juve any more, but she remained so girlish that Donna often wondered if she were brain damaged in some way – between environmental poisoning and gang fight injuries it was pretty likely. She was an ideal candidate for the direct approach.

'Tola, why did Tessera tell the gang you were coming down here?'

'She didn't tell us anything.' Tola looked a little confused by the idea.

'Didn't anyone complain about going down the Abyss?'

It was another unwritten piece of Underhive lore that whenever The Abyss was mentioned someone would refuse to go, quoting the hoary old tales of Down Town and predicting doom for all who did. It was just like juves being irresistibly drawn to trouble, older gangers were irresistibly drawn to avoiding it.

'Ohhh.' Tola's face brightened and she grinned. 'You want to know what Tessera told us to make us come down the Abyss after you!'

Donna swallowed an urge to slap her.

'Yes, Tola!' she said brightly instead.

'Oh, Tessera didn't ask us to come and find you.'

Donna was so surprised that she forgot to be angry. Tessera ruled her gang like a dowager empress, so her next question was born out of pure incredulity.

'Well, who did then?'

'No one.'

'So let me get this right, Tola. Tessera and the gang just happened past? "Let's swing by the abandoned sewage pipes and see if anyone's down there being hunted by monsters and Delaque? Could be someone we know!" Was that it? A chance meeting as they say?'

Tola now looked thoroughly confused and Donna had run out of venom. She thought about starting over but the very idea exhausted her.

'Never mind, Tola,' Donna said, half to herself.

Tola grinned. 'They decided it,' she said. 'The whole gang decided to come, after me and Avvie told them about the fight at the warehouse. We musta told them a good story.'

Donna looked around at the rest of the gang sitting or lying around on the ledge. Some were observing the settlement like her and Tola, others were resting or playing cards. She recognised maybe half of them from her early days – Tessera, Tola, Avignon, Jen and Sara. The rest were new juves and gangers Tessera must have recruited down the years. They were a hard-bitten looking crew. One of the new gangers she didn't know caught her eye as she was looking around and called out to her.

'How soon do we go in, Donna? What's the plan?' Expectant faces turned towards her.

Donna was taken aback again. 'I'm sneaking in on my own. That's the plan. You lot aren't "going in" anywhere,' she retorted quickly.

There was a ripple of discontent from the gang. At first she thought they were getting angry or sullen but, looking around at their faces again, she concluded they were mostly disappointed.

'There's no point in you all getting chopped up by Relli's guns. A frontal rush would be suicide,' she explained. For all their bravado they knew that was true, they had seen the manse defences as well.

'But we can't just frikkin' sit up here while you go alone!' Jen, one of the old school gang, stood up and faced the others. 'We all voted to come, we can't turn back because Relli has a few frikkin' muscleboys guarding his house.'

There were giggles and calls of assent from the gang, and Donna felt the whole situation spiralling out of her control. Where the hell was Tessera? The Escher had come spoiling for a fight and weren't about to be denied one. And what was worse, they seemed to think they were here to help her!

'Look, Jen, you're only here because you and Tessera feel duty bound to look out for me because you brought me down to the Underhive all those years ago. The same goes for Tola and Avignon and Sara, too. When you brought me down from Hive City I left my old family behind and I found a new one with you.'

That made them start listening to Donna again, which was a good start. Now to put the meat in the sandwich.

'But I left the gang because I drew too much fire. Bounty hunters knew just where to come looking for me. That's how Kristi got killed and Faer lost her arm, in stupid fights we didn't need to have, which happened because of me.'

That changed things. The new gang members were looking differently at the old guard now. Donna hoped they were thinking about the realities of bleeding out from a torn artery like Kristi, or being burned like Faer. They were also looking at Donna a bit differently, too.

'Now, I'm here to chase a vendetta, another stupid fight that's no one else's but mine. It means something to me, but it means nothing to you. I'll not have more deaths on my conscience. There're enough there already and, despite rumours to the contrary, I do have a conscience.'

The finishing joke was a bit subtle, but most of the older gangers caught it and smiled. Job done: she'd communicated her perspective to them and made them relax a little. They weren't ready to rush into a fight any more.

Donna turned and walked away along the ledge towards Down Town.

No one followed her.

DONNA HAD GOT maybe a hundred metres along the ledge and was just starting to think about milliasaurs when she heard grating stones behind her. She whipped around with a drawn laspistol to find Jen coming along the ledge after her. Reliable, dumb Jen couldn't take a hint. Donna ignored the vagrant part of her brain that said, 'Just shoot her,' and waited.

Jen came and stood beside Donna, her burly tattooed shoulders making her look petite and demure by comparison.

'Nice try, Mad Donna,' Jen said. She grinned at Donna and flung an arm around her that made her tense at the unaccustomed contact. The only times Donna usually got this close to someone was when she was killing them. 'But you're wrong t' think your fights mean nothing to us. You're a frikkin' legend, girl.'

Donna shrugged to get free of Jen's bear-like grip. 'No no no. I'm just a frik-up, Jen, an aberration, not anybody's frikkin' legend,' she snarled. The embrace suddenly tightened, pinning her closer.

'Now listen up, Donna, and listen frikkin' good,' Jen hissed low and murderously in her ear. Jen looked big and threatening close up, but old habits ensured that Donna didn't flinch.

The words came tumbling out of Jen like she'd been thinking about them for a long time. Maybe she had. She never had been a great orator but her low, urgent voice held such passion it certainly came from the heart.

'You *are* a frikkin' legend,' she hissed, 'and I'll tell you why. People come down here because they want a new start, because they think that Hive City is frikked up and they want to be free of it and there's nowhere else to frikkin' go.

'But there's a lot more who dream of it but never make it – they're too frightened of losing their pict feed or their shower, or their two meals a day, or their friends on the line or their precious frikkin' *routine*.

'But now... now they've got *you*, a frikkin' noblewoman from the frikkin' Spire who made the choice to come down to the Underhive and survived. *You* turned your back on all those comforts, and more privilege than a frikkin' prole in the city can even dream about, but you're still here. So now a lot of people have got to thinking that if you can make it in the Underhive then so can they.'

'I didn't have any choice–' Donna managed to interject but it sounded weak even in her ears. Jen pounced on the statement with almost feral glee.

'Yeah, you did! Yes you so frikkin' had a choice! You coulda stayed in the frikkin' Spire an' your da would've covered things up. In fact, he did as best he could from what you've said. You woulda been forgiven an' ya know it, and I reckon that's half o' why you never looked back. You didn't *want* to go back even if they'd frikkin' let you. You made the brave choice, the one with pride, to go it frikkin' alone. Besides which, I swear there's not a man in Hive Primus who doesn't treat women better because of what you did up there in the Spire. I'll bet even frikkin' Helmawr is nicer.' Jen grinned happily and punched Donna on the shoulder. It hurt.

'So, sorry girl, but you're it, and no one gives a flying, fridge-arsed frik why it happened in the first place. That's all part of the... you're like one of those frikkin' logos in church, y'know, a picture that means something because it's a bit of a story.'

'An... an icon?' Donna managed to stammer.

'Yeah that's it. You're a frikkin' icon. And we aren't going to stand around with our frikkin' thumbs up our butts while someone friks with our icon.'

SHE WOULD ALWAYS *remember that morning. Every detail of it stood out vividly, no matter how hard she tried to forget them.*

It was the morning of her first meeting with her husband-to-be and D'onne was as tense as a strung bow. Sleep had been elusive and she had spent much of the night studying the hereditary rolls of House Ko'iron. They revealed a house that was not exactly the brightest star in the Necromundan firmament, maintaining its position in the Spire courtesy of ownership of several ramshackle Hive City manufactoria districts and a few choice off-world charters.

Sylvanus had proudly informed her that Ko'iron had offered a magnificent bride price, fully three times that anticipated. All D'onne could think was that they must be desperate. A direct tie to house Ulanti meant family contracts and favourable supply rates, so Ko'iron could not help but prosper by it. But they must have virtually bankrupted themselves winning Sylvanus's approval. Did they really believe that their fortunes would be won through her betrothal? D'onne had realised then that she knew Sylvanus better than them, and that his plan was to swallow up their remaining assets and turn them into his puppets. She was bait.

How would he close the trap on them? A succession of loans offered to tide them over? Sureties taken with the promise that they would never be realised? Perhaps he would use a quick and aggressive acquisition of their properties while their stock was unexpectedly weak. All ably assisted by his own spy in their camp, the seemingly demure little D'onne. Sylvanus might decide to secure the reigns of power using the old ways, the ways of blade and poison, and D'onne had trained herself for that eventuality too.

Her gown had been delivered the night before. The morning was spent with servitors jabbing her with blunt needles as they tailored it to her nubile body. It was a fantastic creation of elegantly spun metal and chromium mesh, fit for an industrial queen. It split at the small of her back to reach over her breasts and up to a high collar. Ladder-panels traced the curves of her hips before plunging down her legs to show creamy glimpses of calf and thigh. A fantastic froth of silver tracery was caught at her throat, bust and hem. The metal chimed softly when she walked or talked, adding ethereal music to her every movement.

It was also heavy, chafing, hot where it covered her flesh and cold where it left her back, shoulders and arms uncovered. D'onne hated it before thirty minutes were up.

She had found picts of Marneus Ko'iron, eldest son the house – Count Ko'iron to give him the correct honorific. He had chiselled, granite-like features that looked to have been weathered beneath strange off world suns. His craggy nose and jaw were emphasised rather than softened by his moustache. He looked old to D'onne, although the records showed him as only four decades her senior. Kadotti's Testimonial listed his interests as hunting, metallurgical antiquaria and Saljuk breeding (an offworld ruminant, apparently).

He sounded exactly as D'onne would have expected the first son of a noble house to be. He sounded proud, pompous *and stuffy, like all Spire nobility in fact. She struggled not to let her preconceptions colour her preparations for their first meeting, now only a few hours away. According to formal Spire etiquette, when the suitor and his would-be fiancée were first introduced (with the approval of both families of course) it could be at either a public function or a private one. Some scandalous public episodes in the past had influenced most noble houses towards private meetings as the first chance for both participants in a forthcoming union to get the measure of each other. So, with faux-casualness, Count Ko'iron was to come calling for dinner with D'onne Ulanti at the tower where she had dwelled alone for over a decade. Who said that romance was dead?*

She had selected a light menu that she had hoped he might appreciate, all of it imported foodstuffs free of the chemical tang of local Necromundan fare. She fretted over which perfumes to wear as nimble-fingered servitors wove her hair into a dazzling cascade of gold hung with beads of blood-red ruby, topaz and yellow cats-eye agate. The art of mixing perfumes for the correct occasion had long been acknowledged as one of the finer social graces of the Spire. She desperately wanted the count to know she had studied and practiced it as adroitly as any noblewoman. D'onne chose a simple trinary arrangement in the end: dianthe as a base to give an underlying scent of freshness and sweetness; a cinnamon medium to hint at spice and sexuality; an amarylis catalyst for sophistication.

As the hour approached, she ensured that the table was correctly laid, then swept to the lock in all her finery, awaiting the count's arrival there and trying to remain calm. The appointed hour came, and then went, with no sign of the count. D'onne paced up and down fretting helplessly, but she had no way to know what might have happened to him. An accident perhaps? Or unexpected business? She waited on tenterhooks, not knowing what else to do.

Over an hour after the appointed time the lock slid open.

'Count Ko'iron,' the tower announced laconically.

D'onne's sense of grateful release instantly dissipated as the count exited the lock. He was not alone. Two hulking bodyguards entered the tower with him, still laughing raucously at some jest the count had just made. The first bodyguard insolently eyed D'onne in all her finery and made some crude comment to his compatriot. Ko'iron didn't even bother to look at her.

She curtsied. 'Count Ko'iron, I am honoured by your presence. Thank you for coming.'

The count deigned to notice her for the first time when she spoke. His cold eyes measured her up like a saljuk that he was considering purchasing.

'Indeed, D'onne, the pleasure is all yours,' he slurred. The two lackeys sniggered. D'onne realised the count was drunk.

She fought the urge to scream at him to leave, or to run and lock herself away from this intruder. But Sylvanus had trained her too well for that; she knew she could win this oaf around and a part of her relished the prospect of doing so. So instead of fleeing she smiled and steered the count to the dining chamber with gestures and touches of his elbow.

'I've heard all about this place,' he sneered as they passed along the companionway. 'Haunted they say!' He kicked the wall with an elegantly tooled boot. 'Ho! Spirits! Avaunt!' The bodyguards laughed obediently with him, but D'onne's guts froze. Was he attempting to be as crass as possible? Or was the man himself really so boorish?

They reached the chamber and she ushered him inside. When the two bodyguards moved to follow, it was a measure of her anger that she stood bodily in the doorway to stop them and said, 'Gentlemen, you forget yourselves! This is an engagement for us to acquaint ourselves privately and discreetly, not a drinking club!'

They were surly but wouldn't meet her furious gaze. They retreated outside and D'onne closed the door with a snap. The count was already poking at the sweetmeats on the table with a frown. She crossed to his side in a few quick strides, struggling to control her anger.

'What kind of muck is this?' he muttered petulantly.

'Why, my dear Count, as well travelled as you are I had hoped you might appreciate a taste from distant stars.' *She tried to sound seductive and coquettish but had the uncomfortable feeling her anger edged her voice with too much sarcasm for that. The count appeared not to notice.*

'I have learnt only that foreign muck is always foreign muck,' *he grunted obstinately.*

D'onne took a deep breath and seated herself. Hearing raucous laughter outside the door, she fretted for a moment at what the guards were doing. In truth it was only a welcome distraction from her immediate issues. Count Ko'iron was now sprawled in a chair and brazenly staring at her breasts.

'Not bad,' *he muttered,* 'not bad at all.'

D'onne's heart scrunched up a little bit tighter, more so than she had thought possible even when Sylvanus was tormenting her. She had never felt as trapped and desperate as she did now. She tried talking to the count more, exploring his views, his personality. Each opening gambit was ruthlessly crushed, her opinions derided or dismissed on principle. Unless the count considered himself a complete authority on the subject (which he did about many things with little qualification) it was deemed an irrelevance. D'onne was to be his adornment for social functions, to fawn her appreciation of the great man he apparently thought himself to be. She was a piece of meat that would be used to breed a Ko'iron heir.

It occurred to D'onne that the count had been raised to be nothing other than her polar opposite. Where she had been taught to be cunning and manipulative, he had been trained to be obstinate and stupid. Where she knew only how to woo and persuade, he had learned only how to dismiss and belittle. She saw their life together spanning out into the future, a life filled with eternal battles for supremacy, of infidelity and lies and hate.

DONNA'S MEMORIES LAPSED *there. There were only shreds of reminiscences left, fragments wedged so deep inside her mind that she couldn't shed them entirely. She remembered playfully sitting in his lap and picking at food with a fork. She remembered his hands on her and the hot flash of anger she hid as she turned to him. But the rest was a merciful blank.*

The next thing she clearly remembered was standing in the companionway with a laspistol in her hands, looking back to see the dining chamber carpeted with the sprawled bodies of the count and his two guards. The lock cycled open beside her, making her jump, but, for the first time she could remember, no one was inside it. She ran inside without another backward glance, and a moment later she tasted a freedom she had not known she was a little girl.

Rumour had it that she dug out Ko'iron's eyes with a fish fork. Donna herself didn't know if that was true, but she had certainly attacked him – that much she could be sure of. However, if her memories of that day were true, as she always assured herself that they were, then the bastard most definitely deserved it.

8: THIRTY MINUTES

'Oh, poor old man your Mare will die,
And we say so, and we know so,
Oh, poor old man your Mare will die,
Oh, poor, poor old man,
We'll hoist her up to the main yardarm,
We'll hoist her up to the main yardarm,
Say I old man your Mare will die,
Say I old man your Mare will die,
We'll drop her down to the depths,
And down, down she'll go,
We'll drop her down to the bottom,
And down, down she'll go,
We'll sing her down with a long, long roll,
Where the sharks'll have her body and the
devil have her soul.'

                                       'The Dead Mare Shanty'

STILL WATERS RUN deep. Donna looked at the slick, roiling surface of the sump and felt a moment of sick sensation at realising that something goes much, much deeper than you thought was possible. Jen's words were still ringing in her ears: 'You're a frikkin' icon, Donna.' Here she was at the absolute bottom, both literally and figuratively, a millimetre away from the accumulated waste of a million billion trillion hivers over many, many centuries and she still couldn't escape her rep. Instead she was paddling towards a boat full of armed men with only the vaguest idea of a plan. No wonder they called her mad.

Paddling the flat little skiff she'd stolen was hard work. The peeling flank of Relli's manse was some way off still. Sometimes the sump clung tenaciously to her keel, at others she glided silkily across the poisoned waters. The effort was making her sweat. Acid mist tingled at her skin and the rebreather mask she was wearing struggled to filter out something breathable from the air.

She'd swung out onto the lake at first, gambling that the guards would be watching the shoreline and that any denizens of the deep wouldn't be swimming this close to the settlement. But it was slow going, and time wasn't on her side. Jen's parting words had been unequivocal.

'Thirty minutes, and then we're comin' to get ya out. Thirty minutes to do ye business quiet, an' then it'll get loud.'

She inched across the surface towards the bloated behemoth with agonising slowness. If Donna got spotted at this point she was well and truly screwed, caught in the open with no way to advance or retreat.

The boat-thing looked even bigger when you got close up to it. Whatever Relli's other shortcomings, he'd obviously commanded plenty of credit at some time. Not that he would have bought deeds to this place or anything, but being able to occupy it meant having enough muscle and business sense to keep away rivals.

Right now it looked virtually abandoned, only a few portholes showing any light. It could probably house a hundred times as many people as were aboard it right now, although doubtless a lot of space was given over to cargo storage and defunct machinery.

An eternity of maybe ten minutes brought her beneath the curve of the prow. Her theory, plus what she'd observed from the ledge, seemed to hold true. Those guards who were covering that massive area thought that the sump was impassable so they barely gave it a second glance.

Now came the real fun part.

Tendrils of wire weed were starting to quest at the skiff's low gunwales; she didn't have much time. Donna unwound a hook and line, span it three times and looped it up to the deck high above. It caught fast first try. Only speed and dumb luck would stop her being spotted now, but there was no other way on board.

Donna was still shimmying up the line when a broad, ugly face sporting an orange Mohican peered down at her over the rail and cursed. The wide bore of a gun swiftly followed the ugly face.

'Come a'board girly, yo're expected,' the Goliath guard called jovially. 'Jest keep it nice an' slow nah.'

While hanging on the line there wasn't much Donna could do. It was just too fine to grip one-handed and try shooting it out. She heard a disconsolate plopping sound from below her as wire weed pulled the stolen skiff beneath the surface of the sump. No way out there either.

'Ok, ok,' she said quickly, and rather shakily climbed the rest of the way up. She heard the Goliath call other guards from further along the deck. Donna couldn't fathom how she had so badly underestimated their alertness. While she had been watching from the ledge, the guards had idly wandered about on occasion but mostly stayed below decks. There was only one likely explanation, and it was an ugly one.

One of the Escher had sold her out.

Just why had Tessera really been missing earlier? Surely not? Donna's stomach flip-flopped at the thought.

The Goliath took a step back to let her get on the deck. Out of the corner of Donna's eye she could see pit slaves and another Goliath heading towards them. She was changing hands to grip the railing and vault over when her boot slipped suddenly and sent her teetering backwards over the hideous drop into the sump. The Goliath lunged forward with surprising speed for his muscled bulk and grabbed at her arm to save her from a painful and corrosive demise.

He seemed genuinely shocked when Donna seized his nose ring and used it to haul him over the railing. The Goliath made a piteous shriek before hitting the sump, where he was reduced to hideous gobbling noises as toxic sludge rushed into his open mouth. He was still trying to scream when the wire weed pulled him under.

Donna snorted derisively and vaulted over the railing without a backward glance. The other Goliath started spraying lead at her, the bullets striking sparks and ricocheting wildly along the deck. Donna replied with plasma. She was well past the point of screwing around any more.

The Goliath saw the white lightning gather about the Pig's muzzle and dived aside but the pit slaves were not so lucky, their smoking cybernetics and charred flesh hissing into the sump in a molten cascade, as a survivor fled screaming. The Goliath pounced out of cover to catch Donna defenceless with the Pig discharged and still smoking in her hand. She shot him in the eye with the laspistol in her other hand.

'Where's Relli?!' she yelled. 'We have some business to discuss!' No point in being subtle now. She found herself laughing wildly.

It was an act of mad bravado. She could hear boot heels ringing on the decking all about her. She jumped up and caught the railing to a higher deck tier, intending to swing up to it and gain some height advantage. A hammer swung down at her with piston-driven force – she ducked aside and it crumpled the heavy railing instead of her skull. The transferred shock alone was enough to numb her hand and make her drop back down. There were people waiting for her.

'Alive!' she heard someone shout as they rushed her.

Donna grinned happily. That one got them killed every time. She disappeared beneath a rush of sweaty bodies and grinding bionic limbs for a moment and rolled clear a second later, leaving one dead and two injured behind her. She darted off through an open hatchway while her attackers struggled to disentangle themselves.

Rusting corridor panels flashed past her as she ran along the narrow space beyond the hatch. She came to a ladder and fired off two shots behind her to discourage pursuit before sliding down it. At the bottom she found more narrow corridor, with doors banging and sounds of pursuit all around and closing in. Not enough time for choices and nowhere to hide, so Donna kept running blindly through the guts of the boat.

Inside it was like a maze, a run-down labyrinth of peeling bulkheads and stained floors. Shots splattered the corners as she ran; she was only a turn or two ahead of her pursuers at best. She was fleet of foot but they knew their ground better and kept corralling her into an ever-tighter area, drawing their numbers in around her like a noose.

She ran into a corridor and saw a cluster of figures coming towards her from the opposite direction. Shots started flying in both directions as the ones behind caught up to her again. Donna was soon pinned down in the crossfire and forced to duck into a hatchway for cover.

It was a trap. The room beyond was for storage and had a hatch in the roof as the only other exit. The roof hatch started cranking open, its two halves folding back to allow light to spill in from the deck above. It wasn't a promising sight. Armed figures stood silhouetted in the lights and one of the deck guns, a quad heavy stubber, was pointing menacingly into the hold. If they let fly with that thing every square inch of it would be filled with flying lead in an instant.

'Well, well. Mad Donna.' A familiar whisper floated down mockingly from above. It was Shallej.

Donna leapt towards the hatchway through which she had entered, but it was slammed shut in her face. Derisive laughter came from above.

'Our guest at last.'

Donna tried to see Shallej, but he was staying well hidden.

'That's correct, Shallej, well done, very well done indeed.' This was from a new voice, one high and obsequious but full of faux culture and superiority. Relli.

'What the hell do you want, Relli?' Donna shouted. 'You wanted my attention, well you've got it now! You've got three seconds to explain before I blast my way out of this tub of yours and send you all to the bottom of the sump.'

Shallej snickered.

He could snicker all he liked but it wasn't false bravado this time. Donna reckoned the Pig could eat its way through the deck and down far enough to sink this damn thing before they could finish killing her. Under the circumstances she felt quite prepared to try her theory out.

'No! Nobledam, wait!' Relli squawked.

Well, that was gratifying.

'One!' Donna called with devilment in her heart.

'Nobledam, I was engaged by one who sought to find you, who wishes you well, a friend whom you know from the Spire!'

'I have no friends in the Spire. Two.'

'He said you would be recalcitrant but he bade me… he bade me speak his final words to you from the last time you met. They were: "Remember this moment always, D'onne, for you stand at a threshold few would ever dare pass." And that would tell you all you needed to know!'

The word 'three' died on her lips. Lars was behind this, and with that her last hopes of any good news from the Spire shattered into a million pieces. The fool had followed her down. She felt suddenly very tired and alone.

'Is he here?' she asked quietly.

'In my quarters, nobledam, awaiting your pleasure.'

IT WAS QUICKLY evident that Relli's personal domain was a very different realm to what Donna had seen in the rest of the boat-thing. It lay at the top of sweeping stairways up a central atrium that accessed the upper decks. Here the carpets were clean and the smell was chemically fresh. White painted walls showed artfully chosen paintings (not picts) and no hint of rust, bright lumen bulbs casting a cheery glow over it all through crystal chandeliers high above. Only the occasional creak of the boat's hull or whiff of the sump broke the illusion of quietly palatial splendour.

Shallej and his posse had disappeared below deck again with a sardonic parting bow. The four surviving Goliaths were Relli's personal retinue and had remained. They disarmed Donna (or so they thought), and then marched around, boxing her in at all times. Donna felt creepy knowing that snake Shallej was around and not in plain sight but right now she had more immediate concerns. Judging by their scars, Donna guessed the Goliaths had been working with Relli for a long time. They were certainly pissed at Donna for killing two of their number. They kept jostling her whenever they thought Relli wasn't looking, or drawing their fingers from ear to ear in silent threat of what they would do as soon as they got the chance.

Donna noticed they all had tattoos on their necks that depicted crude, gnashing canine teeth. They were Dog Soldiers. The Grand Dog had been kicked out of the settlement of Filth Pond a long time ago, but his Dog Soldiers still showed up in the most unsavoury parts of the Underhive as guns for hire. These had sunk pretty low if they were working for a guilder, the Grand Dog had always taken a dim view of The Merchant Guild, seeing it as more of a resource to be harvested than a force to be reckoned with.

'Sorry about your two brothers,' she whispered to them as Relli fussed over a door lock. No pit slaves were permitted inside Relli's sanctum, just the Goliaths and a few chosen lickspittles. Obviously Relli was scared that his pit slaves might take it into their heads to kill him and go outlaw.

'Just a case of mistaken identity,' continued Donna. That seemed to mollify them slightly and some of the bunched up tendons around their jaws relaxed slightly. Relli opened the door.

'If I'd known you were Dog Soldiers I would have killed them more slowly,' Donna stage-whispered to them. The Dog Soldiers' eyes glared psychotically and their thick fingers spasmed into hammer fists. Donna stepped through the doorway, laughing at their impotent fury.

The doors opened to reveal a vast hall with arched windows along one side. Donna's mind skipped for a moment as she gazed at the view outside. Streams of high liners and shuttles snaked about the flank of the Spire, etching the skies with their contrails. Thunderheads roiled out from below their feet to the horizon, carpeting the perfect blue vault of the heavens with coarse, black wool. She was back in the Spire.

'Impressive, is it not?' Relli's unctuous gloating was obscene. 'This ekranoplan was outfitted with luxuries fit for the Spire in its time.'

A trick. Holo shutters showing a Pict recording. It made Donna realise how long it had been since she'd seen such a trick. It also made Donna want to kill Relli there and then. She didn't need her blade, she would do it with her bare hands and take pleasure in snapping his fat neck. A warning rumble came from behind her. The largest and ugliest Dog Soldier had entered the hall too. Ironically enough, he was the one carrying her weapons. Even if Relli didn't realise that he stood at death's door the Goliath certainly did, and his truculent gaze challenged her to just try it. Donna smiled sweetly at him instead.

'An ekranoplan? What's that?' she asked Relli smoothly. The Goliath's eyes rolled fractionally upward at the query.

'It is a hybrid of ship and aircraft, nobledam, one which is able to skate across flat surfaces at fantastic speeds. The skill of building them was sadly lost many centuries ago. Now this may be the last example of that wondrous art on all of Necromunda!' Relli's words tumbled out bloated with excitement and immodesty. It was obvious the boat-thing was the guilder's pride and joy. Donna made a mental note to sink it before she left.

'You've been restoring it, I see,' she said. 'It's very impressive.' How easily the lies came, Donna thought. The sight of the Spire-view had obviously brought back old habits.

Relli's face dropped. 'Well, I have had to suspend work for the present, nobledam, which rather neatly brings me to the subject of our current venture.' They were approaching an ormolu door at the end of the hall. 'I have in fact not one, but two noblesires anxious to make your acquaintance…'

Donna had sudden misgivings as Relli reached for the door handle. 'What the hell do you mean, Relli?' she snarled. 'Who else is in there?'

'Ah, he felt it would be best to make his own introductions.'

The door swung open.

Donna wanted to run when she saw who was inside.

AN OVAL TABLE made of crystal that was the colour of oily smoke dominated the centre of the chamber. Four ornate chairs stood around it, two of which were occupied. Donna's eye was instantly drawn to the figure seated on her right. His white armour seemed incongruous in the opulent setting, but his bearing was eminently suitable. He sprawled indolently in the chair as if it were a throne. A cloaked figure stood at his shoulder and was bending as if to whisper in his ear as Donna entered. She could only see the man's face in profile but the sight struck a chill in her heart. It was

Count Ko'iron, the man she had murdered in the Spire, back from the dead.

'So the bitch-queen finally showed up! Well done, Relli.'

The voice was wrong, younger and less assured. As the face turned towards her Donna saw that was wrong too, a crease here and an angle there – similar for sure but not the same. She saw that the cloaked figure wasn't whispering at all, in fact it had skeletal metal fingers like hypodermics inserted in the mans neck. He seemed oblivious to their presence as he addressed her.

'You've caused an intolerable amount of harm, D'onne Ge'Sylvanus, but your little jaunt is over now.'

'Ah,' Relli said. 'Forgive me, noblesir, but please recall our agreement.'

'Quite right, Relli, say your piece and get on with it then.'

The figure slumped back in his seat, the skeletal hand at his neck faithfully following the movement. Donna's scattered thoughts realised that it was a medicae unit, a dedicated nurse, doctor and surgeon rolled into one. The count was being treated for something – an injury or poisoning perhaps? She suddenly remembered the other person at the table.

Lars was looking not a day older than when she had seen him that day in the arboretum. He at least was dressed for dinner in an immaculate chequer coat and cravat. He smiled at Donna uncertainly and she suddenly realised how different she must look to him. He probably barely recognised her at all.

D'onne had seemed petite and demure; Donna had grown tall and imposing like some barbarian queen. D'onne had been a broken, frightened girl; Donna was a fearless gang fighter grown used to life on the knife's edge. Shock was written all over his face, but he looked her resolutely in the face (no doubt with his guts squirming at the sight of her bionic eye) and said, 'I told you I would find you again one day, D'onne.'

'You were a fool to come down here, Lars,' Donna snarled. She turned. 'And just who the hell do you think you are? Because you sure as crap aren't Count Ko'iron.'

'Ah, nobledam, in that respect you are mistaken,' Relli tried to sound conciliatory. 'Please, ah, please be seated so we can talk properly.'

Donna treated him to a contemptuous look and took a seat as far from the alleged count as possible. She noted that Relli's biggest Goliath was now standing in front of the door, blocking the only way out.

She almost laughed when she saw the food laid on the table, high-class fare by Underhive standards – a king's banquet. To nobles from the Spire it was little better than raw sewage, and lay completely untouched. Donna's guts were churning with tension but she grabbed up a roasted haunch of rat to gnaw on in the hopes it would upset the two nobles further. Relli seated himself between Donna and the count.

'Ah, it's a great honour, of course, to have such esteemed persons as yourselves as my guests,' Relli began. Donna glared at him.

'Ah, well, there is a delicate balance at work here, nobledam. I should perhaps explain what has brought us together. I was first approached some time ago by noblesir Polema with an exciting proposition,' he gestured to Lars with fat, ring-encrusted fingers, 'to organise an expedition to a locale known colloquially as "Dead Man's Hole".'

Donna was suddenly back with Hanno again at Dust Falls, peering over his shoulder at the little cogitator screen and trying to understand what DMH stood for in the guilder records. Now she knew. Dead Man's Hole meant two expeditions that had failed to return, twenty-one people lost. There was no need to let Relli know she had uncovered that little tid-bit of information just yet, so Donna kept her mouth shut and waited to see what the guilder would admit to.

'There have been some... difficulties in mounting a successful expedition to the area, as it lies deep within the Badzones and a considerable distance from the nearest settlement. However, the noblesir had convinced me that the rewards of such an undertaking would stand to repay our efforts a thousandfold, and so we turned to thoughts of how to secure our future success.'

Lars was looking from Relli to Donna and back again as if he desperately wanted to say something. Relli ignored him and continued.

'The noblesir had confided in me that the nobledam Ulanti had been known to him through... prior association in the Spire. Knowing of the fearsome reputation you have gained in the Underhive, nobledam, I had thought to locate you in relation to our difficulties and contract your services to assist.'

Donna eyed Relli critically. It sounded plausible enough except for two things.

'Then why the bounty hunters and why him,' she gestured at Ko'iron.

'I had contracted Shallej Bak on a number of previous occasions and he had been assisting me with the expeditions. He told me that he knew how to find you and bring you here – a simple letter in the right language, he said. I apologise for his methods, nobledam, I had no idea they would turn out to be so... direct. This noblesir arrived here barely two shifts ago, nobledam. He has his own reasons for being here as is best explained by his good self.'

Lars was almost bouncing up and down in his chair for attention by now but the count and Relli were ignoring him.

'What's eating at you, Lars?' Donna asked.

'D'onne, I wanted to say I was never in favour of all this scheming,' he said in a rush, 'I told Relli at the outset I should come and find you, that you would listen to me—'

'I would have slapped you silly and sent you back to the Spire. In fact, I may well still do that.' Donna took a bite out the rat haunch. Lars looked crestfallen.

'Alright, that's enough!' The count surged to his feet, and the medicae unit hissed as it struggled to keep up with him.

'I didn't come down this dung hole to listen to all this rubbish.'

He turned on Donna.

'I am Julius Ko'iron, rightful heir of the House Ko'iron and you are D'onne Ulanti who was betrothed to the heir of Ko'iron. I demand you return with me to the Spire and fulfil your family duties.'

Donna laughed in his face.

'So, it's Julius is it? Piss off back to the Spire, Julius, before I kill you like I did your big brother, Marneus.'

'You didn't kill Marneus, you bitch! That would've been kinder!' The count's face was bright red, and the skeletal fingers were rapidly massaging his neck with their needle tips.

'Oh no, eight years fighting before insanity completely overtook him! Even now he hides from the light, locked away in his apartments day and night.' The new Count Ko'iron tottered and slumped back into his chair heavily.

Donna was shocked, her world broken in two. All this time she had been with the murderous scum of the Underhive because she was convinced she belonged there. Hiding and fighting and scraping an existence, all the time convinced she had murdered a noble and so was worse than all the gun-scum and the bounty hunters around her. That's what she had told herself, time and again, that she had joined the other dysfunctional killers in Necromunda down at the bottom, in the Underhive, because there was nowhere else to go.

But was she any better than that really? Julius had said his brother had gone mad, doubtless tormented by the memory of how she had unmanned him – her, a mere woman after all. Somehow she felt now she *was* better than a murderer. What she had done to Marneus was one thing, what he had done to himself afterwards was another. She realised Relli was speaking again and probably had been for a while as she was lost in her thoughts.

'…the count has graciously agreed that given his condition, it may be some while before he returns to the Spire.'

'What condition? What's wrong with him?' Donna snapped.

'The count suffered poisoning from a milliasaur bite as he came down the Abyss, hence the treatment from his chirurgeon. So, as I was saying, nobledam,' Relli seemed a little peeved, like he felt he was losing control of the situation, 'the count has agreed that his claim to your hand can wait sufficiently long for Dead Man's Hole to be investigated with your help, in return for a share of the proceeds. I might add that the count himself has some very talented individuals in his entourage who will vastly improve our chances.'

Relli beamed. Everything obviously made perfect sense to him now they were all sitting down together. To him it was all a simple matter of negotiation. Time to introduce him to a few finer points of negotiation.

'So let me summarise what you're saying, Relli. You want me to go help find Dead Man's Hole and then go back to the Spire and wedded bliss with the good Count Ko'iron here.'

'There'd be no gallivanting around the sewers at all if we weren't still out of pocket from your damn brideprice, Ulanti,' the count muttered bitterly.

'Well I...' Relli could sense the trap waiting for him: he didn't want any of those things, he just wanted bottomless wealth to spend on his ekranoplan. To him the nobles were a way of getting it and their personal entanglements hadn't entered his balance sheets.

'And pray tell what would be in this for me?' Donna swallowed another bite of rat meat.

'Ah, the chance to return to the Spire, nobledam, wealthy enough to repair any old harms.'

Donna arched her brows at Lars. 'Lars, what have you been telling him?'

Lars suddenly found himself at the centre of attention and squirmed visibly. 'I believe that what lies in Dead Man's Hole would significantly alter the market in Hive City,' he said quietly.

'What part of the market, Lars?' Donna asked incredulously. Market forces on Necromunda had been ruthlessly monopolised and jealously protected by the Houses for centuries. Even a slight fluctuation had huge implications for Hive Primus. Proles could find themselves in or out of work by the millions and whole sectors of the city could open up or close down as the finances shifted.

'Energy generation.'

After thousands of years energy had become the most desperately sought-after resource in all of Necromunda. For millennia, engineers had tried unsuccessfully to balance out the massive requirements of the teeming populace and industry of the hive world with the concerns of availability and cost. Their demands had reduced the surface of the planet to a poisoned ash waste and necessitated the building of the first hives so that people could shelter from the cataclysm they had created around their remaining energy reserves. Energy consumption still remained the most significant limiting factor in the growth of any House.

'No kidding.'

Parts of the puzzle were sliding into place. Ko'iron, Lars, Relli – their motivations were all transparent. Relli's was simple: greed. He thought he had found a way of making a fortune and even when it had cost him dearly, he had refused to let go. If anything, he'd only become more desperate and held on tighter. Lars and the count both thought they could take her back to the Spire, Lars armed with nothing more than unrequited love and some harebrained scheme, Julius with pig-headed stubbornness and overweening pride. Frikkin' nobles.

That left only one player unaccounted for. The one, she realised now, who had been manipulating them all from the beginning.

'You don't know much about Shallej Bak do you, Relli?' Donna said casually.

'Ah, I, yes, yes I do. I have dealt with him for years, on and off. He's always been a tremendous help in the past.'

'Well, if you'd ever thought of him as more than a hired gun you might have checked up on his background.' Donna's voice was low but clear, almost hypnotic.

'Bak's clan came down from Hive City en masse about twenty years ago, first as Delaque gangers and then spreading out over the years to become gun-scum, bounty hunters, outlaws, watchmen, settlers. It's got so there isn't a settlement in the Underhive that doesn't have one of the Bak clan around to watch and listen.'

'What are you implying?' Relli asked, white-faced.

'It's an open secret in many places. The Baks do "jobs" for Hive City Delques on a fairly regular basis. Among many others, they form the network of spies, assassins and saboteurs the Delaque have in place to safeguard their interests in the Underhive.'

'Naturally, the Delaque, being slimy, underhanded backstabbers, believe that all the other houses have agents in the Underhive too, including the noble houses.' Donna took a last bite of rat meat and looked at the long, greasy thighbone left in her hand.

'They think I'm an Ulanti agent, and Shallej's been using his bounty hunter status to try and hunt me down for quite some time.'

'Whatever scheme you're pursuing with Dead Man's Hole, you can guarantee the Delaque won't want it to happen. Any shift in energy generation would favour the Orlocks most out of all of the Houses, as they have the most readily available industrial capacity to use it.'

'In Shallej's mind this all makes sense. As an Ulanti agent I would do all I could to assist a scheme that would ultimately benefit the Orlock's biggest patrons – House Ulanti.'

'But, but why would he help bring you here then?' Relli stammered querulously.

Donna could see he already knew the answer. It was written in his fear-filled eyes, but she decided she would spell it out for him anyway. She stood up and snapped the thighbone with a crack that made Lars and Relli jump.

'So he could get us in one place and kill us all at once.'

There was the distant crump of an explosion. The deck lurched beneath Donna's feet, and lumebulbs flickered overhead, blowing like miniature fireworks.

Thirty minutes was up.

THERE WAS BLOOD *on her hands and she couldn't get it off. It didn't matter how hard she rubbed them, the red streaks wouldn't go away. She had come to the arboretum seeking water, somewhere she could wash the blood away, but now that she had found it she couldn't bring herself to get close. Couples and families strolled past obliviously, but she knew if she dipped her hands into the fountain it would run red, and then everyone would see she was a murderer.*

So she sat on a bench with her hands clasped in her armpits and rocked gently back and forth. The fantastic gown she wore rustled and sighed in time with her movements. It was comforting.

'You look a little cold there, nobledam, may I offer you my coat?'

D'onne was so surprised to be spoken to that she almost cried out. She looked up sharply at the one who had addressed her and broken her spell of invisibility. He was a youth of medium height and dark hair, with strong but not unpleasing features. He smiled uncertainly and held out his heavy brocade coat. D'onne realised that she was cold. Her bare arms and neck were like ice. She took the coat and slipped it on, luxuriating in the welcome warmth of its previous occupant. She gazed up at him again, thinking she must look pathetically grateful.

'Thank you.'

'My pleasure. It is a beautiful dress but perhaps better suited to dinner in the Summer House than winter by the fountain?' His eyebrows arched inquiringly, an earnest plea for his gentle foray not to be thought too gauche.

D'onne giggled. 'I didn't intend to come here, my feet just brought me.'

'Ahh, I know that well, all too often I look up only to find myself in places I've reached unbidden.'

'Sire, you mock me.'

'I swear I do not. Why, only this shift past I appeared at my sweetheart's domicile only to discover my sweetheart was my sweetheart no more and her heart was given to another. What man would consciously place himself in the path of such woes? It is all the fault of those wandering feet, I tell you, we would all be happier without them.'

'Oh, I'm so sorry. I did not mean to intrude upon your grief, sire, please be on your way, I should delay you no further.' She grinned wickedly at him and started to shrug off his coat.

'Oh no-no-no, nobledam,' the man said, and seated himself beside her so fast that he almost bounced. 'All grief over my lost love has been eradicated by an altogether brighter star arising in the firmament. Indeed, now I give thanks for what I cursed an hour, even a minute ago.'

'Do you usually reveal your innermost thoughts to strangers so readily, sire?'

'I am moved to desperation by the possibility my new star may be a transient body, liable to leave my own sphere without warning. Hence I give my worship now while I still may, before cruel fate, and perchance cruel feet, remove her from me.'

D'onne laughed again; it was nice to be flattered. They sat quietly for a moment watching the fountain splash into its bowl. The shadows were growing longer and less people were coming by. With his eyes distant, he leaned over and murmured confidentially to her.

'I feel we share a common thread, you and I. Our paths have been brought together by circumstances beyond our knowing, forces beyond our ken.'

D'onne was wary. 'Why do you say such things, noblesir?'

'Because when I saw you I sensed a kindred spirit in mourning. I saw the weight upon your shoulders that I had felt upon mine when I lost my love, though I fear cruel fate has weighed upon you even more so than it has me.'

D'onne could only nod desolately at his words.

'But it is a time for joy, don't you understand? In seeing you here I've felt my heart beat again, even were we to part now and never meet again I would cherish this moment always if only for that.

'I know that to you I'm just a fool in the park but I... I burn with joy that I could even make you laugh and lighten your burden just a little. Thank you for allowing me to live again.'

The man reached out and gently took D'onne by the hand. Caught in the wonder of the moment, she didn't think to pull away. He looked down at her hands and tutted, laying them delicately back in her lap before going over to the fountain. He returned with a moistened kerchief and wiped the red streaks of blood away without a word. He looked up at her face again and smiled.

'Would you grant me a boon to celebrate the event? Allow me to take you to dinner by the lake in spring.'

D'onne smiled back hesitantly. 'That would be nice, but why there?'

'Because spring is a time of new beginnings.'

THEY HAD LUNCHEON by the lake and it was glorious. They sat and ate and talked all the while, with D'onne expecting to be caught at any moment but not caring any more.

His name was Lars Polema. He was of the House of Greim, a minor cousin to the head family, and so little more than a well-connected employee. He was engaged in antiquarian studies of the endless records of Hive Primus from previous centuries that Greim used for its quota forecasting, and laughed about how dull it was. She simply called herself D'onne and he discretely enquired no further.

After luncheon he took her along the arcades near The Wall looking for new clothes. He gently steered her towards the most durable, understated garb they could find: a strong pair of boots and a well tailored pair of slacks, a close fitting jacket with lots of pockets and a hood.

He begged her to wait outside another store while he darted inside and she did, suddenly realising she didn't know what else to do. With a sad feeling she understood that she had to part from him soon, because to stay with him could only bring him to harm when Sylvanus caught up with her.

She looked up to see him standing before her. He held out something to her that was so small that it was cupped in his hand. Puzzled, she opened hers to receive it. Two small white cylinders lay in the palm of her hand.

'D'onne?' Lars asked. 'Have you ever gone into Hive City?'

9: DOG SOLDIERS

'If you can't keep it, then it was never yours.'
Old Underhive saying

RELLI, LARS AND Ko'iron were shocked into paralysis by the detonation, jaws dropping slackly in alarm. Donna was already moving. Ko'iron recovered his wits first.

'That's it, Relli! All bets are off, I'm taking the girl now!' blustered the count as he struggled back to his feet. The surviving lumebulbs flickered and dimmed ominously before brightening again. Donna was suddenly beside him.

'Good enough for one is good enough for both, I say,' she proclaimed and plunged the sharp end of the broken rat bone she was holding into his eye. Count Julius Ko'iron screamed and fell, the medicae unit collapsing over him like a marionette with its wires cut. Relli was backing off against the far wall, blubbering. Donna looked up at Lars.

'You better get out of here, lover,' she said. 'Things are going to get messy.'

Before Lars could answer, Donna ducked aside. A blow from the Goliath bodyguard shattered the edge of the table where she had been standing a second before. She short-kicked the Dog Soldier in the crotch, and then smashed her knee up into his face as he doubled over. The Goliath roared in anger and pain, swinging his iron mace again and sending Donna skipping backwards to avoid it. He lumbered after her with a murderous gleam in his eyes.

This fight could only go one way. Without weapons Donna couldn't hope to best an armed ganger like the Goliath – she could just annoy him for a while. Fortunately, she was not entirely without weapons. Her flat little throwing blade was still secure inside her bodice. She sidled around the table so the Goliath couldn't rush straight at her.

The Dog Soldier's solution was predictably direct. He leapt up onto the tabletop, scattering slime loaves and rat meat everywhere. While the Goliath was still regaining his balance she drew the blade and threw, quick as a snake.

The blade flew straight and true towards the Goliath's thick neck but he twisted aside at the last instant, the sharp sliver burying itself in corded muscle instead of carotid artery. The Dog Soldier just grunted and swatted at the blade as if it were a biting insect. Not good.

The Dog Soldier made to leap at her but slipped in some fungus marinade and half-fell on the table instead. Undaunted, he unleashed a swing at Donna anyway, catching her off-guard with a rib-cracking strike in the chest. She tried to roll but was hurled backwards by the force of the blow. Red flashes of pain shot through her torso as she tried to breathe, a sucking void of oblivion felt close behind her skull. She shook her head groggily.

The Dog Soldier laughed. 'Ahm comin' sweet'eart, soon be ovah!' he called and slid off the table in a shower of hors d'oeuvres.

Imminent death was enough to sharpen her mind considerably. She scrambled to her feet, leaping aside from the Goliath's charge by hair's breadth. An ornate chair was splintered into matchwood in her place. Out of desperation, she snatched up a sharp piece of wood and speared it into the Goliath's arm. He just contemptuously backhanded her away and sent her reeling.

He came in again with the same right-to-left rib-cracking swing that had worked so well last time. Donna was not caught out twice. She ducked under the hurtling iron and darted inside his reach. She knew it was a risky move; he could crush her in a moment if he could bring all of his monstrous strength into play. But that was why Donna needed a weapon.

She seized the hilt of a knife protruding from the Dog Soldier's wide belt, intending to draw it and slash him with it in the process. The damn thing was so heavy it took all her strength and most of her body weight to draw. She staggered backwards, dragging the heavy lump of metal with her, taking it in both hands to avoid dropping it altogether. The Dog Soldier laughed so hard at her that he almost cried.

'Hoo thass fair nah, you got yore weapon an' I got mine, hur-huh.'

'Well, come and get it, fatboy,' Donna snarled. 'Donna's waiting.' The Dog Soldier's knife might be big, unbalanced and stupidly heavy, but it had a wicked edge to it. It might just be sharp enough to carve through even the Goliath's thick skull.

He was more cautious, despite all his bravado. No straight rush and right-left cross this time. He was still slow, only now Donna was almost as slow, even wielding the knife in both hands. She managed to parry his first blow and her arms ached with the shock of impact. She darted past him and put a slash in his flank though he cannily rolled away from it and the wound was shallow. They locked weapons again with the same result, only this time he got completely out of the way of her riposte.

Attack, parry, riposte. The pattern repeated with variations again and again. Donna's hands were too numbed from the impacts of repeatedly parrying the Goliath's mace to do more than simple crosscuts in return. An accurate killing thrust was impossible, so she darted and slashed at the Dog Soldier. This was exactly the kind of fight the Goliath wanted, a slugfest where sooner or later his superior strength and endurance would overcome her skill and agility. She had some successes, producing a nick here and a cut there, getting ever more exhausted in the process.

She dodged away from another swing and bumped into the edge of the table. The Dog Soldier had been backing her towards it all along, obviously not prepared to wait for his victory. The mace swung down like a plunging meteor with all the force of his bulging muscles behind it, impossible for Donna to parry with the heavy knife. At the last instant she abandoned the knife altogether, and once freed of its encumbrance she spun aside, weaponless again.

The mace shattered another chunk out of the table and flying shards of oil-glass nicked Donna's exposed flesh. The sharp kiss gave her an idea. She threw herself at the Goliath, shoulder charging him while he was still off-balance from his missed blow. The Dog Soldier stumbled and fell, his chin crashing into the jagged edge of the table where a hundred crystal knives were waiting for him. Blood splattered spectacularly across the table, the food, overturned chairs, the rich carpet.

Despite his obviously mortal wound, the Goliath gurgled hideously and tried to get up.

'No. You. Don't!' Donna yelled, punctuating each word with a kick at the back of his neck, driving it against the saw-toothed edge. On the third kick the head came free and rolled across the tabletop with the eyelids still flickering as the dying brain tried to focus. The torso flopped grotesquely and sprayed the rest of its contents from the gory stump. The chamber fell suddenly quiet except for the ragged sound of Donna's breathing and the streaming of blood.

Donna quickly retrieved her weapons from the Goliath's corpse, cursing at her cracked ribs as she bent down to take them. Only then did she think to look about her. Lars and Relli were gone. An opening that hadn't been there before had appeared in the back wall – some kind of secret bolt-hole no doubt. Someone must have dragged away Ko'iron during the fight because he was gone too. She stepped towards the opening. As she did so, another explosion shook the deck and Donna heard the chatter of weapon fire in its aftermath.

The Escher were attacking just like Jen had said. If Donna didn't help they would be massacred – she could hear the firing notch up as the quad stubber deck gun kicked in and drowned out the other gunfire. The way it was pumping out rounds made it sound like the Escher were pinned down – long strafing bursts of stubber fire were followed by a few defiant shots barking in return.

Despite her lust for revenge, Donna found her feet carrying her back to the door by which she had entered. Relli could wait for now, she reasoned, but the Escher couldn't. The buzz-saw noise of stubber fire cut the air again, this time followed by fewer return shots.

She started running along the entry hall back towards the atrium. Power fluctuations on the ekranoplan were making the Spire-holos flicker and jump in the windows beside her as she passed.

Relli had thought he could simply tempt her into doing whatever he wanted with a few glimpses of the Spire and some empty promises, that she would be pathetically grateful enough to become his agent. The stupid, bloated egotist. She took malicious pleasure in shattering the holo shutters one by one as she ran, leaving a trail of empty blackness in her wake.

The door to the atrium was partway open, which was odd considering Relli had closed it. She slowed down as she got close to it and covered the gap with her las. Her mind was running through a list of all her foes aboard the ekranoplan and trying to rate them for threat value.

There were the three remaining Dog Soldiers, all pretty hard bastards and ready to kill her on sight. There was a good chance at least one of them was waiting for her in the atrium. There were Relli's pit slaves, who would keep fighting as long as Relli or the Goliaths were around to tell them to, but would probably slink off if they got the chance. On the other hand, they were all trapped onboard the ekranoplan by the Escher attack, so they would probably fight like cornered rats.

Then there was Ko'iron's entourage, 'talented individuals' Rellis had called them. Doubtless they were hungry for revenge too but probably more concerned about how to get the noble Julius back up through The Wall, living or dead.

And then there was Shallej and his posse of Delaque. He could be trying to kill off Relli, Lars and Donna individually or just working on a way to sink the whole damn ekranoplan with all of them still aboard. The explosions she had felt didn't seem big enough to be demolition charges, so they were probably grenades from the Escher. Donna prayed that however much of a fool Relli was, he hadn't shown Shallej the self-destruct button or the plug or whatever else would send the craft and its contents to the bottom of the sump quickly and easily. The fact she was still alive told her that he probably hadn't.

A shadow moved in the doorway. Donna fired her las through the gap and charged. Someone cursed and Donna saw the silhouetted head and shoulders of a man appear before being dazzled by a muzzle flash from something in his hands. An autogun chattered wildly, firing wide of her and smashing one of Relli's holo shutters into a cloud of tinkling shards.

Donna heard the clip run dry on the Dog Soldier's autogun at the same instant she cannoned into the door and sent him staggering back from the threshold. Seventy-six swept down with a hungry snarl but the Goliath blocked it with his gun. The rotating teeth seemed to scream in frustration as they scrabbled at the metal barrier between them and soft flesh. Donna flicked her wrist and sent the chain blade skipping down the gun at the Dog Soldier's fingers. He desperately threw the weapon at her and took his chance to jump backwards as she batted it aside.

Donna heard shouts from down below on the floor of the atrium, followed by a shot. The Goliath flinched back as a chunk of railing vapourised beside him.

'Oi! Watchit ya numbties!' he yelled. Donna risked a sideways glance to see whom he was shouting at.

Two pit slaves were crouching in the lower doorway with stub guns drawn. Two more stub rounds clipped the railing marginally closer to Donna than the

Goliath. The little frikkers didn't care who they hit, she concluded. Apparently reaching the same conclusion, the Dog Soldier jumped as far back from the railing as he could. She put a las-shot into him and clipped his shoulder, barely slowing him as he pulled out an autopistol.

Donna dived down the stairs just as he let rip. The Goliath swung a crescent of hot lead around himself with no aim whatsoever, spraying bullet-pocked arcs across the atrium and various objets d'art with raucous abandon. Donna snapped off a las-shot in return but had her own problems as she fought to keep from going headlong down the stairs and breaking her neck. Another couple of stub rounds smacked into the wall near her, almost unnoticeable in the chatter of autofire but quite distinct because they were vaguely accurate.

Donna snapped off a couple more shots at the doorway and sent the pit slaves scurrying for cover. The autofire stopped and she heard the Dog Soldier changing clips. He was out of sight from her now. Donna decided it was time to start the revolution early.

'Why the hell are you shooting at me you pricks! Relli is dead! You're free!' She shouted to the pit slaves. Okay one little white lie – Relli wasn't dead, yet.

'Thass bullshit, don lissen boys!' The Goliath's angry bellow came over the balcony. At least she had an idea of where he was standing now, and he seemed a bit too quick to respond to be sure about pit slaves' loyalties.

'Like we should believe you, Dog Soldier!' one of the slaves was plucky enough to shout back. 'What if she's right?'

'Yous little frikas!' the Dog Soldier snarled. 'Gerrout an' fight or I'll kills you mehself!'

'Yes, what if I'm right?' Donna taunted. 'No more free dinners, fatboy!' She creased the balcony with a couple more las-shots.

That was all it took to push the Goliath into a murderous rage. He appeared at the balcony and sprayed the doorway with bullets. One of the pit slaves screamed in pain. The other one ducked back out of sight again. Donna bounced up and unleashed a fusillade of shots at the Goliath. Chunks of railing disintegrated under her volley and the Goliath retreated. Her angle was bad here, but going back up on the balcony gave the Dog Soldier an odds-on chance of turning her into a sieve.

Stub gun rounds snapped out from the doorway. Not at her, bless, but at the Goliath. She used the distraction to run back up the stairs and onto the balcony. Auto rounds whipped past her head the instant she came in view. Donna dived and rolled, blasting shots back almost at random. One of her las-bolts caught the Goliath in the thigh, spinning him around. He clung onto the shot-scarred railing for support and levelled his autopistol at her. She put two shots just past his ear and then had to run for cover, still cursing at her inaccuracy as he opened fire again. Bullets pelted around her, ricocheting wildly. Something hit her heel and made her stagger. She span and snapped off a shot at the towering Goliath – another clean miss. He was struggling upright and pulling out a knife with his off-hand, the giant cousin of the one she had tried to use earlier.

A huge red splotch suddenly masked half the Goliath's face, the autopistol dropped from his nerveless fingers and he toppled slowly over the railing to hit the floor of the atrium with a wet thud. A stub round had taken him in the back of the head, a hundred-to-one shot at least – score one for the revolution.

She ran down to the doorway below before the pit slaves got a chance to change their minds. She found both of them still there, one cradling the head of the other as his life leaked out of the holes stitched across his chest by an autopistol burst. There was something tragic and pathetic about the slaves. The crude amputations and mismatched bionics couldn't disguise their very human suffering. Donna had intended to waste them both to make sure they couldn't shoot her when her back was turned. Pity stayed her hand.

'You should get out of here,' she told the survivor softly. He looked up at her desolately.

'Frikking guilders. Friking Hive City. Friking *planet*.' There were tears in the slave's eyes. The ownership stud in his forehead winked in silent mockery of his pain. 'Why do we have to frik things up all the time?'

Donna shrugged. 'It's the natural order of things. Frikked up. For what it's worth, I'm sorry.'

'The guilder's not really dead, is he?'

'Soon,' Donna crooned soothingly. 'Soon.'

DONNA LEFT THE slave to his misery and ran along the maze of narrow corridors. They had caught her here before, but now it was quiet except for gunfire echoing eerily down from the deck above. She came across a freshly bullet-scarred corner – it had been hit when she had been chased through earlier. Looking about her, she found a trail of destruction left by the pursuit and used it to find her way back to the outer hatch through which she had entered. She edged it open carefully and peered out onto the deck.

Flames and strobing muzzle flashes lit the dark surface of the sump outside. Hard black shadows flickered and danced across the deck in time to bursts. Donna could see little of the deck but it looked empty beyond the hatch. With her heart in her mouth she slipped out onto the deck, but no salvo of bullets crashed out from a waiting ambush. Everyone was too busy watching the massacre on the dock.

The deck she stood on was the lowest and ran in a U-shape around the stern of the ekranoplan. The next highest deck lay between the arms of the U and carried the quad-stubber and another deck gun separated by a big tailfin or funnel of some kind. She had seen stairs from there up onto a still higher deck at the front of the craft, up where its stub-wings projected out, presumably making it the location of the bridge or control room. Donna would lay odds that would be where Relli had run to – it was the castle's keep of his little kingdom after all.

She sheathed her weapons, jumped up and caught the railing of the next deck up. She pulled herself up and dropped into crouch. The gun in front of her was a smoking ruin, two pit slaves lay dead around it and the corpse of a Dog Soldier was grotesquely pinned into the wreckage. The roar of the quad-stubber suddenly cut off with a sighing exhalation and Donna got the weird feeling that she was chasing ghosts. She cast a wary look up to the bridge but it was out of sight.

There were gunshots from the deck below her and behind the tailplane ahead. They sounded leisurely, well-aimed, like an audience keeping itself amused while they waited for the big performance to start again. She heard grunts as heavy bullet belts were slotted in place and then she suddenly understood. They had stopped firing the stubber to reload; the audible sigh had come from coolant hissing on the hot barrels. She drew her weapons and crept around the tailplane to get closer.

Another quad-stubber squatted on the deck before her, identical to the one behind her that was now twisted wreckage. Two pit slaves were reloading it and a Dog Soldier sat in a central cage with two of the long guns mounted on each side of it. He was cursing at the slaves to load faster. From here Donna could see more pit slaves at the railing and some on the lower deck close to the rear of the craft, all taking occasional pot shots at the shore.

The gun tower on the dock was in flames. There were bodies scattered at the bottom of the gangplank with bloody drag marks leading off behind a stretch of broken wall nearby. From up here she could easily reconstruct what had happened. The Escher must have knocked out the deck gun and the tower in the first moments of the attack, with a grenade launcher presumably, and some very well calculated shots. They rushed the gang plank then, and cut down the guards at the bottom. Before they could get to the top, the Dog Soldiers got the other quad-stubber firing and drove them back.

The wall at edge of the dock was extensively etched with fresh bullet holes. Donna was guessing that the Escher were still pinned down behind it. She couldn't see how they could escape with the quad-stubber covering them. It had a perfect field of fire. Anyone that tried to run would be cut to pieces within three paces. That was once it was reloaded, of course, and that was something to which Donna decided she was categorically opposed.

Donna waited patiently until they had threaded the last belt in place, listening to the other slaves laugh and shoot while they waited too and hating them for taking pleasure in it. Only then, just as they were about to open fire, did she step out into plain view.

'Hey, Dog Soldier!' she called. 'You're the last one! All your brothers are dead! Come out and face me!'

The Goliath's head snapped round at her challenge and the quad-stubber started turning towards her. For a split second it was lined up with the other pit slaves at the railing, who were also turning in surprise – this wasn't part of the evening's scheduled events for them. She picked that moment to fire the Pig.

The plasma discharge flashed across the deck with blinding fury. It tore voraciously into the stubber's ammo hoppers and cooked off the freshly laid belts of ammunition inside in an instant. The results were nothing short of spectacular.

The quad stubber coughed out streams of bullets that went hosing wildly across the deck and transfixed those poor unfortunates standing at the railing. Then more ammo popped and metal went scything outwards in all directions. Even Donna was taken aback by the violence and darted behind the tailplane for cover.

Impacts and ricochets rang all around her for what seemed a painfully long time. She peered cautiously around the corner as they died away. She saw a fist, and then stars, and then her head cracked on the deck. A crushing weight fell on top of her, pinning her down.

'Yo're gonna die nah bitch!' The Dog Soldier spat in her face.

He was hideously burned all down his left side and one arm had been shrivelled into a twisted stick. Sooty flakes of immolated flesh were dropping on Donna as they struggled. He was trying to get his remaining hand around her throat. Donna flailed desperately but the Goliath was too heavy to dislodge. He clamped his knees tighter and her ribs screamed in protest. Another punch made her see stars, and his big, calloused hand locked around her ivory throat and squeezed.

Donna's vision darkened and she felt neck bones grating ominously. She could only kick and flail feebly. Her flapping hands encountered something on the deck – it was familiar and it was comforting. Her oxygen-starved brain struggled to make sense of what it was. A number; Seventy-six.

She swung the chainblade into the Goliath's arm below the elbow and it chewed into flesh and muscle. The weak blow couldn't do more than cut him. He grunted angrily and kept squeezing. Donna grabbed Seventy-six behind the blade guard with her other hand and pushed it deeper with all her might, sawing it back and forth. The Dog Soldier roared in pain and tried to rear back, as he did so his arm severed and dropped away in a cascade of crimson. Donna took Seventy-six and rammed it into his crotch. She kept pushing upwards until the chain blade protruded between his shoulder blades, just to be sure.

Donna crawled out from beneath the carcass and spat blood out of her mouth. She was starting to remember why she despised Dog Soldiers. They just didn't know when to lie down and quit. Pain and fatigue pulsed through her body as she fought with an almost overwhelming temptation to lie down and rest for a while.

Shots struck sparks from the deck beside her with shocking violence. She was suddenly wide awake and rolling into cover behind the wrecked stubber on nothing more than instincts and adrenaline. Her wits were scattered, but she finally realised that the shots were from somewhere near the bridge. She risked a glance out and almost got her face sawn off by autoguns. There were at least two shooters and they most definitely had her in their sights.

The Pig lay where she'd dropped it, in plain view on the deck not two metres away, but Donna knew that she would never be able to even get a hand on it before she would be cut down. That left her with the noble laspistol, but a simple laspistol just didn't give her enough firepower to go up against riflemen in good positions. A couple more bursts of autofire ricocheted off the wreckage. Donna realised they weren't interested in hitting her, they were just keeping her head down. But what for? Someone sneaking around for a grenade throw or head-shot? Neither prospect made Donna inclined to stay behind the stubber wreckage to find out.

She waited until she reckoned at least one of them was reloading and then sprinted for the edge of the deck. It was a calculated risk, she told herself. She had no way of knowing what she would be dropping into on the deck below, so it was a bit mad, but it had two things in its favour: one, she would be closer to the Escher; and two, it was better than staying where she was. Bullets chased her all the way, whickering through the railing as she vaulted over it.

The lower deck was a vision of chaos lit by the flames of the burning tower. The Escher had come storming up the gangplank as soon as the stubber blew. They were fighting the surviving pit slaves hand-to-hand; the Escher's slender blades clashed against a crude array of hammers, saws, drills and claws. The deck was slick with blood and bodies lay everywhere.

She took all this in during the quarter second it took for her to drop down. Seventy-six was out and slashing even before her feet hit the deck. A pit slave went down with his skull split in two, the twin hemispheres of his brain displayed as neatly as if in a coroner's autopsy. She sheared muscle and sinew from a brawny arm next, then blocked a swinging saw-blade before impaling its owner.

Donna felt no pity or mercy for her opponents now. These were the most vicious slaves in Relli's employ, keen to fight or they would have quit their posts and fled long ago. More than that, these patchwork mannequins of steel and flesh weren't just trying to kill her, they were trying to kill her friends too. A lot of the Escher were people she had never even met but they came to help her anyway. All because for some messed up reason they thought 'Mad Donna' was worth something. She was an icon.

Through a gap in the crush of flailing bodies, she saw an Escher juve go down with her head pulped by a hammer. Jen's face flashed into view with one eye covered in blood. She grinned at Donna and was gone again. Donna felt a surge of hate well up inside her: hatred for Jen, for taking D'onne's misery and making it into a cause for martyrdom; for Tessera for bringing her down here; for Relli, Ko'iron, her father; for all causes, and all manipulators, everywhere.

The one thing she could do was ensure that the Escher didn't have to die for her.

Her hate was unstoppable. She ranged through the lumpen pit slaves with blade and pistol and made them howl. The toughest or stupidest came at her first, thinking to prove their worth by taking her down in close combat. She killed them most cruelly of all, with shorn limbs and torn faces that howled out their agony long after they should have been stilled.

The smart ones came next. They would usually try to put a bullet in her before coming within reach of her blade. They found out that Mad Donna's aim was as deadly as her blade, and the laspistol infinitely quicker. She shot them down where they stood.

The losers were last, too stupid to realise they needed to run until it was too late, and too weak fight. She killed them with contempt verging on boredom.

There was a sudden silence after the clangor and screams of combat. The stench was overpowering: burning, blood, spilt viscera. Donna almost retched when she realised her boot heels were sunk in the soft entrails of a dying pit slave. She looked around wildly. Her first impression was that there was no one left standing at all, that she was alone on a ship of damned. Then she caught sight of the Escher rallying around a triumphant looking Jen. There were half a dozen of them left. Donna's heart froze at the sight of someone she knew among the injured to whom they were tending. Bright arterial blood leaked from her midriff and she was in a bad way.

It was Tessera.

10: TERMINUS

SMOKE WAS SWIRLING across the deck. The hazy figures of the Escher were slipping out of view, only outlined by the occasional gun flash as they chased after the last few of Relli's pit slaves. Donna crouched down beside Tessera disconsolately, feeling her heart grow cold and shrivelled as she watched one of her only friends dying. Three little pieces of metal had pierced her midriff, three insignificant little pieces of metal moving fast enough to rupture organs, shatter bones and cleave arteries. They had tried patching her up as best they could but there was nothing they could do to stop her bleeding internally.

'So... did you find... what you came for... D'onne?' she said weakly. Blood was dribbling from the corner of her mouth.

'No, you're dying for nothing.' Donna voice was flat and bitter, angry.

'Thanks, D'onne,' Tessera smiled up at her beatifically. 'That's been... the story of my life.'

Donna stripped off a glove and took Tessera's hand in her own. Her grip was tight, and the skin felt dry and smooth. She knew what Tessera needed to hear.

'I did what you suggested – I know, I know, but there's a first time for everything – I asked the gang why they came looking for me. I was so sure you'd put them up to it. Jen set me straight.'

Tessera nodded and spoke. 'I've seen it happen before. Someone... survives long enough... gets a... name and there's always some idiots ready to call them... a messiah.'

Tessera's voice was dwindling to a whisper. Donna's mind searched frantically for an answer, some way to save Tessera, or to go back in time, or to change reality to fit with the way it should *really* be. It made no difference, Tessera's heart continued to pump blood relentlessly into the gaping holes that had been torn in her body cavity. In the end, all Donna could do was say how she felt and hope reality would somehow deign to take notice.

'I don't want you to die, Tessera'

'It's alright... I do... I'm too old for this game now... everything hurts... Jen's ready to take on the gang...'

'Dammit, Tessera, I still need you!'

'D'onne, hush... you don't need anyone any more... never did really...'

Donna's heart pulsed suddenly as her brain spat out an answer: Ko'iron's medicae unit! There was nothing they couldn't fix, or at least stabilise long enough to get fixed. Donna's words came out in a headlong rush, tripping over each other. 'Look, just hold on. I know how I can save you, if I can find Ko'iron – he's got a medicae unit. One way or another I'll get it and bring it back. Just don't die!'

'You're... mad... D'onne.'

The grip on Tessera's hand tightened momentarily and then Mad Donna was gone.

DONNA QUICKLY CLAMBERED her way back up onto the gun deck. She chafed at the need for caution as she slunk forward; Tessera lay dying below her and she didn't have time to waste slinking about. She kept telling herself that she couldn't afford to get pegged by some passing gunman now, and a headlong rush would just make her real dead real quick.

Smoke was drifting everywhere, backlit by the orange glow of flames in the wreckage here and there. It sounded like there was a spirited firefight taking place around the U-shaped deck below, but the gun deck she was on and the stairs that led up to the bridge seemed deserted. No sign of the gunmen that had driven her off earlier. She found that faintly disturbing. They'd had a good position – why give it up?

Donna heard a creak close behind her and spun around in an eye blink. Tola and Avignon were hauling themselves over the railing behind her.

'Figured you wouldn't mind some company,' Avignon stage-whispered. Tola giggled.

'You two idiots better not get in my way,' Donna said, though in truth she was glad of the back-up.

'No sweat – ladies first,' Avignon smirked.

'Humph. What's all the shooting about?'

'Jen reckons we've got Bak's little Delaque friends pinned down in the front bit of the boat. She sent us up here to see if we can get an angle on them.' Avignon patted her well-worn autogun meaningfully.

'Alright then. There were two at least up in the bridge with autoguns. I don't know whether they've gone or are just waiting for good shots. Cover me and we'll find out.'

Donna ran, zigzagging between scattered wreckage and body parts. The eviscerated, half-burned corpse of the Dog Soldier she had fought stared up at her accusingly as she passed. She was gambling again, working the theory that Relli had dragged Ko'iron and the servitor away to the bridge. She was also gambling that autofire couldn't cut her down if she ran fast enough.

She threw herself to the side as muzzle flashes stabbed out from the bridge. Bullets lashed the deck behind her like hail. Avignon's autogun chattered out and elicited a cry of pain in response. Donna rolled, covering the bridge with her laspistol, scanning for a target.

She heard Tola running forward and saw a flicker of movement as one of the gunmen raised his rifle to the railing. Her las-bolts slammed into his head at the same instant that he pulled the trigger on Tola. The burst sprayed wildly around the deck, and the gunman's finger clamped in a death grip as he toppled out of sight. Tola shrieked.

'Check on her, Avignon!' Donna called as she sprinted for the steps. She hugged the wall and slithered quietly up while trying to look in all directions at once. She peeked over the edge at the top and saw the gunman sprawled nearby with a scatter of spent shell casings around him. His head was a gory ruin but the long coat and pale skin told her all she needed to know. She'd found the Delaque.

The Delaque Avignon had hit was wounded and trying to crawl away. Donna scanned the open deck she could see at the top of the steps for more enemies. It was bordered along one side by the bridge itself, but there was a long run of windows and doors that could conceal an army of lurking foes.

'Tola's okay, down but not out!' Avignon called from below.

Donna cleared the top of the steps and skipped along sideways facing the bridge. No lights were showing inside, no signs of movement. The wounded

Delaque saw her coming and scrabbled for a pistol at his belt. She closed on him in a couple of long strides and easily kicked it out of his grasp.

'Ahh, you bitch,' he hissed. 'Just kill me and get on with it.'

'You're forgetting something, slick. That's "psycho-bitch" to you,' Donna hissed. 'Where's Bak and Relli? I swear if you don't tell me quick you're going to regret it for the rest of your very short and very painful existence.'

The Delaque squirmed. He knew Mad Donna's reputation as well as any.

'He's–' the world exploded into gunfire and an avalanche of shattering glass. Donna instinctively dived behind the injured Delaque for cover. She felt his body jerk as bullets ploughed into it. The deafening salvo seemed to go on endlessly: breaking glass, bullets whining past, ricochets pinging off metal. A tiny corner of her brain registered Avignon shouting somewhere in the distance.

The firing stuttered and died away, leaving Donna with the whiff of gun smoke in her nostrils and pounding eardrums. A familiar voice cut through the sudden silence.

'Glad you could make it, Donna, I really am.' Bak's sinister whisper was obscenely triumphant. 'You've been everything I had hoped for – a distraction, an assassin, a saboteur. I couldn't have wished for a better partner!'

'Well then, come out here, partner!' Donna called back. 'I want to renegotiate some of our business arrangements.' Donna was scanning the bridge, looking for the shooters, but all she could see was darkness and shards of glass hanging from their frames like broken teeth.

'Oh, I find them eminently suitable for our current relationship,' Bak sniggered.

'I was thinking of something more like that arrangement I had with Cousin Kell, you know? The one where you die screaming and cursing the day you ever heard my name.'

'Oh you poor Ulanti bitch, you think you can bait me over Kell? He was as useless as he was stupid, that's why I put him in Dust Falls to draw you on in the first place.'

'Nice story, Shallej. Is that why you sent men into the sewers after me? To "draw me on?" How many died Shallej? Half of them? All of them? And what about Dead Man's Hole? How many more did you lose there? You know something, Shallej? I think you're a crap leader. I think the only way you stay in charge is by killing off anyone that's better than you, which isn't asking a lot.' Donna figured there was no harm in trying to sow a little dissension in the ranks. Something she said must have stung Shallej. His voice was pure venom when he replied.

'You think what you want! Tell it to the sumpsharks!'

She heard him saying something to the men with him. It sounded like, 'It's done, let's go'. That was worrying.

Donna felt a vibration run through the deck. A high-pitched whine began, coughed out and then restarted. It was picked up and repeated, once, twice, rising in volume each time: three, four, five, six more times. Donna realised the noise was coming from either side of the bridge, so she glanced outwards and saw a sight that froze her heart.

Each of the stub wings to either side of bridge bore the squat shapes of three big engines. She had given them no heed until now, assuming them to be empty husks. As she watched, the engines opened up like flowers. Venturis extended seamlessly and lit with cherry red flames. The engines built up to full power in a rising howl. The ekranoplan lurched and began to slide forward from the dock.

'Take Tola and get out of here, now!' she yelled down to Avignon, not even knowing if she could be heard over the roar of the engines. She heard a fusillade of shots crackling up from the lower decks, Jen was doubtless finding out that the Delaque weren't as pinned down as she'd hoped.

Donna jumped up, charging headlong for the bridge. Muzzle flashes lit like stars in the darkness, driving her back into cover again. She fired back blindly but the flashes were moving targets. Bak's men were pulling out.

Time was running out, and that made Donna more reckless than ever. She dived headlong through a shattered window, tearing her flesh on the knife-like shards. She landed on a table in the darkness and slid awkwardly off it as the ekranoplan lurched. Shots buzzed past her like a swarm of angry insects. Rolling upright, she saw a Delaque silhouetted in a doorway. Donna put two las-shots into his torso and he fell back out of sight.

The firing stopped abruptly. The room was empty. With her bionic eye's crystal vision Donna could see that she was in some kind of chartroom, with a corridor running forward to the bridge proper and doors off at either side. She was starting for the doorway where she had shot the Delaque when a sudden chill at the back of her neck made her spin around.

The room was empty. Nothing moved. The Delaque had all gone. But even now she felt as if something was creeping up on her, something she could see just out of the corner of her eye, but when she looked directly it was gone. The chill feeling at the back of her neck didn't go away. If anything it intensified.

But time was running out and she didn't have time for mysteries. The roar of the engines had steadied and the ekranoplan was wallowing and lurching against its mooring lines like an unruly pack animal. Donna heard the whip-crack sound of a line snapping. Soon the ekranoplan would be heading off into the sump for its final voyage. The room was empty. Nothing moved. She turned back to the doorway.

Something hit her from behind with the force of a sledgehammer and sent her flying. She crashed into a cabinet and fell to the deck. She glimpsed a glitter of chrome hurtling towards her and she lashed out with a blind kick at it. Her boot connected solidly enough to deflect steel-pistoned jaws driving at her throat, but the enforcer hound behind them kept coming. Blade-sheathed claws raked at her legs as it lunged at her again with its jaws snapping.

Donna swung Seventy-six up but it was too close for the blade to connect. She punched the cyber-mastiff's gargoyle-like head aside with the knuckle guard instead. That bought her another second of life. The beast reared back and Donna rolled from beneath it. She was up and onto one knee before it came ravening back at her again. This time her chainblade parry connected squarely, gouging at the polished steel of the mastiff's exoskeleton. Donna took a return cut at the mastiff's foreleg and sent it skittering backwards with a shower of sparks.

It looked like a spectacular hit but Donna wasn't fooled. Any ordinary creature would be shorter by a leg after a blow like that; the enforcer hound barely even slowed down. It dug its claws into the deck and jumped at her. This time Donna darted aside and let the heavy cyborg crash into the cabinet behind her. In the second it took for the mastiff to shake itself free of the wreckage, she darted out of the door.

The door was metal and it was heavy, more of a hatch. Donna threw her weight against it and it swung ponderously shut. She glimpsed the polished metal of the mastiff's skeleton through the closing gap. Then the door jammed only partway shut, and Donna looked down and cursed. The dead Delaque's foot was caught in the doorjamb, and the mastiff crashed against the door. Donna had to fight tooth and claw to keep it from being forced open. Tortured metal shrieked in protest, and the mastiff's muzzle and claws scrabbled in the gap with a whining of servos.

The assault ceased for a moment and Donna instantly thumbed Seventy-six into life. The whirling teeth licked downward through the dead Delaque's ankle and severed it with a spray of blood. Donna threw the door shut in the mastiff's face. Panting and shaking, she glanced down the steps at her side and then out of the small porthole in the door. The mastiff was close by, staring back at her. Now there was another figure in the room with it, one that sent an involuntary chill down Donna's spine. A robed figure, one she had seen what seemed an eternity ago at Cliff Wall – short and rotund-looking, it was swaying as if in time to unheard music. The robe's hood had been cast back to reveal a pale, round face framed by tangled black locks. It was a homely looking face, suited for a nursemaid or a cook, apart from a pair of eyes that twinkled with ages-old malice.

An icy sensation brushed through Donna's skull as she looked at the woman. A bloom of frost appeared on the glass of the porthole and stretched feathery fingers across it. The chilling sensation swelled, becoming cold spears inside her head that stabbed down her spine. The world pitched and darkened before her sight, consciousness dwindling into a shrinking spot of light.

She had failed everyone: Tessera, Tola, Avignon, Hanno, Jen, Lars. Their faces reared out of the darkness at her. They flowed past her in a vivid parade of accusation and disappointment. She had led them all into pain and suffering. Everyone she had ever met had been hurt by knowing her. It would have been better if she had never been born, better if her life were ended now to stop the damage she was doing to everyone and everything around her.

Her head throbbed abominably. Everything went black.

DEAD LEAVES RUSTLED *above her like dry hands. A chill wind caressed her bare back and arms. The arboretum was covered in a light dusting of frost that caught thin polarised rays of light coming through the skylights high above. Blood was on her hands. Her heart hammered in her chest. She would be found soon. She would be caught and taken back to the tower. Imprisoned for life.*

Nobles and their entourages strolled past. Harassed nursemaids shepherded children in unruly flocks. Their faces turned minutely away whenever they came close to her, denying her existence within their ordered world. She could almost hear their thoughts: a girl alone in the Arboretum? Scandalous! She must be insane! But not a word was spoken, not a glance was given. Her solitude remained perfect and unchallenged.

Their movements reminded D'onne of the slow, formal dances her father had insisted she learn, of masquerades where nobility stepped and fought their internal battles of supremacy with gestures and nuances almost too subtle to register. A wave of hopelessness surged through her. She felt hollow, spent, an empty shell filled only by the beating, skipping tremor of her heart.

A shadow fell across her. She looked up into the furious face of her father and her fluttering heart broke.

LOQUI'S OPEN MOUTH *was screaming but the banshee winds snatched the pitiful sound away and tore it apart. Her night robes billowed wildly about her like torn wings, she was spinning, flailing wildly as she flew up into storm-wracked skies. Streamers of cloud whipped past like predatory shoals and arcs of lightning scored the swollen, bruised atmosphere with bright metallic fractures from horizon to horizon. Loqui was swept further out from the creaking spire and started to fall towards the roiling cloud base far, far below. Despite the patent absurdity of it, D'onne believed she could hear her sister's thin, distant scream long after she disappeared from sight.*

Her eldest sister, Corundra, was smiling down at her with full red lips. Her face flickered in and out of the darkness, the actinic glare of the lightning distorting it into a hundred cruel masks. Little D'onne felt herself being lifted by small hands and carried over to the edge of the esplanade. Lightning crashed down about them as they reached the railing.

COUNT KO'IRON'S SWEATY *face leered up close to hers. His hand was gripping her by the throat and he was forcing her onto the table. Her back was bowed back cruelly against the table edge. Crystal goblets scattered and broke with a hysterical tinkling sound. But there was no one there. No one would come to help. She was alone with a predator in her home.*

DONNA KNEW WHAT came next. She didn't want to see this, she'd hidden this deeply a long time ago, so deep that even she didn't see it any more. Why? Why was this memory here?

Ko'iron laughed and raised a bottle to his lips, easily keeping young D'onne pinned with his other hand. He knew his business when it came to forcing himself on women, and making them feel helpless while he did it. She writhed in his grasp, only exciting him further. He pressed his slobbering lips against hers, his waxed moustachios scraping rapaciously at her soft skin and the reek of alcohol gusting into D'onne's nose and mouth.

Something small and hard was clutched in her fist. She smashed it into Ko'iron's leering face without a second's thought. The resulting spray of blood shocked her to the very core. The grip on her throat released at once, and Ko'iron fell back burbling out a thin, high scream and clutching his face. In an instant the tables had turned – a small piece of metal had made Ko'iron stop when a hundred pleas had not. Rage blossomed in D'onne's breast, this was the man she was being sold to, the man her father wanted her to breed with. She smashed the fork in her hand into his other eye, realising at the last instant that Ko'iron's cold grey eyes exactly matched those of her father.

Donna's living eye snapped open. The deck lurched beneath her feet as the ekranoplan surged against its last mooring line. Barely a moment had passed. She could still see the woman, the Wyrd, silhouetted on the other side through the frost-scarred porthole, but the sleek chrome shape of the cyber-mastiff was gone. She yanked the heavy steel door open and stepped out. The robed woman took an involuntary step backwards.

'That's right, witch, your mind games failed. They've just got me seriously pissed off instead.'

The woman looked confused and upset, like a child that has had its toys taken away. She kept backing away towards the other door. Donna brought up her laspistol.

'Where's Ko'iron? I won't be asking twice.'

The woman closed her eyes and Donna's nape hairs prickled. She fired, and the las-bolts cut straight through where the woman stood, although Donna was not sure if she really hit anything. There was the stink of burnt flesh and a spray of blood, but when Donna looked at the spot they seemed to fade away, just like the woman herself. The room was empty. Nothing moved. Pretty soon Donna found herself unable to believe the woman had ever really been there at all.

A snaking trail of viscous fluid led off towards the bridge. Bright score marks showed where steel shod claws had run. Had the mastiff returned to its master? There was one way to be sure, and at least it looked like the brute was hurt, leaking out precious fluids, just like Tessera.

The corridor at the back of the chart room was short, with cabin doors hanging open at either side to give glimpses of cramped quarters. A fresh corpse was sprawled half out of a bunk in one room, and bullet holes were everywhere Donna looked. Bak's men had not been subtle when they took over.

The bridge itself was a complete mess. No lights were left but fires sputtering in the guts of wrecked consoles gave the place a fitful illumination that reminded Donna of a sepulchre. More bodies were strewn around on the floor here. She paid no heed to the dead. She was too numb with pain and exhaustion to give them more than a cursory glance as she walked by.

Some had been riddled with shots but at least two had had their throats cut. The sluggish pools of their life-blood sucked at Donna's boot heels as she passed. Directly ahead of her a skeletal metal stairway disappeared up through the roof. Bright scratches struck exclamation points in the oxidised alloy of the steps – the mastiff had gone up. Now the question was how to follow without one's head being bitten off.

Outside, the last mooring line gave way with a crack like thunder. Donna was almost thrown to the deck by a sudden surge of acceleration. The multi-throated engine noise rose in triumph and the ekranoplan slid majestically forward across the sump. Donna couldn't help but grin – wherever Relli was, he must be pissing in his pants by now.

Anyone up top must be trying to hang on for dear life after that lurch. Whatever she was going to do, the time to do it was now. She bounded up the steps, diving and rolling out from the entry too fast (she hoped) for anyone to draw a bead on her.

She glared around, chainsword and pistol in hand for the expected rush of enemies, but there were none. The steps came up into a groove in the top of the wings that in turn led to the frame of an observation blister that had once been artfully faceted in armoured glass, most of which were now cracked or missing. A perfunctory mast rose in front of the blister at a rakish angle – it had the look of an afterthought placed there only to hang flags on.

The wind whipped past, tugging at Donna's hair and stinging her living eye to tears. She could see a figure up ahead, just beyond the observation blister. It was only a silhouette but the chromium glimmer of the mastiff was at his feet and that left no doubt.

Count Ko'iron was making his last stand beneath the empty flag-pole of a sinking ship. He was surely ignorant of the rich, unconscious symbolism of his choice.

'You've got your own gun, that's a good start,' the old woman had told her as they had made their way along yet another service corridor worming deeper into Escher territory. To D'onne's eyes this 'Tessera' looked older than her mother, but she seemed fit and able enough as she led them down into increasingly filthy and disused-looking areas with a familiarity that was reassuring.

D'onne had been surprised that they knew about the laspistol she was hiding until she thought about it for a moment. Of course they had scanned both her and Hanno for hidden weapons when they entered – it was simply basic security. Hanno probably knew about it too. They didn't bother about the pistol at The Wall because no one cared what was taken out of the Spire and into Hive City, just what got brought back inside. The Escher were probably the same way. D'onne felt naive.

Hanno was still blustering furiously and to no avail.

'You can't just take a noble into the Underhive! Not without personal armour and proper support!'

'She won't be the first noble to get crap on their shoes, enforcer,' Tessera told him. 'Besides, it's the only kind of sanctuary we can offer now. If she stays here, thousands are going to pay for it with their lives.'

'Lord Helmawr can provide her with all the protection she needs! There must be a proper investigation!'

D'onne was getting tired of being treated as an article of baggage to be argued over.

'Enforcer Hanno,' she interjected, quietly but firmly, 'I appreciate your concerns and your dedication to your duty does you credit. However, I fear your optimism in relation to Lord Helmawr's most likely stance is unwarranted. There will be no investigation. If I surrender myself to the ruling house I can either expect to be held as a hostage against House Ulanti's good behaviour for years to come, or, more likely, be traded back to my father for some immediate short term advantage.

'Believe me, Hanno, I know what I'm worth,' she concluded bitterly. 'Coming here was an act of desperation. If Madam Tessera believes I've put these people in danger, then I have to go. And quickly. You can either extend your sense of duty to accompany me for my protection, or go and report back to the proper authorities on what you have witnessed.'

Hanno looked taken aback. Her analysis had been clear and dispassionate, a statement of undeniable fact from someone in a far better position than he to know just what Helmawr would do. Tessera was nodding unconsciously as D'onne spoke but Hanno had been too wrapped up in his own worldview to see it as clearly.

Hanno had looked at the seething, ramshackle Hive City and, like most, blamed its many problems on human incompetence and simple neglect. Only now was he coming to understand that those were just symptoms. The founding fathers of Necromunda had institutionalised corruption, built greed into the city's very foundations and then set themselves as rulers over it all as the noble houses. For millennia they had made it so and nothing was going to change now.

Poor Hanno. D'onne could see the cracks in his belief system yawning into vast gulfs as he learned more about those he served. The lords of Necromunda had no interest in redemption, or the wellbeing of their fellow man. Their populace was an indentured workforce and nothing more. Even their own sons and daughters were bartered and sold on the open market. That didn't fit his worldview at all; it made him into a corrupt servant of a corrupt regime, not the fair-minded arbiter of justice his ego told him to be.

D'onne looked at Tessera and tried to radiate calm and confidence she didn't feel. Her stomach kept knotting tighter and tighter the longer they stood around. Whatever was going to happen, she needed to know what it was going to be and, most of all, she needed it to happen quickly.

'Madam–'

'Just call me Tessera, D'onne, we aren't big on titles here.'

'Tessera, do you believe that we can escape into the Underhive without my father knowing?'

'No, I don't believe we can even escape from House Escher without your father knowing. What's more, the news of where you've gone will hit Hive City about four minutes after we get to the first settlement in the Underhive, but that's what I'm counting on.'

'I don't understand.'

'Oh my dear D'onne, it's all a question of reach. In Hive City there are literally hundreds of thousands of agents House Ulanti can mobilise quickly and easily against any of the industrial houses. Many will work for your father just out of spite and political expediency up here. It's not like that in the Underhive.'

'No, it's a shambolic anarchy of crazed mutants, renegades and criminal gangs from Hive City, which is why my father won't be able to reach me there, presumably.'

Tessera had given her an odd look then, as if re-evaluating.

'That's a little simplistic, but I expect that's exactly what you're taught in the Spire,' she said, perhaps rather archly.

The point was that all the houses have plenty of spies in the Underhive but they have very few agents working for them down there and even less whom they can trust.

'Your father will quickly hear that you have left House Escher for the Underhive, but there will be very little he can do about it, and while he's searching for a way the attacks on House Escher will stop.'

That made her reappraise Tessera too. She was thinking clearly about the best course for her house, and seemed to know plenty about the Underhive too – which made D'onne wonder about those 'criminal gangs' that supposedly plagued the Underhive in such profusion. Could it be that they were all simply shady extensions of the Industrial Houses?

'Well Hanno, what's it going to be?' Tessera asked as they arrived at a hatch that was caked in rust, centuries old. Hanno gave her an icy stare before turning to D'onne.

'Nobledam, I was given permission by my proctor only to accompany you as far as House Escher territory,' Hanno said to D'onne. 'But under the circumstances I think it is clearly my duty to accompany you further if you are determined to go ahead with this plan to enter the Underhive.' He shot a sharp look at Tessera.

Interesting. It seemed Hanno didn't want to go back Hive City. D'onne wondered how much of it was a desire to protect her and how much of it was a desire not to go back and explain what he had heard. Lord Helmawr might well decide it was most expedient to dispose of the earnest Enforcer Hanno once his story had been recounted. Calamitous events in the Spire seldom left a surfeit of live witnesses behind. Dead men tell no tales.

Tessera spun the wheel in the centre of the hatch. It turned remarkably smoothly, considering the apparent decrepitude of its mounting.

'In that case, my dear enforcer,' Tessera said with a wicked grin, 'you might want to lose the body armour before going much further.'

She hauled open the hatch and a wave of hot, humid air surged out. Sweat prickled on D'onne's body as the noisome heat enveloped them.

'Deeper down it gets cooler,' Tessera said conversationally, 'and the condensation isn't half as bad, but for the next few shifts it'll be like this or worse so you want to strip down if you can. Heat stroke can be a killer down here.'

D'onne knew right then that she was going to hate the Underhive.

THE HATCH OPENED into a kind of common room. There were bunk beds, crates, chairs and half a dozen Escher lounging around. Their baroquely shaven heads, tattoos, piercings and plentiful weaponry told D'onne that these were gangers, real Underhive scum. They eyed D'onne and most especially Hanno with studied insolence, the threat of imminent violence floating in the air between them.

'Be nice now', Tessera said. 'These two people need our help. It's not like they're the first to ask and it's not like it's the first time we've said yes. These two are just a bit unusual is all'.

Several of the gangers eyed Tessera with overt scepticism but no-one turned away muttering and none of them challenged her directly. D'onne was fascinated. When Tessera had started talking, D'onne had been convinced that it was some kind of foreign language. It was only by listening carefully that she could make out the weird inflections, the *clipping and lengthening of vowel sounds that were at work mangling the usual prole cant into something entirely different. Tessera had slipped into it easily, shrugging off her formal, upper Hive City accent like a cloak.*

One of the gangers stood up suddenly, a blonde mohawked giant that stood a full head taller than anyone else in the room. She jabbed a blunt, scarred finger at Hanno and declared, 'Me an' the girls say we goin' nowhere with law boy there, until e' drops the armour so we can see that sweet enforcer reargurd!'

The room erupted in hoots and giggles. Hanno went an interesting shade of purple. It was doubtless just the release of tension but D'onne found herself laughing too. She couldn't remember the last time she had laughed without thinking first about whether it was 'appropriate' to do so. Maybe being in the Underhive wouldn't be so bad after all.

Tessera rolled her eyes, turned to D'onne, and whispered with theatrical conspiracy, 'That is "Crazy Kristi," I'm afraid. We would have got rid of her a long time ago but no one's figured out how to kill her yet.'

Crazy Kristi spread her arms like a triumphant pit fighter and lapped up the storm of boos, cat-calls and thrown litter from her fellow gangers. D'onne grinned.

Not so bad at all.

11: SURVIVAL INSTINCT

In the broiling social froth of the Necromundan hives, it is not the strongest individual that survives, nor the most intelligent. It is the one that is the most adaptable to change.

> **Exercept from: Xonariarius the Younger's**
> *Nobilite Pax Imperator – The Triumph of Aristocracy over Democracy.*

THE EKRANOPLAN WAS skimming across the sump lake on its final odyssey. From the top of its upper wing, the dark majesty of the glistening sable expanse spread in all directions, and the pale lights of Down Town were dwindling away behind them with alarming rapidity. Methane fires twisted in their wake and rippled away to black horizons inestimably far off. Gargantuan stalactites hung overhead like inverted mountains, reaching out to touch the surface as if it were a starry night sky and the ekranoplan was racing across the heavens instead of through the roots of the underworld. Donna had never felt so consciously out of her environment as she did upon the sump lake – she could have been in outer space and felt more at home.

This was a truly alien place, inimical to the intrusion of man.

The sharp tang of pollutants was different out here on the lake, not organic and rotten like it was around Down Town but more obviously chemical, caustic and deadly. The whipping wind made by their progress scoured the skin and stung Donna's living eye. She could still make out Ko'iron through the tears. His white armour shone starkly against the fantastic midnight panorama behind him, and the glittering chrome enforcer hound lay silent at his feet. He was the very image of some paladin or angel descended from the places of light into darkness to smite the fallen.

The High Cathedra of Hive Primus is full of such images, armoured warriors selflessly fighting aliens and foul beasts to protect their fellow man. There are even relics of crusades among the stars, and scriptoria filled with ancient accounts of battles against impossible odds now long since forgotten. The faithful always point to these as evidence of an earlier golden age of justice and honour, mankind at its best and bravest as it confronted a new dawn on a million worlds across the galaxy.

Little D'onne had always been dazzled by the shining holo-liths of the cathedra, its secret treasure houses of reliquaries and the halls of tattered, shot-scarred banners won beneath distant suns. The martial pride of the Spyrer hunt had first stirred her interest and then her long sojourn in the tower had later given her ample opportunity to study the subject at her leisure.

Like any good noble, she had studied the careers of her illustrious ancestors first and foremost. By every standard she had been taught they were the only things that really mattered. The results were disappointing, to say the least. Every time she had followed up some epithet or battle history she found the so-called regimental hero had been a hundred kilometres from the battlefront at all times, or the landfall of a battalion on a hostile planet had been bravely 'led' by a noble up in orbit. The family histories wheedled and pleaded on behalf of its paper-thin protagonists but could not conceal their arrogance, ignorance and sloth.

D'onne eventually understood that to her family war was just another business arena, and an unprofitable one at that. It was only commonly proffered as a career to the most wasteful, stupid and myopic family members. Others might toy with it briefly, just long enough to get a few awards and a uniform for attending the correct social events before returning to an undeserved heroes welcome. It seemed those aberrant few that became true, professional, soldiers left Necromunda and never returned. She had been quietly sickened by all matters military after that, and turned her mind to other things.

But nobility still loved to wrap itself in the flag of past glories it had never earned. They spouted martial tradition and rattled their immaculate sabres at every opportunity, and some even went so far as to hunt down in the Underhive. Then they came equipped with weapons beyond the comprehension of their enemies and armour suits that were smarter than those they protected. The suits had stored water and food to nourish the nobles, inbuilt diagnostics to tend to their wounds and inertial maps to guide them to prey located by a suite of sensors. The nobles believed this tradition kept them hardened and honed in readiness in case they were called on to fight for their house or their world.

It was hard to make headway against the wind. Headwind slapped at her, trying to force her back at every footstep. Donna tried not to think about what would happen if she lost her footing altogether and was swept off the top of the wing. She stayed inside the groove to the observation blister and it afforded some shelter. The white armoured figure of the count remained stock-still, gazing forward across the lake while his argent cloak billowed and snapped like a banner behind him.

You could tell from his very stance that Julius Ko'-iron was just such a mock-warrior noble. He embraced the fantasy of the heroic hereditary warrior, those who since ancient times had selflessly protected (read: tyrannised) their people (read: unwilling subjects) in return for their support (read: money) against threats internal and external (read: rebellious subjects and rapacious relatives). He had exterminated vermin in the Underhive and thought himself a man, a great hunter. Well, Donna thought, now the great hunter was going to meet a great predator. She had already taken his eye and now she was coming back for the rest of him.

She was getting tired of fighting against the headwind and trying for stealth. It was making her whole body hurt but most especially her ribs. She had a sneaking suspicion that the count knew she was there anyway, but that he was choosing to prove his superiority by ignoring her until the last possible moment.

'Ahh, there you are Julius,' she called out playfully. 'How's the eye?'

He turned then, and as the argent cloak whipped aside she realised what had become of the medicae unit. It clung to his back like a parasitic child, thin legs clamped around his chest. One steel hand was at his neck and another on his face where it covered the eye she had gouged like a squatting metallic spider. Its dull-eyed face swiveled as Ko'iron turned; it had been watching her all along.

'D'onne Astride Ge'Slyvanus Ulanti,' he yelled over the noise. 'I knew we weren't finished with each other yet.'

'Still thinking you can take me home to do my duty?' Donna's voice dripped with sarcasm.

Ko'iron's face flushed crimson at her insolence as he screamed back at her. 'You stupid, ignorant woman! I didn't come down here to take you back to the Spire. I came down here to erase a mistake, an embarrassment to not just one but two, two houses of the blood. You–'

Donna was laughing. 'Oh Julius, you are quite the charmer, so like your brother in so many ways. You try to make it sounds as if Ulanti and Ko'iron were equals. We both know different, Julius, so you can drop the act with me.'

Ko'iron's jaw worked ineffectually as Donna swept on.

'There's no scandal like an old scandal that just doesn't go away, is there Julius? So you decided to uphold your family's honour, huh? I don't buy that. Nobility is great for talking about honour until their skins are on the line. My father put you up to this, and he sent you down here for a reckoning. I'm guessing he told you that he would write off some of the bride debt you owed, I'd bet –'

'You couldn't just die and sink into obscurity, could you! You had to become a gang fighter! You had to gain notoriety and a name! All because D'onne Ulanti is more important than her family, or her father's promise! You disgust me! Alliances fractured, deals broken. Have you any conception of the mess you've made?'

'That's all crap, Julius. If there's one thing I've learned down here it's that in the Spire alliances and deals are just another way of screwing each other over, all the while dreaming that something can be had for nothing. The families use people as playing pieces in the same old games to try and win more of the pot, which is wasting even while they squabble over it. Know your place, do your part. Words to turn generations into automata while the few decide amongst themselves how to divide what is made by the many.'

'What? That's swing shift heresy! Is there no depth you won't plumb, woman? I don't know what Old 'Sly'vanus thought he was doing with you but it must have been a total failure. How could he have spawned such a heretical prole for a daughter?'

'You should thank me really,' she shouted into the wind. 'There'd be no House Ko'iron left if father had had his way – you'd all be serving drinks and cleaning boots in House Ulanti by now if I hadn't objected so strenuously to the match I was presented with.' That was a bit of a stretch, but the idea seemed to upset Julius a lot.

'Bitch!' he shouted.

Ko'iron's hands came up and Donna dived into cover before she even saw what he was holding.

There was a roar and a miniature meteor howled past, a second and third following it in quick succession. A fourth one clipped the observation blister and exploded, throwing metal and glass outward in a spinning corona of fragments that hissed venomously and rattled off the wing.

He had a bolt gun, a rare sight in the Underhive thanks to their expensive ammo and temperamental reputation. Bounty hunters, gun-scummers, watchman types like Hanno often used the pistol version if they could get their hands on one. The miniature rockets that bolt weapons fired, the 'bolts', could blow off limbs or eviscerate a body with a single hit, or even cripple with a near miss. They were so deadly only plasma gave more chance of a one-shot kill.

Another volley of bolts howled past, tearing shrapnel out of the wing behind her. The ekranoplan lurched slightly, probably coincidence but it did make Donna wonder how long it could survive Julius throwing around mass-reactive bolts near its engines.

Julius started stamping around to get a better angle at her, and Donna rolled up to put a shot into him with her laspistol. He made a big, obvious target in his white armour and fluttering cloak, but when she pulled the trigger, nothing happened. She jerked the trigger again and the pistol's grip suddenly pulsed redhot. She dropped the gun with a curse. Julius laughed.

'Thought you could shoot me with my brother's own gun did you?' he shouted. 'Ha! It remembers its place better than you think.'

He raised the bolt gun and let fly. Donna ducked down into the narrow groove and huddled deeper as bolts rained about her. She felt the impacts of the rockets tearing into the wing above, saw the blinding flashes and heard the hiss of shrapnel over her head. Donna's flesh shrank instinctively from the storm of violence and she wished that she could worm deeper into the metal floor for shelter.

Through the strobing flashes of bolter fire, she glimpsed her laspistol. No, she corrected herself, that was *Ko'iron's* laspistol winking up at her from nearby. She wondered what other in-built protocols it might have that she didn't know about. It could obviously sense somehow if a target was of Ko'iron blood and punish the user if they repeatedly tried to fire on them.

Such technology was difficult, but not impossible, to achieve. Donna had heard of weapons keyed so that only certain individuals could use them and this was some bizarre twist on that arrangement. It was probably intended to prevent Ko'iron siblings from shooting each other in the back. She wondered if it now remembered her as 'bad' and would punish her if she tried to use it again. She eyed the treacherous yet seductive pistol dubiously.

The firing stopped, creating a brief illusion of silence until the roar of the engines and the rush of the wind reasserted itself. Julius shouted something, but Donna's ears were still ringing from the barrage and missed it. She gripped Seventy-six and waited, expecting him to rush to the edge of the trench and sweep it with explosive bolts. In the background, the engine noise of the ekranoplan was getting rougher. One of them stuttered and died away, making the whole wing shudder briefly. The other engines howled louder as they struggled to compensate and keep the craft skimming. Julius did not appear.

'Are you deaf? Come out and take what's coming to you, stop hiding like some miserable prole.'

He must be running low on ammunition, and was trying to needle her pride to make her give away her position. Attacking a noble's pride might work in his world but this was the Underhive and Donna had been taunted by professionals. She kept quiet.

'Or maybe you're hurt, and just lying there slowly bleeding to death, hmmm?'

Yes, indulge your fantasies Julius. Go ahead and think you've already won. She wondered briefly if Tessera was already dead, whether she was even still aboard the ekranoplan – it was almost certain that the Escher would have taken her off if they could when the engines started. If so, she had come on this murder hunt for nothing, and was liable to meet her death at the hands of an over-privileged retard with a big weapons' budget in pursuit of a truly lost cause.

A lead weight of determination settled on Donna's soul. Even if she was going to die, Julius Ko'iron could not be allowed to live. She forced her bruised and battered body to move. On a mad whim, she reached out for the laspistol, and fought down the instinctive flinch she felt as her hand closed around it. There was no pulse of heat, the pistol grip felt perfectly cool and smooth through her torn glove.

Time for the oldest trick in the book – Jen had reliably informed her this one was in use before Necromunda was settled and probably even before that. She took out her filter can and tossed it to the other end of the narrow trench, near the steps. The flick of movement and the tinny clatter it made was all it took to get Julius firing again. Bolts rained down like a meteor swarm, raking the top of the stairs with an inescapable web of shrapnel – inescapable, assuming you were actually under it, of course.

Julius was happily blazing away at shadows, so Donna had plenty of time to peek out, take aim, and unleash an accurate volley of shots at her target. Julius saw the flash of her shots and instinctively flinched back for a second before he started pouring fire on her. He didn't see what she'd hit, and didn't even think about why she'd shot at all until a fraction of a second later. That was when the first engine exploded.

Donna didn't know much about engines, especially not the kind of weird jets mounted on the ekranoplan. But, she reasoned, like most things in life, an engine will stop working if you shoot it often enough in the right places. She hadn't expected the results to be so spectacular.

The innermost engine she'd hit belched flame and then exploded outwards into a ball of red-hot metal shards. Its two brethren gulped down some of the debris and were pierced by more of it, each exploding in turn and ripping off pieces of the stub wing they were attached to. The rest of the wing and bits of engine disappeared aft, trailing smoke and flames, all in the twinkling of an eye.

The ekranoplan shuddered and lurched like a dying animal as its motive power was shorn away on one side. It started wallowing over into a sharply banked turn that pushed Donna against the side of the trench she was hiding in. Stalactite-mountains dipped overhead in mock salute as the ekranoplan tipped over towards the surface of the sump lake. She imagined that she heard Julius scream amidst the tumult of howling engines, but that was probably just wishful thinking.

Splash down. The crippled ekranoplan kissed the pitch-black surface of the sump, bouncing off and skipping across it for a dozen metres before digging in again. This time the ekranoplan gave up its remaining momentum in a spray of effluents and toxins that choked the last of its engines. The craft spun through one-hundred-and-eighty degrees and rose almost vertically before slamming down into the lake.

Donna clung on with every ounce of her strength as the world whirled about her. The heart-stopping fear of being flung overboard into the toxic sump gave her muscles strength like iron, though in her frightened mind they felt like water. The awful, sickening g-force of the crash dragged at her, tried to suck her out of her haven wedged into the trench. At the last moment the ekranoplan seemed determined to tip her out, or to flip over completely and crush her beneath its vast bulk. Then finally, grudgingly, the craft splashed back down and slewed to a halt.

It felt like it took a long time for Donna to realise the motion had stopped, or at least slowed to a drift. She was shaking as she disentangled herself from the now twisted trench. The ekranoplan was lying at an angle with the tip of its remaining, intact stub wing dipped into the sump and the wrecked one held high above the surface like a smoking torch.

The crash must have torn a hole in the ekranoplan's hull because the glistening surface of the lake was creeping higher with each passing moment. Methane fires skated and whirled around the wreck like sylphs. Further off, Donna could see v-shaped wakes patiently circling as the local wildlife tried to decide whether this intruder in their realm was predator or prey. It was certainly crippled and sinking, she sourly concluded, so the ekranoplan couldn't help acting just like prey right now.

No matter which way she looked she couldn't catch sight of the lights of Down Town, the oily expanse of the sump was the only thing visible. She craned to see the rear of the craft, where she had left Tessera, but a pall of smoke and fumes hung about the tilted stern. It was hard to imagine Tessera could have clung on through the crash even if she had been conscious, so Donna had probably killed her too. She couldn't see Ko'iron anywhere either, much as she half-expected to find him clinging to some piece of flotsam and shouting imprecations as he died a horrible death in the sump. That would have been nice.

Thump. Something hit the submerged wing tip. Donna raised her pistol and looked over in time to see a white-bodied, multi-limbed apparition haul itself up onto an engine casing. Black slurry rolled off its jointed legs, silver glittered on its back. But it was all wrong – those were not the sleek limbs of a spider-mare, this was something more twisted, and more familiar.

Count Julius Ko'iron crawled up the wing like some newly metamorphosed insect. The tattered and sodden cloak, once so magnificent, now dragged behind the count like a discarded cocoon. His hair was gone, his exposed skin was red, pockmarked and still bubbling in places. The pristine white armour was cracked and stained, missing parts that had been sloughed away in the crash. The medicae unit on his back looked worse: what little flesh it had before had peeled back like old paper to show the bone, staples and circuitry beneath. It was half-clinging to Ko'iron, half dragging him along, and the count's head was lolling back and forth grotesquely.

It was the servitor's ravaged face that stared back fixedly at Donna. Something in its gaze convinced her that it was the count looking out through its eyes, dragging his slack body forward with the help of the servitor's limbs as some hideous composite being. It struggled fully upright as its jaws worked and some gargling, monstrous attempt at speech came out. Donna had already seen enough.

'What ever it is, I don't need to hear it. You want revenge, meat puppet? Come and give me your best shot. You want help?' She thumbed Seventy-six into life and it purred in anticipation. 'Then I'll give you all the help Donna's got to give, the only kind of help she knows about.'

Seventy-six sang as she swung her arm in an experimental arc. All the pain and weakness she had felt was gone. She felt good.

'I will help you die,' she told him.

Ko'iron wanted revenge. Revenge had driven him into the Underhive, and now his thirst for vengeance had consumed him utterly. His once-white armoured arms rose into a fighter's stance and his gnarled red hands twisted themselves into fists. As they did so, his forearms grew blades, wicked hooks that extruded smoothly from hidden sheaths in the armour.

Donna cocked her head and smiled. 'Oh goody.'

He lurched at her, his butcher's-blades swinging. She parried one and whirled away from the other, disturbed by the glassy-sounding crack she heard when the two blades connected. Seventy-six's whine had a stutter to it now. She backed up the wing a couple of steps, Ko'iron shambling after her on all eight limbs. His blades bit into the engine casing like butter as he hauled himself forward.

She cut at him and he swayed back, trying to hook her chainblade. She countered almost absent-mindedly, flipping the tip of her sword around in a half-circle to cut at his upper arm. The teeth scrabbled at his armour ineffectually so, as an afterthought, she thrust it into the medicae unit on his back. Ko'iron mewled and staggered back a pace.

'Mono-blades, my dear count?' Donna was disparaging. 'Those nasty one molecule cutting edges would mess up Seventy-six a treat if I let you keep hacking at me. I think we won't be having that, oh no.'

She aimed the laspistol at him. Ko'iron tensed, then relaxed as he recognised it. He stood up taller, daring her to try and shoot him with it. She smiled and pointed it at the medicae unit's face. She waited for half a second for the shock to register in Ko'iron's mind, and then she shot it in the eye.

The servitor's head exploded in a shower of flash-fried brains and gore. The rest of its exoskeleton fell back sparking and twitching, slithering off Ko'iron's back. The count himself collapsed onto his knees. Donna didn't give him time to recover hacking off one of his arms at the elbow. She took the other arm off at the shoulder, although Seventy-six screeched in protest at having to carve through his thick shoulder plates.

'Just a little longer baby, then you can rest,' she told Seventy-six. It crooned happily again in response.

Julius had fallen down. His legs were still moving, and his head was twisting back and forth. But now he had no eyes left (the sump had burned out his last real one) and he didn't know which way to crawl, even if he could crawl, which he couldn't really. Donna looked around. The sump was inching its way past the outermost engine now, but there was still plenty of time. She put her foot on his chest and looked down at him for a moment. Her voice cracked when she spoke.

'You... if you had just left it alone, it wouldn't have to be like this. If you could have just...' She shook her head. Her voice was hard when she spoke again.

'I've killed a lot of deserving bastards in my time, Julius, but believe me you've made it to the top of the heap, and in record time too. You were a star, count. I feel better about killing you than anyone I ever met before. Now... go to hell.'

She set Seventy-six chewing at his groin and looked in his face as she shoved it deeper inside, through intestines and organs and up to his foul heart, but he was long gone. Crimson tears leaked from the white armour as she methodically churned his insides into soup.

IT WAS PEACEFUL.

Donna sat with her knees drawn up beneath her chin, watching the surface of the sump get closer. The ekranoplan was settling gradually, its internal spaces filling up one by one as the corrosive effluent seeped in. She watched the methane fires dancing, saw the circling wakes disperse and be replaced by the stilt-legged silhouettes of spider-mares that now skated warily in the distance. She gazed in wonder at the hanging spires overhead with their swirling patterns of metamorphosis and decay.

The sump wasn't even black, she realised, but just like oil it was rainbow hued across its restless surface. In places she saw twisting threads of ochre, vermillion and ultramarine streaking its surface, currents of different substances unable to break down into the general entropic mass.

It was quiet too. It was probably the quietest place she had ever been. Here the silence was broken only by the occasional drip or sigh and hiss of the wind-born flame. No engines, no machines, no air pumps, no filters, no power grids, no talk, no screaming, no gunfire – it was peaceful.

Donna smiled at the irony. She had finally found somewhere she could be at peace because nobody could live here. The very bottom of the hive, the place where the most unwanted waste was dumped had become a place where man couldn't survive, and it had become beautiful because of it. Paradise created by toxicity. That made her laugh.

She was ready for the end. She had climbed up to the tip of the ruined wing and now patiently waited for the sump to get to her. She had every confidence it would, and admired the thorough way the ekranoplan was not only sinking but being corroded and absorbed, piece by piece in the lake.

The count's armour split open like the petals of a flower and floated on the surface briefly before being consumed. It would be her turn soon enough, but she had the laspistol in hand in case it hurt too much. It seemed fitting that it should end like this. She and it had been together since the start.

SOMETHING WAS NAGGING at her. She came out of a half-dazed reverie, staring at the swirling colours on the surface of the sump. There it was again. A sound, something breaking into her circle of perfect quiet and solitude.

'D'onne!'

Donna blinked. She had been called that once, a long time ago in another life. She felt affronted by the reference.

'D'onne!'

There was a youngish-looking man calling to her from the spreading stain where Ko'iron had been. She blinked again, half expecting the apparition to disappear. Instead it resolved itself into a man in a chequered coat standing close by on a motor-skiff. He looked terrified.

'D'onne, get onboard! Quickly!'

'Why the frik would I want to do that, Lars?'

'Because you'll die if you don't!'

She noticed the spider-mares were a good deal closer than before, obviously interested in the motor-skiff. Lars was looking too, but he turned back to her quickly.

'Because I'll die if you don't!'

'Well get going now, before the spider-mares decide you look tasty.'

'But then you'll die.'

'Gold star, Lars, I want to die. Now piss off.'

'D'onne, I'm sorry for everything that's happened. I'm sorry I came down to the Underhive. I'm sorry for it all but please… there's more to life than this.'

'Hate and death is all there is, Lars, and I'm the queen of hate and the mother of death. I've had enough of both.'

'No! You're more than that, D'onne. I remember the girl I met by the fountain–'

'That was a romantic fantasy, Lars. I was half out of my mind with fear and I needed to escape – all you did was play-act a role,' Donna snapped. Lars looked hurt and fell silent. Spider-mares skated a little closer. Much against her better judgment, she felt there was something she had to ask Lars.

'What happened to Tessera?'

'What?'

'Tessera. Hell, you don't even know. What happened to the Escher, did they get away?'

'Yes, I think so. I wasn't really looking once I heard the engines start. I saw Bak and his men make off in skiffs like this, so I stole one, I'm afraid, and came after the ekranoplan.'

'Why?'

'Because I thought you were still onboard and I was right.'

'You wanted to ride in on your white charger and save me?'

'I've always wanted to ride in on my white charger and save you. I'm not a strong man or a proud man, D'onne, but since I first laid eyes on you that has always been true.'

'You flatter yourself.'

'Well, that would be a shame because I'm aiming to flatter *you*.' Lars glanced at the spider mares again and wet his lips. 'D'onne, I just want you to hear me out for a moment, and if you still want me to go then I'll go... Not because I'm afraid for my life, which I am by the way, but because it's what you want me to do.'

'Enough with the damn preamble, Lars. Spit it out and then go, nothing you can say will change my mind. This is the end.'

'Well you see I have a theory that I think is pretty sound, and that's that you aren't going to let yourself die.' Donna glared at him but Lars ploughed on. 'It goes like this: if your own self-loathing and hatred was so great, your disgust powerful enough to make you self-destructive, why didn't you die years ago?'

'What?'

'You came down here and ran with the gangs, D'onne. You've taken all the Underhive could throw at you and lived through it. One misstep here or a hesitation there would have killed you a hundred times over. If you had even the slightest doubt in your mind that you wanted to live you would have died. But you didn't. You lived through it all. I just saw this ekranoplan crash into the sump and yet there was no doubt in my mind that when I got here you would be sitting on the wreckage.

'And what that means, D'onne, is that at some point, maybe not now but soon, you'll want to live again. Perhaps when you're half burned by the sump, maybe earlier, and don't look at that pistol, D'onne – again, if you were going to shoot yourself you wouldn't have waited until now to do it.'

'I hate you, Lars. I ought to kill you.'

'But killing me won't help you survive, and I respect your survival instincts, D'onne. I think you should too.'

He was right. Deep down, a chill at Donna's core told her she would be struggling to survive long before she was even half way submerged. The thought of agonised thrashing consumed her. And, as for the pistol, well it had seemed possible before but now she just couldn't imagine using it on herself. Lars had ruined it all; when he gave her a chance for escape her inner serenity had vanished like smoke. Damn him!

'D'onne, also consider this: if you die now, then your father has won, Ko'iron achieved his mission and everything carries on as if nothing happened. Do you want that?'

There was long pause as Donna ruminated. 'You say there's enough generation potential in Dead Man's Hole to upset the markets?'

'I think so, it wouldn't take much.'

'But enough to hurt the Spire?'

'What are you thinking, D'onne?'

Donna straightened up, ran down the wing and leapt lightly onto the motor skiff. She kissed Lars, who was so surprised he stopped looking terrified for a moment.

'I think I may have found a prospect worth living for,' she told him. Lars beamed happily. 'I want to be around to see your untimely death.'

Lars looked hurt again, and Donna laughed.

ABOUT THE AUTHOR

Andy Chambers is best known as a games designer, having contributed heavily to the development of Warhammer 40,000, Battlefleet Gothic, Necromunda, Epic 40,000 and many other Games Workshop games and supplements over fourteen years. In amongst a steady stream of articles for *White Dwarf*, *Fanatic Magazine* and *Chapter Approved*, two short stories, *Ancient History* and *Deus Ex Mechanicus*, were published in *Inferno!* and have subsequently been reprinted in Black Library anthologies. Now working freelance, Andy has taken his first steps into the literary arena to wrestle with the fearsome beast that is a full-blown novel.

THE BLACK LIBRARY

More action and adventure in the savage underworld of Necromunda:

NECROMUNDA SALVATION
C S GOTO

ISBN 1 84416 189 7

Zefer wanted nothing more than fame, fortune and a quiet life. Well, that's zero for three, then...

Download the first chapter FREE at www.blacklibrary.com!

READ TILL YOU BLEED

Read till you Bleed
Do you have them all?

1. Trollslayer – William King
2. First & Only – Dan Abnett
3. Skavenslayer – William King
4. Into the Maelstrom – Ed. Marc Gascoigne & Andy Jones
5. Daemonslayer – William King
6. Eye of Terror – Barrington J Bayley
7. Space Wolf – William King
8. Realm of Chaos – Ed. Marc Gascoigne & Andy Jones
9. Ghostmaker – Dan Abnett
10. Hammers of Ulric – Dan Abnett, Nik Vincent & James Wallis
11. Ragnar's Claw – William King
12. Status: Deadzone – Ed. Marc Gascoigne & Andy Jones
13. Dragonslayer – William King
14. The Wine of Dreams – Brian Craig
15. Necropolis – Dan Abnett
16. 13th Legion – Gav Thorpe
17. Dark Imperium – Ed. Marc Gascoigne & Andy Jones
18. Beastslayer – William King
19. Gilead's Blood – Abnett & Vincent
20. Pawns of Chaos – Brian Craig
21. Xenos – Dan Abnett
22. Lords of Valour – Ed. Marc Gascoigne & Christian Dunn
23. Execution Hour – Gordon Rennie
24. Honour Guard – Dan Abnett
25. Vampireslayer – William King
26. Kill Team – Gav Thorpe
27. Drachenfels – Jack Yeovil
28. Deathwing – Ed. David Pringle & Neil Jones
29. Zavant – Gordon Rennie
30. Malleus – Dan Abnett
31. Konrad – David Ferring
32. Nightbringer – Graham McNeill
33. Genevieve Undead – Jack Yeovil
34. Grey Hunter – William King
35. Shadowbreed – David Ferring
36. Words of Blood – Ed. Marc Gascoigne & Christian Dunn
37. Zaragoz – Brian Craig
38. The Guns of Tanith – Dan Abnett
39. Warblade – David Ferring
40. Farseer – William King
41. Beasts in Velvet – Jack Yeovil
42. Hereticus – Dan Abnett
43. The Laughter of Dark Gods – Ed. David Pringle
44. Plague Daemon – Brian Craig
45. Storm of Iron – Graham McNeill
46. The Claws of Chaos – Gav Thorpe
47. Draco – Ian Watson
48. Silver Nails – Jack Yeovil
49. Soul Drinker – Ben Counter
50. Harlequin – Ian Watson
51. Storm Warriors – Brian Craig
52. Straight Silver – Dan Abnett
53. Star of Erengrad – Neil McIntosh
54. Chaos Child – Ian Watson
55. The Dead & the Damned – Jonathan Green
56. Shadow Point – Gordon Rennie

WWW.BLACKLIBRARY.COM

57 Blood Money – C L Werner
58 Angels of Darkness – Gav Thorpe
59 Mark of Damnation – James Wallis
60 Warriors of Ultramar – Graham McNeill
61 Riders of the Dead – Dan Abnett
62 Daemon World – Ben Counter
63 Giantslayer – William King
64 Crucible of War – Ed. Marc Gascoigne & Christian Dunn
65 Honour of the Grave – Robin D Laws
66 Crossfire – Matthew Farrer
67 Blood & Steel – C L Werner
68 Crusade for Armageddon – Jonathan Green
69 Way of the Dead – Ed. Marc Gascoigne & Christian Dunn
70 Sabbat Martyr – Dan Abnett
71 Taint of Evil – Neil McIntosh
72 Fire Warrior – Simon Spurrier
73 The Blades of Chaos – Gav Thorpe
74 Gotrek and Felix Omnibus 1 – William King
75 Gaunt's Ghosts: The Founding – Dan Abnett
76 Wolfblade – William King
77 Mark of Heresy – James Wallis
78 For the Emperor – Sandy Mitchell
79 The Ambassador – Graham McNeill
80 The Bleeding Chalice – Ben Counter
81 Caves of Ice – Sandy Mitchell
82 Witch Hunter – C L Werner
83 Ravenor – Dan Abnett
84 Magestorm – Jonathan Green
85 Annihilation Squad – Gav Thorpe
86 Ursun's Teeth – Graham McNeill
87 What Price Victory – Ed. Marc Gascoigne & Christian Dunn
88 The Burning Shore – Robert Earl
89 Grey Knights – Ben Counter
90 Swords of the Empire – Ed. Marc Gascoigne & Christian Dunn
91 Double Eagle – Dan Abnett
92 Sacred Flesh – Robin D Laws
93 Legacy – Matthew Farrer
94 Iron Hands – Jonathan Green
95 The Inquisition War – Ian Watson
96 Blood of the Dragon – C L Werner
97 Traitor General – Dan Abnett
98 The Heart of Chaos – Gav Thorpe
99 Dead Sky, Black Sun – Graham McNeill
100 Wild Kingdoms – Robert Earl
101 Gotrek & Felix Omnibus 2 – William King
102 Gaunt's Ghosts: The Saint – Dan Abnett
103 Dawn of War – CS Goto
104 Forged in Battle – Justin Hunter
105 Blood Angels: Deus Encarmine – James Swallow
106 Eisenhorn – Dan Abnett
107 Valnir's Bane – Nathan Long
108 Lord of the Night – Simon Spurrier
109 Necromancer – Jonathan Green
110 Crimson Tears – Ben Counter
111 Witch Finder – C L Werner
112 Ravenor Returned – Dan Abnett
113 Death's Messenger – Sandy Mitchell
114 Blood Angels: Deus Sanguinus – James Swallow
115 Keepers of the Flame – Neil McIntosh
116 The Konrad Saga – David Ferring
117 The Traitor's Hand – Sandy Mitchell
118 Darkblade: The Daemon's Curse – Dan Abnett & Mike Lee
119 Survival Instinct – Andy Chambers
120 Salvation – CS Goto

Coming Soon...
121 Fifteen Hours – Mitchel Scanlon
122 Grudge Bearer – Gav Thorpe

NEWS, ARTICLES, FREE DOWNLOADS,
NOVEL EXTRACTS, ONLINE STORE, PREVIEWS AND MORE...

WWW.BLACKLIBRARY.COM
READ TILL YOU BLEED